THE WIDOW'S SECRET

Brian Thompson was born in London in 1935 and now lives in Oxford. He has written two award-winning volumes of memoir: *Keeping Mum* (2006), winner of the Costa Prize for Biography and the PEN/Ackerley Prize, and *Clever Girl* (2007), longlisted for the Samuel Johnson Prize. The next Bella Wallis mystery, *The Captain's Table*, will be published in hardback by Chatto & Windus in 2009.

ALSO BY BRIAN THOMPSON

Non-fiction

Keeping Mum
Clever Girl

Fiction

The Captain's Table

ONE

EARLY-MORNING MISTS promised a fine day. There was talk at breakfast of a barge journey along the canal, culminating in a picnic at Stone Saxton where the druids had once danced. But to Arthur Gration's great disappointment these mists refused to rise like a theatre curtain and reveal the estate in all its splendour. Instead, they thickened. In the space of an hour, cows in the low meadow that had seemed to float like ducks disappeared from view altogether. Long before the last guest came down to breakfast, the mist had become emboldened enough to lick at the long windows, nudging aside trees and shrubs as it advanced.

Gration consulted Billings, his butler.

'I doubt we shall see much change, my lord. Tidyman walked up from the village with the day staff and says there it is as thick as porridge, his words for it.'

'What can be done?'

'I should not like to answer for conditions along the canal. But if a picnic is still called for –'

'– it has been promised –'

'– yes, indeed. Then may I suggest we open the ballroom and bring along the paper lanterns and such that went with Lady Celia's birthday last year? They might make a pleasant enough show. And it occurs to me just now, my lord, I could send to Compton for the village band, or the steadier parts of it.'

Gration looked at his butler with the kind of admiration another man might reserve for a Fellow of the Royal Society.

'Billings, you are wasted in service here. You should be an admiral or something of the sort. By land, a major-general.'

'Your lordship is too kind,' Billings said calmly. He was thinking of how to coerce the housekeeper into clearing the ballroom, last used the previous November and generally considered a handy depot for things broken, things unwanted, and any amount of suitcases, steamer trunks and empty tea chests.

Only two people from the breakfast table braved the weather. One of these was Mrs Bella Wallis, a widow, but a very assured one, not at all dismayed by circumstance. She was a striking-looking woman in her late thirties, tall, maybe a little on the buxom side, her undoubted appeal amplified by a humorous mouth and wonderfully grey eyes. The previous evening she had been much admired by the entire house party for her genial common sense and – this from her own sex – a comfortably elegant way with clothes. Men found her entrancing.

Now, when she proposed a walk, the first to jump up was Philip Westland, as agreeable a companion as she could have wished for. She waited for him in the hall, a half-smile on her face, as he banged about looking for his hat, trying it on and then deciding against it.

'You will go bareheaded, Mr Westland?'

'I shall risk being wetted, I think.'

When a servant opened the door for them, the fog rolled in.

'But don't you see, if you only had a hat in your hand you could waft away the weather,' she chided, laughing.

'In the past, I have suceeded in that line with wasps. And have heard it sometimes works with cows.'

He ushered her on to the gravel path that led away from the house and they set off together, boots crunching in unison. They were by no means complete strangers. But they only met on occasions such as this – weekend house parties, dinners for twenty or more, the crush bars of theatres and so forth. It was not in Bella's nature to be flirtatious but she was free with Philip Westland in a way she found difficult with others. Part of the pleasure she found in his company today came from knowing that he sailed for India on Tuesday.

Westland was tall, dark and unhandsome. He walked like a sailor with his arms held apart from his body. His hair was unbrushed, his figure on the portly side already. He had no small talk – or not of the kind that is obligatory for weekends in the country.

'Look!' Bella teased. 'A young girl from the village is waiting to ambush you.'

They paused before a statue depicting a goddess with perfectly round breasts and plump arms, beckoning seductively. A marble skirt clung to the chub of her hips.

'I recognize her,' Westland said. 'She is the stationmaster's daughter. I have warned her of going about naked. But she's headstrong.'

'Shall you miss England?'

'On days like this, yes, I suppose I shall. I know nothing at all about India. It is hot there, I believe.'

Bella laughed.

'You make such determined efforts to be offhand. You'll go, you'll fall in love with some very serious young woman and be happy ever after.'

'It is no use my saying I would rather stand about in the fog with you?' he asked. 'Maybe not here. Maybe in some other place in the world where there is nothing but fog.'

Bella flushed. His meaning was unmistakable. She covered the statue's ears with her palms, feeling her gloves drench. Philip smiled and took her hands away.

'You were born to draw love like a magnet, Bella, but I like you best for hardly being aware of it. Think of me henceforth as Westland, the man who went to India and married the colonel's daughter.'

'Shall we go on?' Bella asked in a shaky voice.

'Good Lord, yes. There are any amount of ditches we can fall into. I shall make you walk until your very unsuitable London boots are filled to the brim with dew.'

She drew his head down and kissed him on the lips.

'I am very nearly forty, my dearest Philip, and about as much use to you as a tea-strainer. Or watering can.'

'Watering can is good,' he said. 'A fellow asked me at billiards last night who the devil you were. Meaning where does she come from, has she any money, et cetera. I said that among women you were the finished article.'

'That was gallant of you.'

'He seemed perplexed. He mentioned the name Broxtowe to me.'

At once, Bella's eyes flashed.

'Did he indeed? I like you less for telling me that. Lord Broxtowe is a friend in the way I should like you to be a friend to me. Who was this billiards player?'

'Bella, please,' Westland murmured.

'You won't tell me? Well, damn country-house weekends. And damn you too for not knocking him to the carpet there and then. Broxtowe has been my particular friend since my husband died. He is old enough to be both my grandfather and yours. Never was a more honourable man.'

'Would I have mentioned a single word of this if I knew it was going to cause you so much anguish?'

'I am not anguished. I am disappointed.'

'In me?'

'In men.'

'I am very sorry to hear it. People do say some very stupid things when playing at billiards. Often it is the brandy that talks.'

'No,' she warned sharply. 'I will not be humoured.'

'Does it really matter who it was who made these remarks?'

'It matters to me.'

Still with the warmth of her lips on his, he capitulated.

'The fellow's name is Freddie –'

Before he could say another word, she clapped her hands together in annoyance.

'That mincing idiot? I have been overhearing his interminable prattle all weekend but I'm surprised to find *you* hobnobbing. How disgusting.'

There was enough of the cynic in Westland to think she was protesting too much, but she turned and set off into the blank fog without another glance. There was a faint cry a few moments later and he found her flat on her back at the bottom of a mown bank. She was either laughing or crying.

She was crying with laughter. Arthur Gration loomed out of the fog.

'My God, Mrs Wallis,' he exclaimed. 'You might have broken your neck! And then where should we be? This is worse than when Mrs Profitt fell into the lake.'

'Hardly worse, surely?'

'Much worse. Who gave a fig for Frances Profitt and her ridiculous verses? Westland, be a good fellow and steer this lady back to the house. Damnation take the English weather. Did you see a boy sent to Compton for the village band?'

'We have seen no one,' Westland said.

'No, and how could you? We might as well be in Patagonia. It is foggy there all the time. Most of the hurricane lamps in the world are bought by the natives to lighten their gloom.'

Bella and Westland exchanged glances.

'I was just saying to Mrs Wallis that I should like to live there, under certain conditions.'

'And is that so? Then you're a bigger fool than I took you for.'

But as he made his dramatic exit, melting back into the gloom like Hamlet's ghost, he smiled warmly at Bella, his lips finishing in a knowing purse, halfway to a kiss.

The ballroom picnic was judged a great success. Giant paper parasols had been set up and cushions fetched from all over the house. The Compton band played country tunes and a village child sang unaccompanied airs of such sweetness that one or two of the house-guests felt their eyelids prickle. Gration was delighted with the whole effect.

'This was a very good idea of mine, Billings,' he said to his butler.

'I must congratulate you, sir,' Billings said with his habitual gravity. 'I could never have thought of it for myself, I am sure.'

'What's the matter with that shit, Freddie Bolsover?' Gration asked, pointing. Billings gently drew down his master's arm, as though smoothing out the line of a coat, or giving a last touch to a tablecloth.

'I believe his lordship is talking to Mrs Wallis,' he murmured.

'I can see that. Why is her face bright red? That's my point, Billings.'

Bright red was an exaggeration but certainly Bella's cheeks had begun to flush. In matters touching her own honour, she believed in coming straight to the point; and so it was now.

'I understand that at billiards last night you were anxious to know where I came from, Lord Bolsover. And expressed some curiousity about a very valued friend of mine.'

'Did I appear anxious?' he bantered. 'As for being curious, in the sense you intend, I am seldom guilty of that. Who you know is of not the slightest interest to me, madam. Gossip is very dull.'

'I am pleased to hear you say so. Nevertheless. Neither subject is any of your business, as I'm sure you will acknowledge.'

He seemed surprised by the quiet vehemence with which she spoke.

'Well, well, Mrs Whatever-your-name-is,' he drawled. 'I see I am being given a lesson in etiquette.'

'I think you must mean manners, my lord.'

His eyes widened and a muscle in his cheek twitched. Belle felt a stab of fear at the momentary transformation in his face, which bespoke, not irritation, but pure hatred. And not of her particularly, but women generally. All women.

Bolsover was tall and heavy-jowled. Some earls liked to be addressed as examples of God's benign intentions towards the social order: this one clearly thought of himself in more rakish terms. His clothes were perfectly cut but of a faintly theatrical nature, as for example the turned-back cuffs to his sleeves, finished with a thin silver brocade. The weight that he wore round his shoulders and gut was a sign of dissolute living, as was the crooked smile he gave her, revealing crooked teeth.

'You have said nothing, sir.'

'I am trying to eat a bun, madam,' he retorted, holding his plate up for inspection. Someone nearby giggled.

Bella was rescued by Philip Westland.

'I have found the book we were talking about.' He smiled, holding up a calf-bound volume from Gration's library. 'If you will excuse us,' he added, taking Bella by the elbow.

But the odious man had already turned and sauntered away, handing his plate of crumbs to an astonished young curate from Milfield.

'I believe I can fight my own battles,' Bella said, red in the face.

'Of course you can.'

She opened the book he proffered and burst out laughing. It was *Scenes descriptive of the Manners & Customs of the Inhabitants of Tierra del Fuego, together with a Scheme for the Abatement of Vice in that Country*.

There was a sudden delighted cry from Arthur Gration: the fog was lifting and now nothing would do but a contest of archery for those who were in no hurry to get away. The long-suffering Billings could be seen through the long windows, supervising the erection of the targets on the South Lawn.

'We could stay another evening,' Westland suggested. 'I have already spoken to Gration.'

'Between bows and arrows and the London train there can be no contest,' Bella said, feeling her heart lurch at the gratitude that shone in his face.

And the decision to remain when carriages took others to the station turned out beautifully. A slant sun poured over Gration's elms and his neighbours stayed on in enough numbers to make the archery into a genuine contest. Westland and the curate from Milfield shot it out for the grand prize, a dozen of claret recklessly donated by their host.

'By God, Westland!' Lord Gration cried. 'Cupid himself could not do better. Although, yes, now that I recall –'

Bella's rich laugh floated out across the lawn.

Next day, travelling back to London, Philip Westland plucked up the courage to ask Bella an obvious question.

'Did you know we were to meet at Arthur Gration's?'

'I knew you were invited.'

'And as a consequence you invited yourself?'

Bella had been looking out of the window in an abstracted sort of way. She turned her head and studied Westland with her fine grey eyes.

'Well, I don't think it works exactly like that, does it?'

'You can be cruel, Bella.'

'I wanted to say goodbye,' she explained gently. 'I shall miss you terribly.'

'I know that isn't true.'

'Why do you say that? Any man that can win a dozen of claret with such a negligent display of prowess –'

But she stopped when she saw how much more serious the moment was for him. Westland was smiling but his eyes were troubled.

'I wanted to say goodbye to a dear friend in the nicest way I knew how,' she insisted. 'And as to that, when we come into St Pancras, better we part at once, as though India was, I don't know, no further than Margate.'

'As you wish. There are so many things I don't know about you, Bella.'

'Now whatever can they be, I wonder?' she chided. He easily detected the tiny tremor of warning in her remark.

'I don't mean whether you have ever eaten whelks, or snore when you sleep on trains. Darker things.'

'Do I have dark things about me?'

'You are wrapped in mysteries.'

'Ah that! Very well. I am a Home Office spy,' she suggested lightly.

'I can almost believe you.'

'Such nonsense! I am an old London gossip, my dear. Look, I will show you my place of work.' She smiled, drawing him to the carriage window.

They were running through suburbs of harsh new brick. But on the horizon, mixed in with church steeples, were a hundred tall chimneys poking up into the sky. Westland stared. In the pleasant afternoon haze, they did a little resemble gossip factories. He took her hand and kissed it.

'Then I have wasted my last weekend in England paying court to an awful old gossip without a heart of her own.'

'That is how it is,' she agreed, pulling down his head and kissing him full on the lips.

At St Pancras, they did as she wished. Westland had style. After putting her into a cab, he turned and did not look back.

At eleven that evening, Bella Wallis could be found in her house in Orange Street, writing in quirkily irregular script, a brandy at her elbow, a cheroot smouldering in its saucer. Neither Westland, nor Arthur Gration, nor anyone else was on her mind. Instead, her pen chased the previous day's fog, trying to describe the delicacy of its colour and the strange texture it had, like water rearranged and stretched fine for inspection. The hurdy-gurdy man was playing in Leicester Square, the notes carried by a trick of the wind. A mouse scratched disobligingly behind the wainscot. Bella wrote on, patient and unhurried.

TWO

WESTLAND WAS GONE, save for a faint echo received by postcard from Gibraltar. In its entirety, the news from the Rock was this: *Sad want of fog.* There was no signature. After a little hesitation, Bella did not add the card to the morning-room fire but tucked it under a cushion, feeling uncomfortably schoolgirlish about it, too. Then she marched upstairs to the bathroom, banging and entering in one bad-tempered sweep of her hips.

Lying in the bath was a pale young woman wearing a white linen mobcap to guard her hair. Her skin was the colour of pearl, as though at any moment it would become completely translucent, which only served to emphasize how delicately formed she was, how angelically perfect. There was not a single blemish on her nakedness save one – a mole that kept coy company with her navel. But Bella was in no mood for aesthetic ecstasies.

'Do you think it is fair to Mrs Venn to have her fetch you hot water all damn morning when she has better and more important things to do?'

The girl in the bath stared up at Bella.

'You are going out,' she said, making an accusation of it.

'Yes, I am going out and you, *ma petite,* are leaving this bathroom in the next thirty seconds.'

'With whom do you go?'

'Is that really any concern of yours?'

'You are in a foul mood.'

'Your grasp of idiom is improving. I am going downstairs to calm myself with a pot of coffee, then I am being fetched by a ridiculous man and taken to one of London's most romantic locations. And now,' she bellowed, 'if you don't get out of that bath I shall drown you in it.'

And so, by mid-morning cab to the Royal Agricultural Hall in Upper Street. The horse was mettlesome and the cabbie young and eager, his plum-coloured coat and brass buttons as good as livery. Bella was used to surly men who smoked or spat, exchanged ribaldries or the time of day with their friends in the trade; in short, hard-bitten Londoners. This one still had the blush of the novice about him. Bella guessed that driving up the Pentonville Road at such a good lick was for him a metaphor for setting out in life.

As to the occasion, she had given some thought as to what to wear, settling on a sprigged dress and a hat that might be seen by some to have associations with the countryside. The wing feather of a pheasant (she supposed) perked up at a jaunty angle and she wore the brim low over her eyes. Of her two parasols, she chose the sage green.

'I say, you look most awfully pretty,' Henry Pattison said, as they rattled along. 'Quite the thing, in fact.'

'Thank you. And shall we see some of your own beasts today?'

His face fell and he gripped his cane with something like anguish.

'Oh Bella,' he cried. 'I see I have not made myself clear. It is the Royal Agricultural to be sure but there will be no cattle. We are on our way to an exhibition of farm machinery. The new and improved drain cutter – I thought I had mentioned it – of Dutch manufacture –'

Bella laid her gloved hand on his.

'Dear Henry, please be easy about it. It is all new to me. And I imagine as unlike Gloucestershire as anywhere in London.'

'That much is true,' Pattison agreed gloomily.

In the Great Hall, she walked about with her arm tucked inside his, a tall and buxom figure, with a decidedly full jaw he had never noticed previously. What had entranced him when they first met was her eyes – intelligent, searching eyes – and the air of mystery that hung about her. She was a widow who never spoke of her late husband. But she had such an alluring presence that Henry was torn between wishing to throw himself into the principal exhibit (a steam threshing machine) and blurting out the contents of his heart.

'It's all rather like a railway station,' Bella observed, pointing to the glass canopy, where pigeons squabbled with sparrows. She was secretly impressed by the number of bluff men with reddened cheeks and veiny noses who wished to raise their hats to Pattison.

'You are being most incredibly game about it all, I know,' he groaned. 'And I accept, there are more romantic locations.'

But Bella had a directness that had unsettled better men than him.

'I don't think we came here for romance,' she snapped, just a fraction too tart. Then relented and patted his arm.

'I have never been to Islington before, if that's where we are. And everything is interesting to an open mind, is it not? For example, that steam engine, such a potent symbol of progress, as you have described, is making a devil of a lot of old-fashioned smuts and cinders. Look.'

She held out the sleeve of her dress for his inspection and laughed. And in that instant Henry knew he had lost her.

They had met a week since at a musical soirée in Bedford Square and people had warned Henry she was a tricky fish to land. There was some fellow called Westland she had toyed with and then packed off to India with a broken heart. There were rumours that she smoked, a thing Henry associated with men: if with women at all, then Irish biddies sitting with clay pipes on the steps of caravans when the travelling people came to pester the margins of his property. Otherwise, smoking went with billiards; or brandy.

Though he was staggeringly rich, Pattison knew little of London, or widows, or courtship. He was not young any longer but neither was he particularly wise. He took a London musical soirée to be much the same as a vicarage tea or a weekend shooting party at home – that is, along with everything else a display case of eligible young women. Not for the first time in his life he had gravely misread the manners of the capital city. That night he would go back down to Bromhead Gate, the ancestral seat, wishing himself dead.

'Who is the gentleman tending the new and improved thresher? He is remarkably well dressed for an engineer.'

'That is Lord Yelverton,' Henry said through gritted teeth. 'He has four thousand acres in Somerset. The machine is of his design.'

Bella merely nodded.

They inspected everything: they took a not very good lunch: Bella saw by how much she had unintentionally hurt him.

'My dear,' she murmured, 'I would not have missed this, truly I wouldn't. But I do not go about much and it was the purest accident that we met at Lady Cornford's. That is how it is. And that is all it is.'

'I had hoped we might be friends.'

'Were I ever to live in Gloucestershire, perhaps we might. Neighbours are generally friends in the countryside, I understand.'

'And that is it?'

'That is it.'

'I shall never understand London,' Pattison cried spitefully.

'Nor I,' agreed Bella, who was born there.

On the journey back from Islington, he several times apologized for the scenery. He meant in addition the people in the landscape, dressed in black, stunted, stuttering in their way of moving, their heads swinging this way and that, the faces louring and suspicious. Their dogs raced to greet the cab.

'Mongrels,' Pattison exclaimed in disgust.

Bella raised her eyebrows and let them fall. The truth was, she was already forgetting her companion, his innocence and waif-like insecurity. Her mind was on work, but such work as Mr Henry Pattison could never have imagined.

'You may set me down in the Strand, if you will,' she murmured.

'I shall take you to your door,' he insisted.

The house in Orange Street astonished him. He had some sense of what constituted a good address in London and this was not it. The roadway was none too clean and he was astonished to find a legless beggar right outside Bella's front door, his rump protected from the pavement by a flattened carton. He was smoking and reading.

'Do come in for a moment,' Bella said without too much enthusiasm.

'I am quite comfy here, ma'am,' the beggar replied wittily.

Pattison was irritated by this. Legless beggars should not read. Apples should not be left to roll about the gutter, nor newspapers cling to the railings. As for the house itself, an unpromising façade should not conceal an interior of such casual elegance. Nor was he used to being offered wine at four in the afternoon.

'You have no servants,' he observed.

'Well, I hardly think I would call one to pour two small glasses of Madeira.'

'Did I happen to see your daughter peering over the top of the stairs when we came in?'

'I have no children,' Bella replied offhandedly.

And that was it! Pattison thought with sudden exhilaration: she is a demirep and the girl is her maid. I am in a house of harlotry. He was planning how to go forward with this discovery when he caught Bella's withering and mind-reading gaze and blushed from his waistcoat to his hairline.

'Such a pretty little sitting room,' he mumbled, feeling his legs tremble under him. If the truth were known, he was seeing it as one looks at the sun from the bottom of a lagoon, shortly after falling out of the native canoe. He sat down far too heavily.

'I think you were about to say something else, Mr Pattison,' Bella suggested icily.

'I assure you,' he protested.

'Say what was in your heart.'

Pattison looked at her imploringly.

'Perhaps – you will understand I mean no offence in saying this – it was in my mind that you are a woman of mystery, Bella.'

Poor fellow. He realized at once that he had said exactly the wrong thing. She set down her glass and rose. Her face was like stone.

'How very perceptive of you,' she murmured, handing him his gloves and hat.

Only much later, on his way home to Bromhead Gate, did it occur to him that he may have said something very significant touching Mrs Bella Wallis. But being Henry Pattison, he could not pinpoint what it was.

THREE

A HUNDRED YARDS OR so away, in Haymarket, the sort of whores Pattison had in mind were assembling for their evening parade – well-dressed and grave young women who kept up the kind of manners likely to seduce impressionable subalterns, country squires and the more unworldly lawyers and judges. They sauntered up and down in twos and threes, chatting and giggling behind their gloved hands. Sex came in a package that included supper at Thenevon's in Glasshouse Street or Air Street; or, if the mark looked promising enough, the Café Royal. Girls who a year or so ago had been milking cows or cutting hay were now engaged on more lucrative forms of farming. Their selling point was a quite staggering self-assurance.

Mallet's, halfway along this daily promenade, had once been a small hotel. The man whose name it bore borrowed from future clients to turn it into a club, suitable for gentlemen who never for a moment supposed the strolling Araminta to be a bishop's daughter or Lou a refugee from Hungary, but who could recognize them at once as Molly from the Fens of Cambridgeshire, or Jane from Liverpool.

Lord Bolsover liked Mallet's for its male-only ambience and quite colossal snobbery. It was famously said that when Sir Charles Dilke tried to dine there he was turned away by a uniformed doorman with the memorable remark, 'Your name is not known to me, chum.' The club rooms were small and uncomfortable and Bolsover liked that about the place, too. The food was schoolroom fare. Only the cellar was in any way exceptional. Mallet knew wine far better than he knew himself.

Lord Bolsover was happy to make this crusty and over-mannered man his crony. That afternoon they sat drinking Krug in Mallet's tiny first-floor sitting room, boasting a window that overlooked the street.

'The girl in black striped silk really is what she says she is,' he observed. 'Her father is the most crashing bore but was indeed at one time Consul to some godforsaken Balkan outpost. She was raised on the banks of the Danube. Pa thought to save her from sin and mosquitoes by sending her home, a kindness she has repaid most ungenerously.'

'Name?' Bolsover enquired indolently.

'His name? Pelligrew. The sister married that Irish oaf, Mont Styal. Big house out in the peat bogs somewhere. Very good horses. The girl is called Pauletta, a piece of nonsense wished on her by the mother.'

'You surprise me by knowing as much about this young pox-box as you do.'

'Pox-box?'

'She is a slut, George dearest.'

Mallet smiled. 'I know an amazing amount about a great many people.'

For example, he thought secretly, how you came home early last night with your shirt-front black with blood. But Bolsover waved away the remark.

'Women are sewers. I have yet to meet one who wasn't. I dine my German here tonight, by the way.'

'The gallant Colonel. You might tell me: how did he come by his extraordinary wounds?'

'By standing too close to the flames.' Bolsover laughed, lumbering to his feet. 'That is his unhappy story. One must be nimble, George. Fearless, of course. But nimble!'

Vircow-Ucquart was indeed an awful sight, even when disguised in evening dress. It took courage to look him in his remaining eye and to ignore the ancient ruination of the rest of his face. He sat at table with a ramrod back, breaking a bread roll with blunt fingers.

'Never again a thing such as last night, Freddie,' he warned in a booming whisper, even before he picked up his soup spoon. Bolsover laughed.

'Don't be so foolish. Life is appetite, or it is nothing.'

'But I must tell you –'

'Must? *Must?* You are overreaching yourself, my dear. We are not on the parade ground now; and while I find some of your orders thrilling, you will confine them to the bedroom. Or some dark Teutonic wood. A shooting lodge, perhaps, tended by a pretty boy of both our choosing.'

Vircow-Ucquart realized tardily that his host was already too drunk to eat.

'You have caused our Oxford friend a great deal of anxiety,' he grumbled.

'Do you know what?' Bolsover said suddenly. 'This is a very boring topic. I do not tolerate being spoken of behind my back and I will not be told what I must and must not do. The waiter's name is Charles. He will see to your meal. Good evening to you.'

And with that he pushed back his chair with the greatest possible show of petulance and stalked from the room. Vircow-Ucquart was left with a spoonful of soup halfway to his lips. He laid it back into his plate and wiped his mouth. Mallet appeared as if from nowhere.

'Dear, dear,' he sniggered. 'Whatever can have upset him?'

Bella was also engaged for supper that night but made a small detour into the Strand, having the cab drop her off at Fleur de Lys Court. There was still plenty of light left in the sky and the evening was balmy. The cabbie watched her walk into the narrow entrance of the court, interested enough to produce a low whistle. It was not the most obvious destination for a well-set-up judy in a sweeping lilac dress. But no sooner had she disappeared than a bully-boy of a man came out and hauled himself into the cab.

'Bit of a to-do in there, is there, guvnor?'

'Parrot,' the man said obscurely. 'Take me up to Holborn.'

'A parrot, you say?'

'Listen,' the new fare said with dangerous reasonableness, 'just drive the bloody horse.'

Fleur de Lys Court was small and dark, the walls plastered with advertising. Nobody lived there. What had once been artisan hovels were now lock-up premises. Two were empty, their windows so filthy that little of anything could be seen inside. Three more were offices, of a kind.

Pushing past a gaggle of ragged onlookers, all of them gazing upwards, Bella came across Captain Quigley, who nodded to her, his brown teeth clamped on a reeking cigar.

'There is your problem,' he explained, pointing. 'The bird has been chained at the leg and when it flitted, took the chain with it. Which we now see tangled in the bars of old Solomon's top window.'

Quigley: troubled, uncertain, a blustering man with an actor's painful facetiousness. In his own way of describing it (but only as it applied to others) a classic fourpenny-bit. Twenty or more years ago he had been thrown from a troop transport on his way to the Crimea, pitched over the rail by his disgusted comrades. So ended a private soldier's service that had lasted just nineteen weeks, from the time he turned up drunk at Dover Barracks to flying arse over tip into the inky dark of the Mediterranean. That was Quigley's principal absurdity. He was as much a Captain of Dragoons as Bella was a Chinese washerwoman.

Forty feet above the ground, yet more securely fastened than ever it had been in the public of the Duke of Connaught, the parrot alternately flapped upwards with frantic wingbeats and swung exhausted and upside down like a green clock pendulum. Little feathers drifted down and were caught by street Arabs with outstretched hands.

'O' course, it could have been a cow,' the Captain chuckled, who was not supposed to know where Bella had been that day. But then that was his value to her – his unsleeping interference in other people's business.

'What can be done for the creature?' Bella asked with as much haughtiness as she could muster.

'They have sent for Hampsy, the egg collector. Nimble youth, cleft palate, ginger hair, lives across the river by the Shot Tower. Can climb cliffs of all sizes. Collects eggs for the gentry, who take him to Scotland and other parts.'

'He's going to climb Solomon's warehouse?' Bella asked.

'He's fearless but he's not the human fly. Nah. Boost him up on to the tiles and have him shinny down a rope of some kind.'

He waved his arm at the crowd, indicating that it was this they had come to see. Standing to one side was old Solomon himself, swamped by an ankle-length overcoat that had once been a fashionable dove grey. Though it was his property on which the parrot was entangled, it never occurred to anyone to ask him to walk up to the top floor of his premises and open or smash the window.

'Which he never would, no-how,' Captain Quigley explained. 'Useless to ask him, point firmly established. Not a Christian. Understood.'

The previous night, a young prostitute called Welsh Alice had been found with her throat cut behind some scaffolding in Maiden Lane, only a hundred yards away. Her murder had not created half the excitement generated by the parrot – in fact, even now one of the prime suspects was among the crowd shouting advice and encouragement to the bird.

Bella might have watched longer but when a small girl crouched and extruded a pale, glistening turd almost at her feet, one that curled as it fell, she grimaced, struck the man in front of her with her green parasol and pushed her way deeper into the Court, where lay the door to an office.

'Or Temple of Vanities,' Quigley smirked cheerfully, opening the sticking door for her by throwing his shoulder against the woodwork. His supper lay on the topmost page of a heap of manuscript in the centre of a good, once excellent rosewood table.

'You and I must come to a reckoning,' Bella cried, vexed.

'Who is this talking now – Mrs Bella Wallis? Or that mighty wordsmith, Henry Ellis Margam?'

Bella winced. Though he liked to fancy himself as arch, Quigley had all the finesse of a coal hammer.

'Why not take a megaphone and shout that name up and down the Strand?'

For that was the secret she had withheld from Philip Westland, the one that Henry Pattison could not have guessed at in a hundred years. She was indeed Henry Ellis Margam, writer of sensational novels.

It happened that both men had read a Margam novel. Westland had skimmed a few chapters and thrown his copy into the sea with an indulgent laugh. Pattison read his in a first-class railway carriage, feeling uncomfortable stirrings in the trouser department. Asking cautiously around at his club, he discovered this was by no means unusual.

'Piffle, of course,' the aged and decrepit General Chalmers observed, 'but then you have to hand it to the fellow. He knows women.'

Margam was one of those lucky authors whose reputation grows by stealth. Only a very few people in London knew of his real identity and Bella had never heard his name mentioned by readers otherwise only too anxious to discuss, for example, Wilkie Collins. Bella had once heard Collins described with reverence as a troubled aspen: Henry Ellis Margam was, by comparison, hardly more troubled than a trench of asparagus. He wrote fluently and expressively about sex and betrayal, money and lust as it affected the kind of men – and the readers were nearly always men – who came from Bella's own class. In that one narrow sense, the stories were high-flying adventures; and they had their own eerie style. But they made no pretensions to literature and this was the greatest part of their appeal. They were guilty pleasures for gentlemen who associated pleasure with guilt.

'Quigley, I employ you with more or less cheerfulness,' Bella said now. 'But sometimes your impudence can go too far.'

'My dear madam,' Quigley blustered, clearing his plate by the simple expedient of tossing the ruined contents through the front door. 'Your secret is safe with me. And I ask myself sometimes – in fact, I'll ask myself now – who sought out who? Did I come round your gaff in Orange Street begging for help? I think not. So don't go topping it the society lady, oh no, no thank you. I am here to oblige Henry Ellis Margam. I flatter myself I have done that great weaver of dreams some service.'

'This is his office,' Bella countered. 'His – my – place of work.'

'I understand.'

'I wonder sometimes if you do,' she said, fanning the door to remove the frowst of the Captain's overnight occupancy. Quigley, the great baby of the world, did her the honour of blushing. A thought occurred to her, producing a smile. Pattison, coming across Captain Quigley anywhere at all on his rolling acres, would have despatched him, left and right barrels, without a second thought.

'You have found some humour in our situation,' the Captain suggested.

'This is the smile of quiet desperation.'

'Poetry!' Captain Quigley exclaimed gallantly.

There was a sudden joyous shout from outside. The simpleton boy Hampsy had arrived on Solomon's roof and was hanging upside down from the gutters, his ratty face cracked open by a grin.

'A guinea says he breaks his neck,' a sporting parson up from Wiltshire cried. But then his foot slipped on something soft and upon examining his boot he found he had stepped a fraction too far into the exciting life of the London poor. He retreated into the Strand, wiping his feet on the flagstones, the sweat of humiliation wetting his back and belly.

Henry Ellis Margam derived his plots from weak men like Henry Pattison, whom he turned into monsters of depravity. His work attracted no serious reviews and the books sold by word of mouth – sold in their thousands. His readers shared a common itch. As a genre, sensationalist fiction depended upon weary devices like heirs hidden away at birth, octoroon Misses who dabbled in voodoo, wills that cast down the villain and raised in his place the remittance man roaming the veldt. The women in these stories were termagant foreigners who were discovered to be dead shots with a pistol; titled society whores; girls hardly out of their childhood tied to trees by ropes that bit into their firm young flesh.

What Margam could do was realize these fantasies and locate them. He could scratch the itch. That Mexican beauty with the cruel mouth and pearl-handled pistol, for example. Was she not unlike the sulky Italian woman glimpsed at Harrogate, strolling in the grounds of the Old Swan Hotel? The fictional Lady Witney was surely the actual Lady Eynsham, the hateful snob who once cut the reader's wife stone dead at a charity dinner? As for the damsel in distress with her hands tied behind her, every man with a daughter felt a shameful prod at her predicament. It was Celia semi-naked, watched through the bathroom keyhole by a daddy with sweating palms.

Very, very few of Margam's readers imagined that the book they held in their hand was written by a woman. Nor that the story began its life in a dusty and largely sunless courtyard off the Strand. Margam was a bookseller in Tetbury. He was an attaché at the Paris Embassy. He was a hopeless alcoholic hanging on by his fingertips in Constantinople. He was almost anybody but Mrs Bella Wallis.

FOUR

'WELL, AND DID the boy fall?' the ancient and papery Lord Broxtowe wanted to know. His lordship was entertaining Bella that same night at dining rooms in a far kinder part of London. The surroundings fitted the old man perfectly, for it was the kind of place that lay off the beaten track and persisted in a decidedly old-fashioned way of going on. Among the diners there was hardly anyone younger than sixty and they ate their chops and fresh peas in an almost sepulchral gloom. The oak wainscotting smelled agreeably of many coatings of beeswax, the first laid down in the days when that monster Napoleon mastered Europe.

'The boy survived,' Bella smiled. 'The parrot died of shock, however.'

'Poor creature,' his lordship whispered, flicking his thumb out from his closed fist a few times. And then shrugged humorously, his faded blue eyes fixed fast on Bella's face.

'What great adventures you have,' the old man said. 'What life there is in *your* life.'

'Fie, my lord,' she reproached him.

Bella sometimes wondered whether Lord Broxtowe, whose estates were in Yorkshire, was not above a little slumming when he came to town, and whether she was not a part of those pleasures. On the other hand, he treated her with the effortless manners of an earlier age and would have been horrified to hear her voice what she occasionally thought.

'And tell me,' he asked. 'How does it stand with the agricultural fellow? Mr Pattison?'

'He has gone home to his rolling acres.'

'Which are not inconsiderable, together with a pretty little house and deer park. But I cannot say you have missed a trick there. His conversation is all cogs and drive-shafts. We met at Bowood once.'

'I had no idea you knew of our connection, however slight.'

'My dear child, a musical soirée is nothing if it is not a rumour mill. Lady Cornford was quite sure you were made for one another.'

'That was forward of her. I hardly know the gentleman.'

'Then it is a story about Cissie Cornford,' Lord Broxtowe said with a smile. 'I do seriously mistrust a woman of her advanced years who keeps up with pale mauve mittens.'

They regarded each other very fondly across the table and on an impulse she reached out and sought his papery hand.

'What a friend you are,' she murmurred.

'And you a most beautiful woman, Bella,' he returned.

Broxtowe was much nearer eighty than seventy. He had inherited from his uncle at the age of fourteen, when George IV was on the throne. Broxtowe Hall, where, as he put it, he rattled around, was set in a dale painted by

Turner. In one particular work by the artist, if one peered through what seemed like a gale of sleet lit by a sudden explosion of red in the sky – 'rather like the reflection of the accursed Bradford getting its comeuppance' – if one stared intently enough, the Hall could be seen in the low foreground as a liquid slash of grey.

'The fellow came to stay with us while he was daubing, you know,' he mused aloud. 'I have seen blind beggars with stronger eyesight.'

'Turner?' Bella guessed, well used to her friend's habit of continuing in speech what a second before had been a private reverie. Broxtowe smiled.

'How clever you are, how good for me. Tell me what is troubling you.'

'Margam is troubling me.'

He looked up sharply.

'You haven't told this Pattison fellow –?'

'No, of course not.' Bella smiled. 'You and perhaps half a dozen others know the identity of Henry Ellis Margam. Some through necessity. And some –' she inclined her head towards him – 'for other and better reasons.'

'I saw a parson on the train yesterday. He was reading *Lady Nugent's Letter* with the greatest enthusiasm. A mere boy in appearance, though I thought he blushed prettily.'

He summoned the waiter by a lift of his eyebrow.

'Your lordship?'

'A second bottle of the hock if you will, Joe. And perhaps, in a little while, a plate of glazed pears.'

Broxtowe studied his companion amiably.

'This is Margam's seventh novel, I believe.'

'Curse him.'

'Some say he is a well-placed member of the government, some a bitter old stick like me. I have never met anyone that supposes he is the invention of the remarkable woman I see before me now.'

'He is just another novelist.'

'But what a fellow, all the same. In his latest, Lady Nugent is perfectly recognizable but who else could have invented Henshawe, the implacable Henshawe? What a grudge the man has! And what a place to nurture it, working half naked in the opal mines, coming out only to have his eyes ruined by the cruel Australian sunlight. Those blue spectacles! Spinning in the mill-race below Nugent Hall!'

Bella laughed.

'I like what you write,' Broxtowe protested equably. 'Fellow tried to sell me some French pornography once. It's very poor stuff, you know. I always think about pornography that it only works in certain situations. For example, discovering a single copy of some lubricious convent doings hidden away in the Dean of Windsor's library would be wonderful. One such work is always profoundly erotic, wherever you come across it. Yet two or more are, as I say, dull.'

'I would not know.'

'Stuff!' Broxtowe retorted. 'The thing about Mr Margam's work is that the stories are strictly – how shall we say – improper but they uncover and identify the evil in society. You are a moralist, Bella.'

She considered, her hand still in his. If London society were to be believed, her friend had not been completely untouched by sin in the days of his youth, sin redder than any pillar box. Only his great wealth had protected him then. Now extreme old age placed him beyond reproach.

'I write these books in the first instance for pleasure,' she murmured. 'You are kind to say they have a moral dimension. Yet were my husband still to be alive . . .'

'Oh yes,' Broxtowe said with a kindly smile. 'Things would be very different for you, I am sure. I am sorry never to have met him.'

There was a delicate pause. Just once had he asked her a direct question about who Garnett Wallis was and how he had died. But even to him she refused to divulge even the slightest information. The two friends sat back as Joe the waiter brought them their bottle.

Bella defused the slight embarrassment caused by the direction the conversation had taken. 'Were you really able to guess at the true identity of Lady Nugent?' she asked.

'I met the original at a ball in York quite recently. She is of course furious with the infamous Margam, enough to have engaged private detectives to hunt him down. I directed her attention to a rather squalid set of rooms in Paris. And a man who had been turned out as a butler in Eaton Square some five years since.'

Bella laughed.

'It is you who should be the fictionalist.'

'No, but such a man *was* shown the door by the Countess of Thame and *does* now live in Paris. La Nugent thanked me profusely and rushed home to set her myrmidons on his trail. I should imagine he is having the cravat applied liberally to his back at this very moment.'

'What is his name?'

'Burrell. Born for the horsewhip.'

His keen blue eyes studied hers.

'There is more. A poor fellow called Hearnshaw but not Henshawe has resigned his commission in the Kent Militia and fled the country into Germany. Unluckily for him, he bragged to his fellow officers once too often about owning shares in an opal mine in Cooperpedie. They took him to be the remorseless devil who drove Lady Nugent's daughter into the madhouse.'

'Oh fie!' Bella exclaimed. 'By appearing to the girl as half-man, half-lizard? Are people so very credulous?'

'When it touches their own dark desires, yes. Who would not secretly wish to be the Henshawe of the tale, gazing down on the virginal Lydia Nugent, her breast rising and falling with such palpable innocence?'

'Palpable was good,' Bella admitted, blushing.

'All London has heard of Mr Philip Hearnshaw and his daemonic lust, so thinly disguised in name by that sensational novelist, Mr Henry Margam.'

'Poor devil.'

'A member of the Garrick,' Broxtowe sniffed.

Bella said nothing to this because if the truth were told she was already acquainted with Hearnshaw's fate. When she told the very few people who knew of her second life that she wrote for pleasure, she did not add that part of that pleasure was to do down her enemies. In this instance there was enough of Hearnshaw in Henshawe to seal his fate: his tattooed arm, his laundress mother, his touchiness when it came to matters of social slight. A dozen tiny details confirmed him as the model for a fictional character who came halfway round the world to seduce a mother and her daughter in a frenzy of lust.

'You have not yet said why you are out of love with the estimable novelist,' Broxtowe prompted gently.

'Making parsons blush is all too easy,' Bella said.

The Fifth Earl seldom laughed out loud, but when he did it sounded like a musical peal.

'The real Lady Nugent, as we might term her, prostituted an ugly and not very intelligent daughter for the chance to acquire a coal pit in Derbyshire. I would say a handsome cloak of fiction was thrown over these poor details. Is that so very easy?'

'Easier than you think.'

'Maybe so,' Broxtowe said. He laid his spoon gently on the rim of the plate in the old-fashioned manner. When he sat back, his face was disturbingly out of the light, so that she could not read his expression.

'You are disgusted by Margam, Bella. And you think it demeaning in some way to stamp your foot on such cockroaches as Hearnshaw. I think not. Mr Margam is an important man. What does he look like, by the by?'

'Small,' Bella said, who had given the matter some thought. 'Small and plump, like Napoleon. Earnest. Pontificating. With hands like a mole. You would not wish to touch the dampness of his skin, nor to breathe the roaring stink that comes out of his clothes. Not the gentleman, Broxtowe.'

'Does he have to be a gentleman at all?' his lordship objected, but in such a reflective way that the remark followed her home.

*

The house in Orange Street welcomed her and calmed her nerves. Its principal room was papered blue-grey, a colour that reminded Bella of France, interrupted by gilt-framed oils, none of them contemporary and all rescued from the sort of dealers known to Captain Quigley – that is to say, stolen, or in the Captain's more neutral way of putting it, recently acquired.

At the end of the drawing room were windows that framed a huge and sprawling fig, suggesting secret gardens beyond. But in truth, this foliage concealed a blank wall only a few feet from the end of the property and the fig's stem rose from an ancient pavement of broken York stone. The screen of green she looked out on now was, Bella acknowledged with a sigh, yet another deception. She flung herself into a chair and kicked off her shoes.

And so she slept, until roused by the click of the door latch. Standing on the threshold was her companion and perhaps the consolation of her life, Marie Claude d'Anville. Nearly twenty years younger than Bella, hardly more than five feet tall, Marie Claude was in her nightgown, her hair braided into a single plait.

'Where have you been?' the girl asked with her habitual downturned lips.

'Don't be angry,' Bella chided.

'This is not the way to be happy,' Marie Claude said.

And Bella laughed, jumping up to embrace her in the doorway.

'This way of life? The habit of sleeping in chairs? Before I left him tonight, Lord Broxtowe sent you his love. And that made me very happy. Come, Marie Claude. Look into my face. Do you not see a happy woman?'

'You are hard to love.'

'Ah well,' Bella said. 'That is a completely different matter.'

Captain Quigley had made some efforts to tidy the office – in fact, his employer caught him sweeping it out with a borrowed broom, billows of dust at his feet. Moreover, he was wearing the better of his two tunic jackets and a pair of canvas trousers that concertina-ed slightly less than usual. Bella peered. The gallant Captain had shaved, or been shaved, the razor skirting his mutton-chop whiskers and greying moustache. His skin glistened red.

'There is work,' he explained briefly. 'The cove they took up last night for Welsh Alice's murder has been released. Boiler-plate alibi. Was in Poplar the night of the crime, having been run over by a dray. Eight witnesses, one of them a justice of the peace.'

'What was he doing in Poplar?'

'Drinking,' Quigley said.

'And how is this become work for us?'

The Captain fiddled in his tunic pocket and produced a leather cigar case. He passed it to her with an elaborate flourish. It was empty, save for half a dozen green breast feathers.

'And how did the police miss this?'

'On account it was nicked by the first to arrive at the scene.'

'Who was?'

Quigley whistled, as if for a dog. After a moment or two, the same little girl who had defecated at her feet the previous day appeared. She was clutching in both arms a ruined applewood crate. Bella peered. Inside were a handful of crushed and mangled potatoes and a single carrot.

'What is your name?'

'Can't speak,' Quigley advised. 'Has spoken, used to speak. But not now. A good girl, however. Name of Betsy.'

'You've been shopping, Betsy.'

'Scratting. Up at the market. Gutter work,' the Captain explained.

'And this little case you found. It's for your treasures, is it? Like the parrot feathers?'

Betsy nodded.

'And where did you find it?'

To point, she had to set down her gleanings from the Covent Garden gutters. Her stick-like arm indicated the general direction of Maiden Lane, where the body had been discovered. Quigley caught Bella's eye.

'Story stands up. Found the body, found the case, ran into the Strand, found a bluebottle. Subsequent hue and cry. Betsy bunked off. Smart girl,' he added approvingly.

Bella tipped the feathers into the palm of her hand. A small gilt crest became apparent, embossed in the bottom of the case.

'Just so,' Captain Quigley observed quietly.

'Do you recognize it?'

The Captain shrugged. 'I thought you might. Now this here Betsy was wondering if you would like to buy her cigar case for a consideration. And o' course, somewhere new to keep her feathers.'

'Well now, would this sweetie tin be a good place to keep them safe?'

Betsy held out her hand. Depicted on the lid of the tin a child no older than herself stood by a sundial, surrounded by lupins. A little way off an indulgent grandfather stood with a hoe in his hand. We were in Mummersetshire, where things are ordered differently.

'What do you say, Betsy?'

'That, and a florin. Made up of little silver joeys,' Quigley proposed, ruffling the urchin's hair.

'And how long would she hang on to that?' Bella wondered.

For answer, Betsy spat in both palms and held her dukes up, chin bristling.

'I am not a police reporter,' Bella said, an hour or so later. She was feeling sour: something in the way Quigley cosseted her was proving repellent. But the Captain knew her moods and lounged against the doorpost, picking his teeth with a bristle from the broom.

'Have you told the French Missie about Lieutenant Hearnshaw?' he asked, opening a new line of conversation.

'Not yet.' Something in his expression alerted her. 'Why? Is there further news?'

'Tried to blow his brains out in Germany. Missed, took off an ear and most of his jaw. In quarters now at Brussels. Very low.'

Bella's eyes glittered.

'How many times has Quigley offered to fight your fights for you?' the Captain asked gently. 'I would have cut the young gentleman so that he never walked again, leave alone presented arms down a dark alley to a respectable young Frenchwoman. Your way better. The living death of literature. Excellent. But it's taking something out of you, dear lady.'

'Will he live?' Bella asked.

'After a fashion.'

She rose and paced the room for a moment or two, her hands trembling.

'Are you my conscience now, Quigley?'

'We must hope not.'

'But this is about Welsh Alice, all the same?'

'I draw your attention to it, is all.'

'I knew nothing about her in life,' she muttered. 'Was she an honest, kindly girl?'

'She was a shilling whore. But who followed her out of the market and slit her throat, just because he thought he could?'

Bella considered and then held out her hand for the cigar case with the armorial crest. Quigley was right: it was work, of a kind. Her books always began with a modest discovery, like walking into a dark and trackless forest and finding a single pearl earring hanging from a twig. That was the opening scene of *Belinda Hetherington*, which, for the purposes of the plot, took place in Ceylon, an island Bella had never visited. The earring was her own, however, and the villain whose vanity and sexual cruelty was unmasked by its discovery was equally real.

FIVE

FRANCE: BOULOGNE. THE tide has filled and the Gare Maritime is afflicted with the smoke that announces the arrival of the packet from England. The best hotels have sent carriages to the landing stage; humbler citizens who have rooms to let are jostling each other at the foot of the gangway.

It is midday. By standing order of the garrison commander, Lieutenant Mercier has marched a file of soldiers out from the post guarding the Bassin Loubet. It is exercise for them and a mild demonstration of the might of the Third Republic to the flustered and ill-tempered rosbifs who are alighting from Folkestone.

From Mercier's point of view it is also an utter waste of time, as well as an insult to his rank. He has written the adjutant three letters on the subject. To show the might of the Republic it would surely be better to have a mounted officer at the head of the column? The adjutant is his cousin and generously overlooks the tone of these letters, in one of which Mercier complains of being made to walk about like a postman.

Colonel Duprat, the garrison commander, takes a different view: he dislikes his junior officers almost as much as he detests his posting. While Mercier trudges back to his post on foot, Duprat sips an anis and leafs through a book on the antiquities of Asia Minor. Examining himself at the shaving mirror that morning, he has concluded he is still a devilish handsome man, even if one without immediate prospects of promotion. He lays aside his book and lights a Turkish cigarette.

The novels of Henry Ellis Margam were published by the firm of Naismith & Frean in a list that included the ramblings of Indian Army veterinary surgeons; grim old men who understood the workings of the Lunacy Laws; and pederastical schoolmasters. Composite title: *Diseases of the Young Mind in Tropical Climates, by an Army Surgeon*. The fiction in the catalogue, until the partners discovered Bella, was likewise on the whimsical side. For sixteen years past, a Mrs Toaze-Bonnett had supplied an annual story of the American Plains, peopled by such characters as Old Seth, Sheriff Jinks, and the mysterious and shape-changing Redstick Indian, Dancing Feet.

It was always broodingly hot in Mrs Toaze-Bonnett's world and the rattlesnakes exhibited more impudence in her pages than ever they do in life. In *Tall Tales from Tolliver Creek*, Jim Dalloway astonishes the company at a church social by shooting the knitting bag out from under Lilian Fairbrother's chair. The despicable fortune hunter Colonel Mortimer is all for having Jim horsewhipped there and then but when the tapestry bag is opened, a rattler is revealed coiled in Lilian's skeins of wool. Romance ensues. 'I'm a rough diamond,' Jim explains, 'but many a second son has turned out likewise.'

The cheerful and undemanding Naismith, who oversaw the outpourings of Mrs Toaze-Bonnett's pen, dropped dead under the Euston Arch one frosty morning on his way to see the lady, who lived at Pinner. The surviving partner, the much more various Elias Frean, retreated, as he had always planned, to a house a little way from Boulogne. There he lived alone, save for a young male companion of lissom good looks. And to that place, before the commencement of any new Henry Ellis Margam novel, he liked to summon Bella Wallis.

Though in the fullness of his years, Frean was no taller than a child. His bald head and beaked nose gave him an unwanted resemblance to the handle of a lady's umbrella – was he ever likely to forgive General Sir George Milman's supposition that he slept for the most part in the hall, with walking sticks for companions? Bella liked him for his incurable avarice. Even among publishers, he was stinginess personified.

'You stay at the Boule d'Or, I believe?'

'As always, Mr Frean.'

His chuckle was that of a glass being emptied of stale water.

'Decidedly expensive. Ruinously so. But then, ah yes, the artistic temperament . . .'

They were smoking Dutch cheroots either side of an octagonal rattan table on which lay the firm's most recent publications, all too obviously unread. Frean had an uncertain taste when it came to interior design: the little table was of a piece with several huge fretted vessels in brass and a low-relief panel depicting native boys swimming. The floor was scattered with Baluchistan rugs. There were three sofas, so low to the ground that only the most romantic of minds would consider abandoning themselves to them.

Though he would have died to admit it, Frean was a little in awe of his top-selling author. Bustiman's *A Young Boy's Make-up* had sold well year on year – to a largely disappointed readership – but its sales figures were as nothing to the novels of Henry Ellis Margam. Frean had accidentally struck gold – and if he tiptoed around the problem of keeping Bella sweet, it was not just that he was, on the whole, a woman hater. After all, he knew next to nothing about the sex and had never, in a long life, seen one naked. What made Frean nervous was that he was dealing with intellect, something a decent publishing house avoided like the plague.

'You have an idea for your next book?' he suggested, after the usual civilities. Bella passed him the cigar case from Maiden Lane.

'Ha!' he cried, inspecting the crest within, 'what people won't do for armorial bearings. In my day the government was right to raise tax on them. Have you taken this to the College of Arms, at all?'

'I have not. The case was found on a gentleman murdered in Maiden Lane a fortnight since. His assassin was a young woman called Alice Protheroe.'

Bella watched him closely. It was her habit to take actual events and twist them to her purpose. The poor drab known as Welsh Alice had thus become a governess newly returned from India and the man who killed her was reinvented as the victim. It seemed unlikely that Frean, preoccupied with his life in Boulogne, would know of the real events witnessed by the mute girl, Betsy. And so it proved.

'And this is your plot?'

'It is the opening to my story,' Bella corrected.

'What is the name of this gentleman?'

'I propose to call him Colonel Abbs.'

'Oh, a very bad name for a soldier. Oh dear, no.'

'You may have a better suggestion.'

'He should be called Luckhurst,' Frean said at once. 'Or possibly Luckless. Luckless is good. He too is from India? I do hope he isn't from India.'

'From Bad Gastein. Where he has a small set of rooms in the Hotel d'Angleterre.'

She watched Frean's lips move, as though he were chewing on the idea and had discovered a morsel of gristle. He shrugged.

'And how did the lady do for him?'

'With a hatpin to the carotid artery. Only an expert could have been sure of her mark.'

Frean touched his own neck with fluttering fingers.

'Well,' he muttered.

'That is how the story begins,' Bella concluded briskly. 'I am looking for my usual terms, Mr Frean. You may have the manuscript six months from today's date.'

'Yes, but a governess,' he objected. 'I'm not sure –'

'Miss Protheroe is merely the instrument of someone else's vengeance. Someone of an even darker hue.'

'And who might that be?'

But Bella understood the workings of a publisher's mind only too well. Captain Quigley had once summed up the ideal strategy for meetings like this: go in, make your pitch and leave. It was a lesson learned from his own dealings with the police and other authorities.

'Relevant papers lodged at Chatham. Their business to trace. Material witness now in lodgings at Portsmouth. Statements must be sought. Always remember, dear lady, the more you explain, the more you have to explain.'

With these wise words from an expert echoing in her ears, Bella held out her hand for the cigar case. Frean hung on to it, peering closely at the crest.

'If you will send your standard contract to the hotel for signature,' she pressed gently, 'I shall be in Boulogne one more afternoon. I leave for England tomorrow morning.'

'Yes, but – this vexing little detail here –'

'It is my experience, as it is yours, that the world is filling up with false coats of arms. We can say, if you like, this particular one is the invention of Colonel Abbs. Or Luckless.'

But Frean was by no means as stupid as he sometimes appeared.

'Colonel Luckless, as I understand it, is a figment of your fecund imagination. However, this cigar case exists in the real world. And, according to you, was found at the scene of an actual murder. Or have I misunderstood you?'

'No,' Bella said slowly. 'All that is true.'

'Then, would it not be helpful to know whose crest it is?'

He picked up a copper cowbell and shook it. After a minute or so, his companion Pardew glided into the room. Bella gawped. The Oriental décor had got to Billy Pardew in a big way: he was wearing a clinging muslin gown and had dyed his hair a marmalade orange. His fingernails were painted silver.

'Mrs Wallis,' he lisped. 'How lovely. I see you come up the path from my bedroom.'

The last time she had seen the light of Frean's life, he was a faintly podgy youth in white flannels and a rowing vest. Clearly, he was now striking out on his own. When he reached for Bella's hand it was to bow low, kiss it lightly and then lay the back of it against his forehead.

'How nice to see you again, Mr Pardew,' she murmured.

'Should you like some iced sherbet?' he asked solicitously.

'I think not. Is that henna on your feet?'

He plucked up the hem of his gown.

'These are my henna socks,' he giggled. 'Mr Frean disapproves. Don't you, Mr Frean?'

'Billy, tell us what you can about this,' his master muttered, passing him the cigar case. 'The crest therein.'

Pardew opened the case and peered, a half-smile on his luscious lips.

'Well, blow me,' he exclaimed. 'Ancient heraldry. Or perhaps not so ancient. I don't think we'd see *this* on a knight's shield. Dear me, no.'

'You recognize it?'

'Well, I'm not exactly Garter King of Arms, am I!' he shrilled. 'It rings a bell, Mrs Wallis, I'll say no more than that. It stirs a memory. But now you're making me blush.'

'You *should* blush,' Frean said. 'I have seen this crest before. To be bold about it, on a pair of cufflinks you have in your room, from a time before you took to henna socks.'

'Oh!' Billy cried petulantly. 'My room is my room, I thought we agreed. Have you taken to snooping again, Mr Frean? Have you no trust at all left in you? Fie and for shame!'

Bella wondered why Frean had never taken this impudent telegram boy, as he was in former life, and chained him to the wall with his feet in a bucket of scorpions.

'Either you do recognize it or you don't,' she said tersely.

For a second, all the play actor in Pardew disappeared and he looked at her with a flash of his old aboriginal self. He turned away and minced out of the room.

'*He* is not the man we're looking for,' Frean laughed uncertainly.

'I imagine not,' Bella snapped.

'These cufflinks –'

'You need not explain how he came by them.'

It was a remark she immediately wished she could take back: Frean's face crumpled. When she took a step towards him, he flapped his hand and turned his back on her.

She caught up with Billy on the terrace, where his muslin gown was flattened against his body by the wind. He stood under a trellis, his henna-ed feet plunged into white and pink rose petals. He pouted sulkily.

'I don't have to tell you nothing, I believe, Mrs Wallis.'

'You have already told me something, you little fool. Whose crest is it?'

He chewed on his lower lip, trying to think his way past the yawning pit that lay in his path.

'I seen something similar on the arch over a door in Oxford once.'

'A college?'

'Big house. Just happened to notice it. In passing.'

'Of course.'

'You're wondering if I'm telling you the truth.'

'I am wondering whether to box your ears.'

'A very cool remark, I must say.'

'An arch over a doorway?'

'I just told you.'

'And the cufflinks?'

'You don't own me, neither of you,' Pardew screeched. 'It is the same crest that I seen over the door. While I was waiting for a gentleman.'

'The crest wasn't his?'

'Him!' he hooted. 'I should say so, I don't think! And now I've said all I'm going to say.'

Bella raked him with one last glance and then walked back indoors to say goodbye to Frean. His head barely came as high as her chest and his hand, when it was offered, had the touch of forest mushrooms. Bella resisted a mischievous impulse to further ruin his morning by hugging him.

'My best regards to Mademoiselle d'Anville,' Frean whispered, peering up past her bust at her grave and composed face. Unconsciously, but still horrible for all that, he licked his lips. 'Such a pretty little thing.'

'I shall be sure to tell her so,' Bella replied.

'And as for Billy, I shall speak sharply to him, you may bank on it.'

'You would do better to kick his backside.'

She walked away down his gravel path, her parasol on her shoulder. There was a view of a sea no more troubled than a silk bedsheet. The French flag wagged over the roof of the *mairie* and somewhere a band was playing airs from Suppé. In that instant, she resolved to cashier Colonel Abbs, or Luckless. By the time the manuscript was delivered,

Frean would have forgotten all about him. The very idea of soldiers disgusted her more than she could say.

The walk back into Boulogne lay along a modest enough esplanade with the sea on one side and houses like Mr Frean's on the other. In places, the way was paved and in others last year's high tides had dumped drifts of sand that were churned to a powdery grey. Holidaymakers walked out here for the very French thrill of being at least ten minutes from a decent restaurant: there were a few telescopes flourished at the fishing boats coming on the tide. A rich papa with a mahogany and brass plate camera was trying to arrange a photograph of his wife and daughter and pleading with mama to look less like a fisherwoman with a grudge against life. Out of courtesy, Bella stopped for a moment to allow him to expose his plate.

Standing in her path, his hat hanging loose in his hand, was a pale man she could see at a glance was English. There was something about the abject modesty with which he acknowledged her, his silver hair unkempt and ruffled by the breeze, his eyes soft and downcast, that tugged at Bella's memory. When he saw that she did not immediately recognize him, he smiled ruefully.

'Charles Urmiston, Mrs Wallis,' he murmured. 'I knew your husband a little.'

Bella let out a sharp and genuine little cry and extended her hand.

'What must you think of me, Mr Urmiston?' she exclaimed. 'My mind was quite elsewhere.'

Look at the boots if you want to find a gentleman's balance at the bank, was one of Captain Quigley's rules of thumb. Urmiston was wearing ridiculously yellow boots, their toes scuffed. His suit was in a too loud, far too ancient check and the collar to his shirt rumpled and none too clean. Bella guessed that each item, even down to the shirt, had come from the Caledonian Market.

'And Mrs Urmiston? How is she?' she asked, remembering a tall thin woman with a long nose, on whom her husband doted.

'She had such fond memories of Boulogne. And asked to be brought here in her final illness. I buried her yesterday,' he added, his voice trembling. He looked into Bella's face with such sweet simplicity that now she had him. This ruined man had once been a land agent to the Great Western Railway, with a pretty house on Campden Hill and a carriage of his own. There was some story of a calamitous court case, the details of which she could not bring to the front of her mind.

'Mr Urmiston, my husband had such high opinions of you both. I am deeply grieved to hear of your loss. Where do you stay in London?'

'Just at the moment, I am across the river in Lambeth,' he replied uneasily.

'And whereabouts, particularly?'

'Does it matter?' he asked with a feeble spark of testiness. But then repented, blushing.

'Do you know the Black Prince Road?'

Enough to realize you're a man on his uppers, she thought, feeling a hot rush of sympathy. From Campden Hill to Black Prince Road was a journey as painful as falling out of a balloon on to spiked railings.

'I stay at the Boule d'Or here in Boulogne. Will you not walk that way with me? I shall very much like it if we can take lunch together.'

Urmiston plucked at the fabric to his jacket, his eyes filling with tears. Bella immediately understood.

'Come now,' she said, perhaps a little too sharply. 'Friendship does not stand upon the tailoring of a suit. You shall be my guest and we will talk of better times, happier times.'

To her complete dismay, Urmiston turned and ran, an ungainly and clumsy Englishman scattering children in his path. An irate French papa raised his cane and cracked it across the poor man's shoulders. The sob he gave was hideous to hear. He leapt a low wall and landed on hands and knees in dirty sand. People on the beach stopped their promenades to stare at him in amazement.

The rest of the day should have been filled with reflections on the absurd Billy Pardew and his transformation from a frog into an Eastern princess. But instead she could not rid her mind of Charles Urmiston and his flight. Using hotel stationery, she tried to capture the essence of their meeting.

In her fiction, it was generally women who fell from grace. Lucy Akehurst defended Captain Williamson from charges of fraud and embezzlement, only to discover that the plausible captain, with his rolling sea gait and piercing blue eyes, was a pirate when it came to women. She was undone by girlish innocence and the refusal to face facts until it was too late. Hedley Martineau, who might have saved her, drew back at the last moment. Lucy was left high and dry in Alexandria, lodging with Margarita Busoni, her cats and parakeets. Her bedroom window looked out over the souk and when she woke in the morning, her floor was peppered with flowers and little screws of coloured paper. The reader was left in no doubt. If there was a fate worse than death for the guileless Lucy, La Busoni was planning it.

Charles Urmiston was the first man Bella had come across to be so comprehensively unhorsed in the same way. You could not live in London and not meet ruined gentlemen who had gambled away their inheritance or married the wrong woman. Yet by and large their disgrace was softened by the circumstance of their birth. The best houses might refuse them but they had enough cousinage to see them through. Urmiston, by contrast, had no one. Another man, offered a free lunch by an unattached woman, might have leapt at the offer. Urmiston, the gangling fool, had bolted.

Next day, she looked for him on the boat, but he was not to be found.

'Not a college?'

'Billy says not.'

Quigley shrugged. 'That is good for us. That narrows the field.'

'I thought so too,' Bella said.

'Cigar case not a souvenir of happy days spent construing the Greek. Some mutton-chopped old goat at the head of the class. Stained-glass windows and college port. Rowing. Possibly a bit of hunting to hounds. Nothing of that.'

'You know your Oxford,' Bella exclaimed, with as much sarcasm as would sink the average Thames steamer.

'I do,' the Captain acknowledged, blithe.

'Can you find the place that Billy was talking about, however?'

'I should say so,' he replied judiciously. 'It would seem likely. They are slow down there but if a thing is put simply enough, they can be made to understand.'

'There is one other thing before you set off. In Boulogne, I met a man called Urmiston.'

'Yes?' Quigley leered.

'A Mr Charles Urmiston, late of Campden Hill. A gentleman I would like to help.'

To her surprise, the Captain flinched slightly at the name.

'You know him?' she asked, startled.

'This address in Campden Hill: magnolia in the front? Householder some sort of gent with connections to the railway?'

'I believe so.'

'There is a problem.'

'I'd like to know what that is.'

'You have a picture in your house, of a foreign-looking dinah, a bit on the plump side. Not a stitch on her and looking out the window at some palm trees adjacent. With altogether somewhat of a pensive air, you might say.'

Bella passed this painting on the staircase every morning. She stared into Quigley's face, her eyes narrowing with dreadful suspicion.

'And?'

'It belongs to this Urmiston cove.'

'You sold me a stolen painting?'

'Did I say I stole it? I come by it in the normal way.'

'Which is to say theft. Do I have anything else of his acquired in the same way?'

'I was offered the work at a knock-down price –'

'You received stolen goods.'

'This can go on all day,' the Captain blustered. 'I'll hook it out of your gaff before I set off for the dreaming spires.'

'You will have it removed this afternoon. Mr Urmiston was a friend of my late husband. To say I am angry is to understate the case: I am furious.'

'If I was to meet the gentleman and explain an honest mistake –'

'You will have first to find him. He lives somewhere along the Black Prince Road –'

'A neighbourhood known to me,' Quigley supplied hastily. 'I could nip across the river –'

'What is the name of your associate, the cross-eyed man with a horse and cart?'

'Murch.'

'You will find Mr Murch, go to my house and remove that painting. Right now. Indeed, at once.'

'And Black Prince Road?'

'I will attend to that myself.'

It was a little on Quigley's mind to issue a general weather warning about the Borough of Lambeth, as though there it rained soot and disaster; but the pale fury in Bella's face deterred him. Instead of saying anything, he smoothed down his moustaches with one hand, and jingled the change in his pocket with the other. Murch the carter a reliable sort of cove. No art lover, but then again that did not come into it.

SIX

THIS, INCLUDED IN a small parcel franked with French stamps to an address in Oxford, the paper reeking of patchouli, one edge decorated with a henna thumbprint:

Hoping that I find you well and that you remember a cheeky boy you once knew and I hope you have not forgot. Enclosed please find something that I confess might have been nicked from you once though it was done out of desperation. But now I find my circumstances much changed and for the better, the sea air agrees with me, haha! A lady I won't name was round at my domicile asking questions and you can be sure I sent her off with a flea in her ear. Nothing serious but I thought you ought to know. Please don't try to trace me though I know you never would anyway. The moving finger writes and having writ moves on. This green ink is tres joli, n'est pas? From yours A Friend.

Vircow-Ucquart was something of a crack shot. He and Bolsover lay out on the roof of the earl's Berkshire seat, picnicking on chicken and cold lamb cutlets. From time to time, the German applied his one good eye to the back sight of a long-barrelled game rifle, aimed down the lawn and blew another unfortunate rook into eternity. Bolsover was delighted: the birds did not simply expire but became a sudden puff of feathers and guts. They disintegrated.

There were estate workers clustered at one side of the carriage drive, elderly men with veiny arms who were cleaning out the brook that ran alongside.

'Oh how I wish that fucking breech would blow back in his face,' Claude Atkins muttered.

'Why, m' oldun, time hangs heavy when you'm waiting for nightfall.'

'And what happens at nightfall?'

'They turn into them chaps with the sharp teeth.'

'Vampires,' someone supplied.

'Those are the boys. Vampires, hot and strong.'

There was laughter: but it was uneasy. Another shot, another black snowball of feathers and guts.

'If you were to shoot one of those men down there,' Bolsover wondered idly, 'would they make as pretty a mess, do you think?'

'About this, you should not joke,' the German said.

'Would they blow to pieces?'

'Freddie, listen to me. You are wise to come down here to the country. I will find things to amuse you, provided it is done discreetly. But no more London adventures for a while. We live quiet, we eat well, we stay calm.'

'I am always calm,' Bolsover said. 'I leave panic to others. You have been talking to a certain clerical gentleman in Oxford, I detect.'

Vircow-Ucquart frowned.

'He is concerned for you. You would expect as much from an old friend. He has only your well-being at heart.'

'Well, God damn him for his solicitude,' Bolsover shouted.

He snatched up the rifle and levelled it at the German and closed his finger round the trigger. But the weapon was not loaded and all that resulted was a dry click. Lord Bolsover's manic laugh floated out over the lawns and was caught by the estate workers below.

'Now what?' Claude Atkins demanded.

'The Prussian has said something comical, doubtless.'

Bella was in Lambeth. Persuading a cab to cross the river had involved a conference in the cab shelter by the gardens in Leicester Square.

'Money is money,' she protested.

'Lord love you,' an excitable cabbie exclaimed. 'The way we see it, time is money. That is our trade. I say nothing against the people over there – my old woman was one of them, in her day. But you want me to take you there, have me hang about while you make some enquiries and then bring you back. That's going on for two hours. I could be up and down Regent Street a dozen times for that – *and* run a body to Victoria or Euston. Or into Knightsbridge, say.'

'I will take you,' a frail old man interrupted. There was a roar of laughter.

'That horse of your'n 'll get as far as Lambeth Bridge and then give hisself up to the nearest copper. He ain't got the strength left in his body enough to blow a decent fart, begging your presence, madam.'

And the horse, who was called Perce, did seem in the autumn of his years. But Mossman, whose horse he was, whispered a few encouraging words, and they set off at a leisurely pace. Indeed, so slowly did they progress, the terrors of the Black Prince Road seemed lessened as they drew towards them.

'Do you have a house number?' Mossman called in encouragement as they crossed the crown of Lambeth Bridge.

'Are we close by?'

'Not exactly as such,' the cabbie conceded. They drew up just beyond the Doulton factory for a conference.

'The fact is, I am here to search for a man. I do not have his exact address, nor can I be sure it is in Black Prince Road, even. But the man I am looking for is mild-mannered enough and a gentleman. Albeit one down on his luck.'

Mossman had intelligent eyes and listened in silence.

'You do not have a servant who could do this work on foot?'

'I do not. Is there a problem?'

'There might be. If your gentleman is a black gentleman or a Chinee, that might make things easier. But a great many clerkly-looking chaps live along that road. Which is nothing much to write home about, to be sure. But is not the poorest place in Lambeth. He's not black, the cove?'

'He is tall and thin, with a refined air about him.'

Mossman's smile was tiny but carried enough reproof about it to make Bella blush.

'We can do no more than try,' he said. 'Does he have a name?'

'His name is Charles Urmiston.'

'Better than Smith, then,' the cabbie said, speaking to Perce as much as to his fare.

The search began badly. Though Black Prince Road was cheerless, it was recognizable enough to Bella as a poor but proud street of houses, not all of them subdivided into lodgings. It was true that what had been a pleasant zephyr on the far side of the river was here a sharp and gritty wind, blowing dust and papers up into the air; and though Mossman had the place set down as a bolt-hole for clerks and the better sort of warehousemen, almost the first thing Bella saw was a woman her own age stretched out in the roadway, either unconscious or dead. Her black straw bonnet was rolling gently towards them.

'Stop the cab,' she cried and leapt down to help. On the pavement, five men were fighting each other. While Bella knelt by the woman, dozens of people appeared as if from nowhere and a general milling ensued.

'Take me to Tait's,' the woman mumbled through bloody teeth.

'Tait's?'

'The dairy.'

Mr Tait, if he was the man who gave his name to the premises, was outside, feverishly putting up chocolate-brown shutters. As if in a fairy tale, the five who had been fighting had multiplied to more than fifty: when Bella glanced back, she saw Mossman on foot, dragging Perce round by the head and leading him away.

'Get her in the shop,' Tait shouted.

Once inside, the woman collapsed on to the sanded floor.

'I'm done for,' she sighed.

'No, you're not,' Bella said in the gloom. 'But you've been stabbed, I think. I am going to undo your blouse and stays.'

When Tait came in, locking the door behind him, she glanced up and asked him to fetch his wife.

'This is my wife,' he said, bleak.

'Then fetch me some clean linen and a bowl of hot water.'

'Are you a doctor?'

'Just do as I say.'

The wound, when it was discovered, was superficial. Mrs Tait was cut across the breast and in the fleshy part of her arm. Her husband watched uneasily as Bella swabbed the paper-white flesh and dressed the cut with a bandage torn from a sheet that was by comparison a dirty grey.

'Who are you?' the victim whispered.

'I came down here to find a man called Urmiston.'

'Him as lost his wife recent?'

'You know him?' Bella exclaimed.

'On a better day, I sell him his milk,' Mrs Tait replied.

There was a knock on the door. Mossman's face peered in.

Back in Orange Street Bella reviled herself for not staying in Lambeth a moment longer than it took to jump into Mossman's cab and shrink back against the horsehair upholstery. She had no idea what all the fighting had been about nor who had stabbed Mrs Tait. Much more to the point, she had done nothing to track down Urmiston to his lair. Only when the cab was wheeling her up Whitehall – a wonderfully comforting and orderly Whitehall – did she regret bolting.

The answer was to write to him. There was a terse and faintly aggressive side to all Bella's correspondence. In the end, she sent him no more than a note, inviting him to call on Fleur de Lys at his convenience. For an hour or more this single sheet of paper and its dozen or so words lay on her desk. In this time, Urmiston's future hung in the balance. Bella grimaced, she smoked, she read. On an impulse, she went upstairs and changed her clothes. She wished she had sent Quigley to Lambeth and gone in his place to Oxford. She resolved to take Marie Claude to supper at Fracatelli's and changed her mind.

Only then did she bundle the note into an envelope and find a stamp. There was a postbox fifty yards from the house and she walked there with complete indifference to Charles Urmiston's fate in her heart. He could do as he wished. She could hardly care less. However, even thinking that vexed her. She felt like kicking someone.

SEVEN

Captain Quigley knew some parts of Oxford better than others. For a time, before he took up with Mrs Bella Wallis (as he liked to phrase it), he had lived in a hut by the canal, indulged in his every whim by a stout woman from Norfolk, who left his bed each morning to unload barges. Big Barbara had once won a substantial wager by tossing a hundredweight sack of coal over a five-foot fence from a mark drawn in the mud of the towpath. Her challenger had been the stroke of the Merton boat, who stripped to his white waistcoat to attempt the feat, employing the press-and-lift method, which took the sack above his head, showering dust on to his blond curls. He failed, injuring his groin into the bargain. Barbs won the day by snuggling the coal to her waist and then tossing it clean across the fence, with the same sort of economy lesser women would have employed in emptying their aprons of peapods.

Which story the Captain was now retelling in the snug of the Eagle and Child, every detail closely followed by Mr Blossom, a sweating tub of lard, porter to the missionary gentlemen along the Banbury Road. Blossom, as he had already confessed, was an eight-pint man of an evening, every one of which was needed to look after his flock without himself going mad or running amok.

'A rum lot of coves, are they?'

'Not in the sense you might intend. Not so to say rum as you and I might understand. For a start there's on'y sixteen of them.'

'Brutes, though?' Quigley suggested, who knew very well what their character was, having observed their comings and goings for two days.

'Brutes? A bunch of mollies if you ask me.'

'You don't say!'

'Gentlemen who want to missionarize the heathen,' Blossom explained. 'Who have received in their undergraduate years a call for that sort of thing and now nothing will satisfy them but that they go to some poor benighted country and pester the life out of the savages there.'

'Know the type,' Quigley confirmed. 'Forever close to tears. Handshake wetter than lettuce.'

'You have them off to a T,' Blossom said, admiringly.

'Is there a guvnor to this place at all?'

'Mr Hagley,' the porter responded. 'The Reverend Mr Anthony Hagley.

'Himself a missionary once, I wager.'

'Him!' Blossom cried. 'I doubt he's been further east than Paddington Station. Or,' he added, tapping his nose significantly, 'maybe certain parts of Moorfields, eh?'

The porter had a laugh that could shake plaster loose. Quigley feared for his new friend's life as what was intended as genial punctuation turned to paroxysm. Drink called for. A small gold watch accepted, which Blossom swallowed off, chasing it with a pint of the ditchwater passing as Best Bitter. The porter had raised a considerable wad of phlegm that he disposed of by opening the window and hawking vigorously into the night. There followed a more orderly conversation about the qualities required in a missionary, chief of which was that a Christian soldier should know how to biff.

'A good clout first and let the word of God follow after. I don't say it is always called for, but often enough. Now these gentlemen of mine could not crack a walnut without wincing.'

Quigley began to like Mr Blossom.

'You were handy once,' he guessed.

'I call to mind an occasion in Malta. Hot there, and it makes the locals bad-tempered. As it happens, a very religious island, you understand, but all of them left-footers. However. One night I had the necessity to square up to an Arab sort of cove trying to sell me pomegranates. Which is no kind of a fruit at all. He was an evil bugger with a blue scar down across his eye, like this. So I said to him, I said –'

'Not to interrupt, old son, but aren't those some of your gentlemen in the saloon? Just walked in?'

Three young men were standing awkwardly at the bar, trying to decide how to order a pint without announcing themselves to the world as the tares among the wheat.

'Them three poor buggers are off to the Zambezi,' Blossom said, with grim satisfaction. 'They sail at midnight on Friday to certain death. Goners, each and every one.'

'Then I must buy them a pint,' Quigley declared exuberantly.

'And the more fool you,' the porter retorted.

But the Captain's move into the parlour bar was a shrewd one, for in this way he found the answer to a question that had exercised his mind for two days and two nights. What was a bunch of religious nellies, sincere though they might be, doing with crested knick-knacks like cigar cases? For the house with the decorated keystone over the porch was where these poor devils lived.

'For me, gentlemen, the Cross was my blazon. Fashioned from twigs, tied with seagrass, held high aloft. Accompanied by psalms, hymns, the whole bang shoot.'

It was the concluding trope of an inspirational account of how he had walked the desert beaches of North Africa in search of another Christian soul, a yarn all the more persuasive for happening to be true. He omitted to say how he came to be in such a quarter of the world and how far he had swum to get there.

Two of his listeners had the abstracted air of men who could already foresee death coming at them like the train from Didcot, but the slightly more garrulous Tobias Ross-Whymper offered what the Captain was seeking.

'Our Hall, you must understand, is no part of the University,' he volunteered, as if giving the Captain his due as a man of the world.

'Well it wouldn't be, would it?' Quigley agreed cheerfully.

Ross-Whymper stared him down. 'I myself am a former Christ Church scholar, however.'

Quigley adjusted sights hastily.

'I could see that at a glance. But to be clear, the old crest over the door. That's your badge of honour, so to speak?'

'You could say so.'

'I mention this because a curious thing happened in London recently. Fellow punts me a cigar case with those same arms emblazoned.'

'He punts you it?' Ross-Whymper asked, bemused.

'Beggar type. Offers the case for sale.'

'A cigar case?'

'The same. My curiosity was sorely piqued,' Quigley added, borrowing a line from *Lady Nugent's Letter*.

'Some of the fellows smoke. But hardly cigars. Do you have the case with you?'

'My dear sir,' the Captain protested gently, 'it was my clear and bounden duty to run the scoundrel and his swag to the nearest constable.'

But Ross-Whymper wasn't listening. He turned to his neighbour.

'I say, Ralph. Who do we know in B.H. who smokes cigars?'

'Only Principal Hagley,' Ralph replied, obliging Quigley greatly. He wished the gentlemen well of their voyage, made his excuses, and left.

It was natural in him to walk a hundred yards up the Banbury Road and study the crest one last time. The book-lined room he had noticed on a previous reconnaissance, the one to the right of the entrance, had also given up its secrets. The man lighting a reading lamp was clearly the guvnor, the Reverend Mr Hagley. If he looked spooky, it was because Quigley wished this character upon him.

'You didn't meet him?' Bella asked.

'No, but easily done. The gentleman's not going nowhere. Lives at the Hall, skates about the town all day in clerical dress. However, your obedient ess, finding himself strapped for cash, forced to retire. Has returned to aitch-coo for further orders.'

'You seriously believe a minister of religion, such as you describe, capable of murder? Of slitting a girl's throat?'

'I'm only telling you what I found out. This cove Blossom —'

'Yes, Blossom. An utterly reliable witness I am quite sure —'

Quigley gave her the old level stare, the one that turneth away wrath.

'This Blossom says the Reverend has mislaid his case and searched for it high and low. Thinks he may have left it on the train.'

'We can say he was in London that night?' Bella asked swiftly.

'Not much of a story if he wasn't. Yes, he was out and about that night. Why not say it? He was in Maiden Lane when Welsh Alice was done.'

'And it was he who killed her?'

'Never in a million years,' Quigley said blithely. 'Unless of course,' he added, 'you want to make it so.'

Bella slapped her palm down on the rosewood table that served as her writing desk. To say that she was exasperated with the Captain was to understate the case. It was no use admitting that part of his usefulness to her was just this habit of cheery insolence. It stung: but it made her think. He was the wasp at her picnic.

'He was there,' Quigley repeated. 'But I don't reckon him for a killer. I made it my business to come alongside and give him the hard glance when he was walking down St Giles, they call it. That's —'

'I know where St Giles is in Oxford.'

'So like I say I give him the once-over. Head to toe. And what do I conclude? Not capable of the dastardly deed. Twittish.'

'Then what?'

'Why,' Quigley crowed, 'just afore I left, I'm having a swiftie with Blossom before setting out for the station, when he ups and says that Mr Hagley has found his cigar case after all. My eye.'

All this while, the Captain was practising at the Indian clubs, the wooden billets occasionally crashing into the wall. He had the idea that he would, within a day or so, exercise a few pounds of fat from his bones. His face was an alarming purple. Bella watched him from behind her writing desk.

'Telling Blossom he had found the case was a lie?'

'You can bet your Christmas goose on it. He was there all right but there was others with him. The plot thickens, Mr Margam, sir.'

One of the clubs came loose from the Captain's grip and sailed out of the open door, carooming off the building opposite. Vexed, he threw the other after it.

'What self-respecting Indian ever jigged about with this nonsense?' he muttered. 'Hadn't the time. Served the mem her cucumber sandwiches. Painted the flagpole. Dug the occasional useful ditch.'

'This weight thing is bothering you, I take it?'

'I was called a fat bastard in the Bag o' Nails last evening. Remonstrations. Quarrel taken outside at the request of the landlord. Opponent: Stoker Miller of Gosport. Honours even but it led to a period of quiet reflection.'

'Are you forever going to be quoting from me, Captain Quigley?'

'I am one with an infinite capacity for easeful contemplation,' he countered adroitly, lifting a line she wished she had not written in the otherwise heated pages of *Deveril's Disgrace*. 'I should add, by the way, Stoker Miller very anxious to tender his services to the firm.'

'I thought he was in the Navy?'

'If they ever catch up with him again, yes, that would be so.'

'I think we have enough military genius to cope with, without Stoker Miller.'

'You are in the right of it, as always,' the Captain agreed comfortably.

Charles Urmiston turned up at Fleur de Lys Court two days later. Though he had made a great effort with the clothes brush and a pail of soapy water from the landlady in which to wash his shirt, he still looked decidedly frowsty. He had walked to the Strand in a light shower of rain. Poverty came off him like the smell of a dog's wet fur. When he asked after Mrs Wallis, he was told she had yet to come in. He looked around him with some anxiety.

'I do have the right address, I hope.'

'This is the place all right. And, knowing that you were coming, I have stirred my stumps, Mr Urmiston. I believe this here picture is yours.'

Urmiston stared in amazement as the harem scene was unveiled.

'How on earth –?'

'Quigley has means,' the Captain asserted grandly. 'Has contacts with the fraternity, you might say. The lady was warehoused in a hooky kind of gaff behind Paddington Lock. I took the liberty of making some enquiries. Among art-lovers, the picture valued at twenty sovs.'

These art-lovers were in fact the people who had stolen the painting in the first place. It was one of the Captain's better wheezes. He and Murch had removed the work from Bella's staircase, driven it round to Paddington, offered it for resale (a tenner, topsides) but lingered long enough to identify a portrait by G. F. Watts, lifted only a fortnight earlier from a house in Belgravia. That changed matters to a cove with his wits about him. That is to say, someone like the Captain. Negotiations took a sudden new turn.

'How about this, then?' Quigley suggested jovially. 'A straight swap. The fat china showing all she's got for the lady in the red hat.'

'Pull the other one, Captain,' Frenchie Thomas said. 'This here likeness is a work of genius by one of our greatest living portraitists.'

'And what a crying shame if the law sniffed out where it was and asked how it come to be lodged in your garden shed.'

Thomas narrowed his eyes.

'Dangerous talk.'

'We are men of the world, Frenchie. We both play the long game.'

'How much?' the fence demanded. And then, a moment later, incredulous, '*How* much?'

'Think of it as the price of silence. And of course, an expression of unbroken goodwill between friends.'

Urmiston stared at the painting leaning against the back wall of Bella's office with something like a child's amazement. Quigley smiled.

'Your picture was stolen, do you see? I have extracted twenty sovereigns from the thieves, money that I have in this here handkerchief.'

'Captain Quigley,' Urmiston said, embracing him, 'you are a man of business, sir. I put myself under your command.'

'A rough-and-ready soldier is all,' the Captain smirked.

'Then count me as a very willing recruit. May I offer you a finder's fee from my unexpected windfall?'

'Do you drink at all?' his new friend asked hopefully.

'A glass of something with you by all means! And perhaps a pie. The excitement has whetted my appetite.'

'The Coal Hole the very place, sir. Or maybe, nearer still, the Cyder Cellars.'

'Whatever will please you best.'

Which was how Bella came to find them later in the day, at their ease in her office, feet on the desk, smoking shilling cigars. Captain Quigley waved her into their presence.

'Mr Urmiston has already earned his corn, dear lady. Tell her, Charlie.'

'Anthony Hagley is the living incarnation of the devil who helped lose me my place with the Great Western. The biggest humbug in Christendom, I would style him. Such a cad as is seldom produced in England, even among the aristocracy.'

'And is he such a one?'

'Such a one what?'

'You are drunk, Mr Urmiston,' Bella said wonderingly.

'I probably am. Now there's a less than honest answer – I *am* drunk. But if it's Hagley you're after – that wicked man hiding beneath clerical dress, that Ananias –'

Quigley patted him comfortingly on the sleeve. He rose from his seat – not without difficulty – and walked to the door, where he let fly a huge and stentorian 'Oi!' After a moment or two a boy of ten or so appeared, wiping his nose on his sleeve and in the same flourish saluting the Captain.

'Nip to Tonio's and ask him for a can of fresh coffee. Fresh, you understand. And a couple of biscuits for yourself. Chop chop, double quick.'

EIGHT

Urmiston's story began with a curiously drab view of Berkshire, like a snatched glimpse of nothing in particular seen through a railway-carriage window. The image was not of that dereliction and emptiness that seems to crowd the trackside of mainline routes, as if the homeless have come to watch the rich ride by: all that could be seen were densely packed trees, their trunks glistening. Trees and fallen boughs, emerald moss and a darker carpet of brambles. All set in the sort of unromantic gloom that carries with it a faint air of menace.

In 1869, a little to the west of Wallingford Road Station on the Great Western line from London to Bristol, the company sought a minor alteration to the permanent way. In a fold of woodland, engineers making a routine inspection discovered early indicators of ground subsidence, caused by a particularly wet summer and boisterous autumn.

Their report began to creep its way through the GWR management, accumulating additional papers and memoranda as it went. At a directors' meeting in Swindon, it was agreed that the problem was serious enough to recommend the building of stone revetments along forty yards of track and – most importantly – the provision of a three-hundred-foot run-off channel, to be built in brick, ending in a twenty-foot sump. They sent Urmiston to negotiate terms for the work.

'This is not uncommon?' Bella interrupted. 'I mean from time to time there will be unavoidable repair works to the permanent way?'

'The company has a statutory duty to inspect for just those contingencies when they arise, yes.'

'Then where was the problem?'

Urmiston sipped at his coffee. Bella and Quigley waited while he gathered his thoughts. Though his hands shook, the shabby clothes he was wearing seemed to have fallen from him and in their place he was dressed as the man he had once been. He was back in the moment, speaking the language he had once used. But it gave him no joy.

'Sometimes the repairs are limited to the ground on which the rails actually run – that's to say, the property of the operating company, in this case Great Western. But to build our run-off, we had to seek permission from the man who owned the woods.'

'Makes good sense,' encouraged the impatient Quigley, nodding vigorously all the while. He knew – or thought he knew – how the story came out. Urmiston studied him for a long moment.

'Just so. In this case, the landowner refused point-blank to let us set foot on his property. Not one foot.'

The Captain tugged on his moustaches.

'An awkward cove,' he prompted.

'For the sake of clarity,' Bella intervened, 'I wonder if Mr Urmiston can be allowed to tell this story in his own way, without your contributions.'

'I will come to the point,' Urmiston said. 'Because of this prohibition – which was of course highly unusual – the regional engineering superintendent and I were obliged to walk out along the permanent way to the point where the work was to be done.'

'And how far was that?'

'Just under three miles. In heavy rain and a blustery gale. The site was in a valley, almost a tunnel of trees –'

He spread his hands helplessly.

'You were able to see at once what was at fault,' Bella suggested.

'Oh, there was time and enough for that. We were kept waiting nearly an hour for the arrival of the landowner's representative.'

'Now we're getting to it,' the incorrigible Quigley chortled. 'Now we're nearly there. Tell her what happened next.'

'Normally, such a person would be a lawyer, perhaps a local solicitor –'

'– No, but tell her!' Quigley insisted happily.

'In time, a party came down through the woods, led by a man in clerical dress. Who introduced himself to us as the Reverend Anthony James Hagley, vicar of Brailston.'

Bella stared.

'Hagley was the agent for this business?'

'He had a letter with him granting him full powers of negotiation.'

'A *vicar*?'

'Exactly. From that first moment, there was not the slightest chance of a reconciliation between the two parties. The Regional Superintendent and I were forced to walk a little way off and confer. The situation was unprecedented.'

Bella was picturing the scene – the sluicing rain, the discomforted GWR party, the gale rattling the trees all around. And Hagley, the vicar of Brailston, under his umbrella. A thought occurred to her.

'You say there were others in Hagley's party?'

'There were two gamekeepers with shotguns. I don't know them to have been gamekeepers for a fact – but anyway, men with sacks over their shoulders to keep off the rain and with guns under their arms.'

'Breeches broken, though,' Quigley prompted. 'Safety observed, I don't doubt.'

'No, it was not. The first thing this Hagley said was that if we attempted to step one inch off the company's property, he would order his men to prevent us. Tufton – the engineering superintendent – was a country man. He saw the guns were loaded.'

'This is an incredible story, Mr Urmiston.'

'I can't tell you how offensive Hagley was, how arrogant and aggressive.'

'Now why was that?'

'Why? He was spokesman for an equally vicious and arrogant master.'

'And this man? Who was he?' Bella asked gently.

'The woods and all about belonged to a Lord Bolsover,' Urmiston replied in all innocence.

It was as if he had thrown a grenade. Even Quigley was startled by Bella's reaction. She jumped up and rummaged in the drawers of a battered military chest, a piece of furniture the Captain liked to assure his more gullible cronies was his own. At last she found what she was looking for.

'Is this his crest?'

Urmiston took the cigar case from her and examined its interior.

'Yes,' he said wonderingly. 'But how did you come by it?'

'You are quite sure the crest is part of Lord Bolsover's arms?'

'I am certain.'

Bella glanced at Quigley, who had the decency to look as consternated as she felt. Out in the Strand, the evening traffic grumbled.

'What have I said?' Urmiston asked, confused.

'I want you to go for a walk for a few minutes, Mr Urmiston, the better to gather your thoughts. Perhaps you might walk as far as Temple Bar and back.'

'I am in full charge of myself, Mrs Wallis.'

'I am sure you are. But I am not. I shall be grateful for time to think. Captain Quigley will send out for a bite of supper. Let us meet again in ten minutes.'

They resumed over a plate of mutton and a can of beer each. There was still some light in the sky but hardly any of it percolated to Fleur de Lys Court. They ate by candlelight. The only people to enter the court were men, passers-by who came to relieve themselves against walls scabbed with theatre posters and advertisements for patent medicines.

'What else happened at that meeting?' Bella asked at last.

'I tried to talk Hagley into walking back to Wallingford with us, where we could discuss things in a more businesslike manner. I even offered him dinner that night at the Woolpack. He just laughed in my face.'

'You explained your difficulty in dealing with him as Bolsover's agent?'

'In the most offhand manner, he said that the company should not bother to send another clerk after him. He had served his notice on us and that was the end of the matter. Then he and his bullies turned their backs on us and walked off.'

'And then what?'

Urmiston's smile was bleak as midnight.

'You must remember that I was at the time something more distinguished than how you find me tonight. I was a senior man from the London office, acting on behalf of a very great public enterprise. In the normal course of things I travelled first class, was put up at the best hotels. I went back to town later that afternoon and wrote a short report, the intention of which was to pass the matter up to the most senior levels.'

He thought for a moment and Bella was astonished to see tears in his eyes.

'I had gone straight from Paddington to my house and I wrote this note at my own desk in Campden Hill. What was needed was advice from counsel, obviously. That was my recommendation. I have wished a thousand times the story ended there.'

'But something else happened?'

'Yes,' Urmiston said heavily. 'Marguerite – my wife – said that I should fight them. That I should not be so –' he glanced round – 'I am not ashamed to use her words for it – that I should not be so passive.'

'You do not have to tell us this,' Bella said in her gentlest voice.

'No, but I do. She was ill, to be sure, but her infirmity forced the truth from her. That night, I reviewed the whole calamity – Hagley's contempt, the engineering superintendent's barely disguised disgust, my own sense of bewilderment – and resolved to fight them.'

'You mean to fight Bolsover. He was surely the principal.'

'I never met Lord Bolsover. The management sent me to see him both in London and at his house in Berkshire but he would not admit me. The fight was between me and Hagley. The thing became something of an office joke; here's old Urmiston run off the rails by a country vicar. You should go down to Berkshire and kick his arse from here to Christmas Eve, Charles. Or send your wife, perhaps.'

'And so, in the end?'

'Yes,' Urmiston said, grim. 'In the end, they broke me. They knew they would have to concede eventually but it gave them pleasure meanwhile to stretch me on the rack. After a year of quite indescribable agitation and confusion, I was summoned to a meeting of the directors and dismissed. Very foolishly, I attempted to sue the company. Within another year, I was as good as destitute.'

'But these alterations were essential to public safety, surely? Weren't they covered by Acts of Parliament?'

'Oh, his lordship had no choice in the matter, as he knew from the start.'

'Then what was his game?' Quigley asked, indignant.

'His game?'

'You never met him, he never met you. What stroke was he trying to pull, for all love?'

Urmiston made a face. 'Maybe he found it amusing.'

This was not at all an answer to Captain Quigley's taste. He cleared the greasy plates by banging them together and throwing knives and forks into the tin dish covers. The tray on which the meal had been delivered went out of the door like a sled.

'I do not like these buggers,' he said. 'This Bolsover bird I know nothing about, but you know that the Reverend Hagley is poncing round Oxford this very night in all his clerical glory as Principal of some tuppenny-ha'penny mission to the heathen?'

'You told me this earlier.'

'Well, I don't like it. By God I don't.'

Bella stood and held out both hands to Urmiston.

'I understand you have some money from Captain Quigley for the recovery of your painting. In place of walking back to Lambeth tonight, let him find you a room nearby. Merton's Hotel is small but clean. It will do until something else is found. I will bother you with one last question before the Captain takes you there.'

'I am at your service,' Urmiston muttered.

'Why do you think Bolsover appointed Hagley to look after his interests? No, I will sharpen the question. Did you form any idea of the kind of relationship there was between these two men?'

'They were intimates,' he replied, blushing. 'The Captain asked me what their game was. That was it: to take a mild-mannered man such as me and humiliate him. I was not as they were.'

That night, Bella lay in bed with Marie Claude, stroking her lover's hair and, after a while, patting her back gently, as one would pacify a fractious child. The Frenchwoman had been out earlier in the evening, to the Aquarium, and endured her usual chapter of insults. A waiter had been rude in his address; at a neighbouring table someone had said something unkind about her hat. Certain young men had looked at her in a leering sort of way and one – a bold blond in a mint-green suit – had the temerity to speak to her in French. It was useless to protest that none of these things mattered; Marie Claude was as sensitive as a snail.

'I should have been with you,' Bella said. 'Your friend Miss Titcombe was no defence at all, I see.'

'She is an idiot,' Marie Claude confirmed gloomily. 'Tonight she was dressed in clothes I would not wear for a ballooning trip.'

In spite of herself, Bella laughed out loud. The manly side of Miss Titcombe led her into many a mistake. One of these was a penchant for tweed, which when draped across her ample bosom gave her a decidedly aldermanic look. On her only visit to the house in Orange Street she had astonished Bella by smoking a pipe; not a comely sort of a pipe at all but one with a long stem and tiny bowl, like a caricature or child's drawing of the object.

Bella kissed her companion on the neck.

'Shall we go ballooning one day, you and I? Over the Alps, perhaps, or along some Norwegian fiord?'

Marie Claude raised her head from Bella's breast.

'Yes, now you make fun of me. I am so very unhappy.'

'I would not have you any other way.'

'You should write my story.'

'Easily done! A beautiful but sad girl lives in a cottage under the walls of a castle. People come from all around to hear her cry, which is a sound like the north wind sighing. Her tears are collected in little glass phials, made in Venice. Many men fall in love with her and wish to dance and flirt with her under the castle's chandeliers. But every evening, as the sun sets, she walks into the wood and becomes a silver birch. Only the moon knows where she is.'

Marie Claude considered.

'It is a story for children,' she said.

'Can there be anything more truthful than that?'

'So then, these other things you write, stories about only stupid people, why do you waste your time on them?'

'They are important to me.' Bella pushed her away. 'Go to your own room now. The next time you visit the Aquarium, I shall come with you.'

'And Lydia Titcombe?'

'Can stay at home and cobble her boots, or wax her moustache.'

Marie Claude smiled, a rare event. After she left, Bella lay on her back, gazing at the ceiling. She was picturing four or five men standing in a dank wood, their capes heavy with rain, while the express to Paddington thundered past on the up-line. That one of them was Urmiston was almost, but not quite, beside the point. What attracted her to the image was its sombre monochrome, relieved only by the glint of light on the rails and – she added a further touch – the rags of steam left hanging in the branches of the trees.

On the ground, her naked neck and breast as white as paper, her disordered hair mingling with the mud, lay Welsh Alice. Her eyes were open and her body unmarked. It bore a disturbing resemblance to Marie Claude's. Bella felt a shudder run through her, enough to make her sit up abruptly, her fingers plucking the hem of the sheet. The true beginning to her next novel had presented itself, implacable and as stern as headstones in a graveyard.

As to where these horrors might lead, she had no idea. That was the particular reason she rented the place in Fleur de Lys Court. Otherwise, the images she had just conjured would dissipate like the spring snow. She sat up abruptly and lit a cigarette, something she had promised Marie Claude never to do in the upstairs rooms. With a little twinge of guilt she opened a window. It helped. Cool air slipped into the room and dried her moist hair.

What else was a well-appointed house for, if not to keep such nightmares at bay? Why else choose this curtain fabric over that, or place such-and-such an ornament there and nowhere else? The house in Orange Street was her home, to be sure, but it was also an elaborated spell. Quite recently Bella had bought a massive sponge for the bathroom, quite as big as a small cat. It was a toy for Marie Claude to play with but also in some obscure way a means of fending off disaster. It went along with Bella's collection of glass paperweights, the eighteenth-century rummers, the naval chest that stood in the hall and all the rest of it.

There was a simpler reason still for the office in Fleur de Lys Court. It was where Henry Ellis Margam lived and worked. Even its crabby accommodations were too grand for the monster she had created. He was being punished for his ugliness. Ideally, Bella would like Margam to live in a hollow log out in the woods and drink from puddles. He would run on all fours like a dog.

She rose early enough to walk to Merton's and find Charles Urmiston at breakfast. He looked up guiltily from a steak with a poached egg balanced on it.

'Money has made me reckless,' he said.

He smelled of soap and his face was close shaved. His dreadful old suit had been taken away during the night and sponged and pressed. Merton, who had a keen eye, had sent his daughter round to Jaworski's in Henrietta Street, and that amiable bear of a man had opened early to furnish some fresh linen and a yellow cravat. Urmiston was still the unfinished sketch but a night's sleep and twenty sovereigns in his pocket had made a dramatic change in him.

'You are on your way somewhere, perhaps?' he asked, proffering Bella a bit of toast and the marmalade dish.

'To Fleur de Lys Court.'

'I must ask you: what exactly is it that goes on there?'

'Mischief,' she teased. But Urmiston brushed the remark away.

'You have some complaint of your own against Mr Hagley, perhaps?'

There was no one else in the breakfast room, the windows of which were wide open to the street. Londoners passed by, most of them with the peculiar air of abstraction that people have in the early morning, as if listening to interior voices, or ghostly music. Bella hesitated and then told him what she knew of Hagley and Bolsover and the suspicion she had that they were both implicated in some way in the murder of a drab called Welsh Alice. Urmiston looked out of the window, nodding, watching the world go by, asking no questions.

'I will never be your bravest ally, Mrs Wallis, but if you are about seeing these two villains done down, I would like to be of your party.'

There was more agreeable business to conduct first. Driven by Quigley's friend, the laconic Murch, Charles Urmiston took his newly recovered painting to an address in Shepherd's Bush. Penny, Murch's elderly mare, drew their cart along through early-morning sunshine that had, from the amount of dust hanging in the air, the texture of gauze. Murch pointed out one or two landmarks with his ribboned whip, a thing never to be used on Penny and carried only as a badge of office and as punctuation in disputes with other road-users.

'You are not a London man then, sir?'

'As it happens, I am, Mr Murch.'

'Well, down this here road, afore we go much farther, we shall see sheep and thatch. Is all my meaning.'

'This is hardly beyond Bayswater, Mr Murch. The natives are rich and friendly. As you see, many of them wear trousers in the Christian way and their womenfolk are as chaste as rounds of cheese.'

'I ain't lost,' Murch replied, niggled.

Their destination was a picture dealer called Cussins, someone known to Urmiston slightly, a calm and comforting presence wearing a frogged velvet jacket and smoking a carved meerschaum. He had the pleasant habit of bouncing lightly on the balls of his feet when talking.

'This is a Venneke,' he said of the painting. 'And quite a good one. But of course you know that, Mr Urmiston, for it was I that sold it to you some years past – yes, that's it, the pretty little house on Campden Hill, I remember it well – and now here it is again. Venneke of course has fled – you didn't know that? – fled the country, yes, and is living in Rome, the reprobate, on the Spanish Steps if you please. With a *very* young creature not at all in the likeness of our Turkish lady here. The model for her was a splendid woman, not at all some guttersnipe child, no, but a landlady to a public house in Ladbroke Grove – what was her name now? – ah, yes, Mrs Hill.'

'I had no idea,' Urmiston said faintly.

'Well, I would not have told you such homely details when you were the prospective purchaser, oh dear no. But now, of course, you wish to sell. I suggest a hundred and twenty guineas.'

The deal was struck over a glass of Marsala and little cakes. Cussins looked thoughtfully at his former client.

'I should mention, by the by, how saddened I was to hear of your dismissal at the hands of the Great Western. A shabby affair and you have my sympathies. May Lord Bolsover repent of his sins at leisure.'

But for all his earlier protestations to Bella, Urmiston barely registered the name. He was moonstruck. In the space of twenty-four hours he was richer by a hundred and forty sovereigns, a wonderful sum, a gift as it might be from heaven itself. He forced himself to meet Cussins' curious gaze.

'Lord Bolsover will get his comeuppance, you may be sure of it,' he said with what he hoped was not too foolish a grin. 'I am with new people nowadays.'

They looked up at the sound of an altercation just outside the window. At the back of Murch's cart was a rolled tarpaulin and some unwary chancer had taken it into his head to steal it. While Penny munched placidly on her mid-morning oats, Murch had seized this thief in a headlock and run him full tilt into Mr Cussins' gatepost. The man staggered to his feet and groped about like the victim in a game of blind man's bluff. He found a pillar box in his path and embraced it feebly before sinking to the pavement.

'My best wishes to you, Mr Urmiston,' Cussins said reverently.

'And mine to you, sir.'

NINE

Lord broxtowe was giving Bella lunch at Lord's, comprising chicken and game pie served from a wicker hamper and an excellent Niersteiner. A match was taking place but his lordship could not say who the visitors were, nor did he attend overmuch to the score. He was there in his capacity as a committee member of the Marylebone Cricket Club, a faintly dizzying honour he had held off and on his entire adult life.

'In 1844,' he said, pointing with a wavery gesture, 'we had some Red Indians out in the middle, dancing and stamping, and giving displays of archery. A rum business. Good shots, but surly buggers, I thought them. Feathers and so forth. You may believe this or not, but some of their trousers had no backside to them.'

He smiled. 'Could you not work that story into one of your tales?'

'Where had they come from?'

'You mean who brought them here? I have no idea. Perhaps they came in canoes, of their own accord.'

There were other ladies present, some of them suspiciously young, though none so radiant as Bella. The picnic they were having began to attract glances.

'These other gentlemen nearby, they are also committee members?' she asked in a quiet aside.

'Some of them are from the Middlesex Club, who would like to make this their permanent ground. A piece of damned impertinence if you ask me.'

'What I wished to ask you, Broxtowe, was whether you knew a family called Bolsover.'

'Knew the Second Earl – he played here in the Eton–Harrow match I can't remember how many years ago. Before the Red Indians, probably. He married my cousin Lydgate, who had but one leg. The other she left in a public garden in Mentone, which gives you a good idea of the morals of that unhappy branch of the family.'

'But losing her leg was surely an accident? Some beast attacked her, I imagine. A savage dog, perhaps.'

'A dancing bear. What a disgusting thing for a young girl to wish to witness in the first place.'

He proffered her his serviette with which to wipe her chin.

'You want to know about the Third Earl, of course. An out-and-out snake, my dear. There is a small house of some kind in the Thames Valley. I dined there in his father's time. A gentleman would not keep his dogs in the south wing, which is where I was put to bed. Elizabethan, they claimed.'

He hesitated.

'You are a sanguine enough creature, Bella, and so I will tell you. The boy – Freddie, his doting mother called him – played wife to a hulking great servant they had, a footman of some sort. You understand me sufficiently, I think.'

There was a shout and a ball clattered on the steps to the newly erected pavilion. Lord Broxtowe was the only man present not to applaud, merely adjusting his top hat to a more comfortable tilt.

'The man's altogether a subject worthy of your pen, I'd say. Reckless, notoriously so. Vulgar. The very devil when it comes to an argument. Lacking altogether in gentlemanly conduct. Some say he is deranged.'

'Have you heard his name in connection with a man called Anthony Hagley?'

'The parson fellow? Didn't he set him up in Oxford a year or so back? Some nonsense about missionarizing the heathen. My neighbour Fullerton sent his son there. The boy wanted to Christianize China. Was given Tahiti, I think it was.'

'What happened?'

'I imagine they ate him. Are there cannibals on Tahiti?'

Bella had no idea.

'Quite the most stupid boy in Yorkshire, anyway. Resigned his commission, went to Tahiti – if it was Tahiti – never been heard of since. And I must say,' Broxtowe added, warming to his theme, 'the world is littered with the graves of these poor devils. As soon as the quinine and the tinned sausages run out, pfft. Harry Fullerton commissioned a fellow to go out there and photograph his son's grave. A very foolish act of piety.'

'Did the man come home with anything?'

'He has never been heard of since. Also eaten, I daresay. But we were talking about Bolsover. A goddamn monster, Bella. Fifty anvils would not weigh that fellow down. Want me to ask around about him?'

'If you would.'

'Care to say why?'

'Monsters make good reading,' she said evasively.

He patted her hand.

'If we had only met when I was younger,' he declared gallantly, and loud enough to disconcert a gaitered bishop sitting nearby. 'That bodice. How many little buttons does it have, now?'

The bishop inclined his head eagerly.

'Forty, my lord,' Bella said smiling. 'But not all of them are functional. Otherwise, where would we be in the mornings?'

Lord Broxtowe's shouted laugh floated out across the ground just at the moment the receiving batsman was playing forward to a fast delivery. He edged the ball to slip and then stood disbelievingly as it was gathered in.

'Mr Copley has been dismissed, my lord,' the servant provided by Broxtowe's hotel explained. 'On a score of ninety-eight at that.'

'Two buttons short,' Broxtowe murmured, causing the bishop to convulse in silent laughter.

Meanwhile, Quigley was playing the part of adjutant, a role he greatly enjoyed. He was taking a pot of tea with Mrs Bardsoe in Shelton Street, a little below Seven Dials. That is to say, she had offered and he had graciously accepted. His feet were planted square on what had once been a very good Indian carpet, his arm laid along the lace tablecloth. The Laughing Cavalier, no less. Moustaches tweaked from time to time, eyes (he hoped) twinkling.

''E's not an actor, is he?' Hannah Bardsoe asked suddenly.

'He is a gentleman, ma. I already told you.'

'Well, if he's a gentleman, what's he doing wanting to come round here?'

The house was tall and narrow, the ground floor given over to a little shop selling herbal remedies and the more explosive kinds of proprietary medicines. There was a steady trade in Hensher's Bile Pills and Dr Eagleton's Linctus for the Throat and Chest; but the front window also advertised open jars of quinine bark, liquorice sticks, the dried flowers of feverfew, cinnamon, cloves and – some people swore by it – nettle tea.

'He is a gentleman who has recently buried his wife. Poor woman planted on foreign soil, leading to a grief too deep for words.'

'Are you still messing with that Mrs Wallis?' Mrs Bardsoe wanted to know suspiciously.

'Don't change the subject. Urmiston's the name. Doesn't hardly smoke, drinks no more'n a hummingbird, the very figure of a saint.'

'And a bit on the shy side I'd say,' she added. 'And for why? Because he ain't here is for why!'

'I left a note for Billy Murch to fetch him round.'

'Billy Murch!' Mrs Bardsoe exclaimed fondly. 'Is he still with us?'

'He's not fifty yet,' Quigley retorted.

'He and my Harry had some times together, so they did. Well, if he's Billy's mate, that puts a different complexion on the thing. That's putting a bow on the dog all right. I thought you was trying to palm off some friend of your'n, Captain. Which is to say, trouble in trousers.'

Urmiston arrived shortly after and was shown three rooms on the top floor. The presence of Mrs Bardsoe gave a useful scale: she was almost as broad as a door.

'A sunny aspect,' Urmiston observed politely, indicating a bar of sunshine not much wider than a tea tray.

'There's a good half an hour of that,' she observed. 'But I make no claims, sir – it *is* a gloomy sort of house. Bardsoe was from Sussex, originally. He found it terrible going here in winter-time. Though we took our Christmas regular with his people and the wind from the sea down there would take your leg off.'

'Your late husband was a herbalist by profession, I think?'

'Profession is ripe, very ripe. No, he was a bit on the slow side, to speak frankly. The little business you see downstairs was my idea.'

'And are you at heart a countrywoman, Mrs Bardsoe?'

'However did you guess?' she asked, pleased. 'From Uxbridge.'

She left him alone to explore the accommodation and he felt a sharp pang of yearning to hear a woman's tread on the stairs, even one so formidably clunky as Mrs Bardsoe's. As for the house and its location, Urmiston could not say that this was as low as he had ever fallen, for measured by the single room he rented in Lambeth, he was on the way up. Though the floorboards sank as he moved over them and the walls were none too straight, the place was scrupulously clean and smelled faintly of apples.

When he went back downstairs, Murch and the Captain had gone. Urmiston had the strong impression that something had been cooked up during his absence. Mrs Bardsoe passed him what he took to be a cordial but which turned out to be best Martinique rum.

'Now you listen here, sir,' she said. 'You won't find a shrewder judge of character than me, you can go to Timbuktu to search for one. And I say this: you will do. I am a respectable widow woman and while there are some in this street that are no better than they ought to be, you will find me straight.'

'An impression I have already formed, Mrs Bardsoe.'

'As may be,' she said. 'As to terms, I would take it well if you was to have some breakfast with me of a morning, but I do not intend to cook for you, nor do your wash. You can come and go as you please and for the rest, kiss my arse – I beg pardon – if I won't look after you a treat.'

'What would you like to know about me, Mrs Bardsoe?'

'Bless you, sir, I already said, I read you like an open book. Your are friends with Mrs Wallis?'

'I knew her late husband well.'

'Then we shall have no trouble, Mr Urmiston.'

'I shall need to buy a few sticks of furniture.'

She laughed, a wonderful round bell-like sound.

'The Captain is your man for that. Good Lord, yes. None better, the thieving old rogue.'

'He has been very kind to me, Mrs B.'

'They do say Dick Turpin was kind,' Mrs Bardsoe pointed out, though blushing for pleasure at the way her name had been shortened to almost an endearment. To Urmiston's amazement, when he extended his hand she brushed it aside and kissed him lightly on the cheek.

'You'll do for me,' she said briskly. 'We ain't going to stand on no ceremony here, I do hope.'

Urmiston was saved by the single clack of the shop bell. A young woman in a shawl stood there, and when he walked out with Mrs Bardsoe from her parlour, waited for him to leave before she consulted with the widowed herbalist on a topic unfit for a man's ears.

'She seems to know you,' Urmiston said of his new landlady, an hour or so later. Bella was smoking a cheroot, with her feet up on a second chair.

'Tell me,' she asked. 'Do you think the Middlesex Club should play at Lord's on a permanent basis?'

'Of course.'

'Do you have reasons to say so?'

Urmiston considered.

'Progress,' he said. 'Or inevitability, if you like.'

'I like the word progress better,' Bella decided. 'As to Mrs Bardsoe, yes, I know her a little through Quigley. I seem to know half London by that conduit. But here's a thing, Charles. The other London, the one that you and I were born to, knows nothing of it. I could sit outside Mrs Bardsoe's little shop, smoking a pipe and spitting into the gutter, and not one friend from that other place would be any the wiser.'

'Yet it seems a world filled with kindness.'

'Oh, what nonsense. Everyone you have met since we came across each other in Boulogne is standing at the edge of a black swamp of cruelty and despair. About which we can never speak.'

'Not even Quigley?'

'Not even he.'

'And me, Bella? Where does that leave me?'

'You must find your own place. But a little moral instruction from a friend never goes amiss and I should welcome that. Without ever having met the Reverend Mr Hagley and exchanging few words with Lord Bolsover, I find I hate them with a passion. You must stop me from poisoning myself.'

Though she spoke lightly, her eyes were dark. Impulsively, he took her hand and so they sat until the return of Captain Quigley. He was carrying a plush chair on his head. Murch followed with a rolled carpet.

'Before we takes this round to Shelton Street,' the Captain asked, 'will you be needing a desk of any kind?'

'A desk? I don't believe I shall be writing anything.'

'You'll leave that to the experts, will you?'

It was the ghastly knowing wink that did it. Urmiston turned to Bella enquiringly.

'There is something I have to tell you about myself,' she said with a sigh.

But it made no difference to Urmiston. He had never heard of Henry Ellis Margam and though he made all the polite expressions of wonder and congratulation, such as authors pretend to disdain but love to hear, she saw that the day had been altogether too joyful for him to care. When she had finished explaining her purely literary interest in Lord Frederick Augustus Bolsover and the Reverend Mr Hagley, she waited for a response. He fiddled with a pencil he picked up from the rosewood table, his lower lip thrust out in thought.

'Mrs Bardsoe seems a very pleasant woman,' he said dreamily.

Bella laughed.

'Urmiston, I have just confided to you my most precious secret.'

'That you write books? Excellent. Should I read one, do you think? Well, I should: it would be a kindness.'

'What do you read normally?'

'Ah,' he said, awkward. 'I have a fitful interest in travel books. There's a fellow called Oliphant who's done some daring things – he rode into Sevastapol disguised as a merchant just before we went to war in the Crimea and –' his voice trailed off to be replaced by a shy smile. 'As you can see, your secret's very safe with me.'

'What did you want to ask me about Mrs Bardsoe?' Bella murmured.

'Oh,' he said, flustered. 'There is one thing, perhaps. I was going to ask you whether I was not compromising her good name by being her sole lodger. You know, a strange man about the house.'

'What exquisite manners you have,' Bella complimented him, keeping her face straight by a superhuman effort. 'I would say she is very pleased to have the company.'

'Yes,' Urmiston said gratefully. 'Yes, of course. That is the way to look at it.'

Bella's hooted laughter followed him out into the Strand. Ears burning, he turned up into Southampton Street and, passing along the edge of the Market, bought his landlady a sheaf of roses. When he got them home, the look of astonishment on Mrs Bardsoe's face sent him scampering upstairs as red as a beetroot. And there he stayed, his hands between his knees, staring at the pattern on his new carpet.

TEN

Captain quigley went back to Oxford. For three days he dogged the Reverend Hagley through the strets, meeting many interesting and entirely irrelevant people along the way. In his own mind he moved about as unnoticed as the shadow of leaves upon the pavement; or perhaps something in the Chinese way of things, silent, pattering, inscrutable and remorseless.

Luckily for these fantasies, Hagley was an easy man to follow. In the early mornings he went for a constitutional in Christ Church Meadows. Clergymen were as plentiful there as rooks in a cornfield, but none of them with Hagley's haughty swoop. On the way home he undertook what Quigley thought of as a town patrol, raising his mortarboard to as many dons and scholars as he met. Some he acknowledged in a curt way, some with greater elaboration. Very few were seized with a desire to engage him in conversation. Nothing abashed, he made his way home for lunch and in the afternoon walked one or other of his young gentlemen up the Banbury Road and down again. Their conversation was entirely theological.

In the evenings, Hagley dined as a guest in this or that college, allowing the Captain ample drinking time in the King's Arms, the pub he made his headquarters.

A conversation with a porter from New College established how long the gentlemen's snouts would be in the trough. It seemed to depend on how generous Fellows were with their wine. Wadham scored highly.

'I have seen McIlvanie of Worcester brought away by wheelbarrow from there,' the porter said. 'Hertford is a more abstemious place these last few years. Dr Pike the exception to the rule. That is Pike there in the back bar.'

Quigley saw a man apparently with two beards, one overlaying the other, fashioning the idea of a cider press or perhaps a bilge pump with his hands. These gestures accompanied a harsh and grating monologue, from which occasional key words flew like rocketing pheasants. A semi-comatose cleric listened, a wineglass balanced on his stomach. Quigley edged within hearing. The subject of Dr Pike's address was not mechanical engineering but certain field stones in Littondale and their misinterpretation by the thrice-cursed Summerscale, Prebendary Dean of Ripon Cathedral.

'What are field stones?' Quigley asked the New College porter.

'They are stones, matey. That is the in and the out of it.'

On the last evening of his surveillance, Quigley drank off his pint and sauntered out past the Radcliffe and across the High to wait for Hagley in Oriel Square. The dusk had that appealing mauve colour: he watched appreciatively as a young man walked towards him down Merton Street in white flannels and a rowing blazer, transformed from an oaf to a wavering will-o'-the-wisp.

Quigley himself had little poetry in him, but the light and the location provided the magic. His cigar was drawing well and for a moment or two he seriously contemplated joining the University in some capacity or other. One of his chance acquaintances of the last two nights' drinking had been a servant of the Bodleian Library, a job he described as light work in a largely unsupervised environment. It was true that this particular man had been given the old heave-ho for accidentally locking Stebbings of Keble in the Divinity Schools the previous Christmas Day but the point held. There was an actor asleep inside Quigley and here was a city full of them, with a stage large enough for all their ill-assorted vanities.

The boy in the rowing blazer came abreast of the Captain, who was startled to see blood spattered on his sleeve and shirt.

'There's a fellow down there that needs your help,' he said in a stiff voice. Quigley peered.

In the gloom, a gentleman in black was sitting on the cobbles outside Merton, his head on his chest. Dignity prevented him from howling – that and a broken nose. As Quigley drew closer, he saw that it was none other than the Reverend Anthony Hagley himself. Frisked up by a final glass of the Oriel port, he had come out into the alluring dusk and said the wrong thing to the wrong man.

'I have stumbled and fallen,' Hagley said.

'Generously put, sir, but the scoundrel that struck you passed me not two minutes ago.'

Hagley considered for a moment and then nodded, spraying the cobbles with gobs of bloody snot.

'An unprovoked attack. I was asking directions.'

'Why, Mr Hagley sir, you know this city like the back of your hand,' Quigley chided. 'Ah! I see you have broke your nose. If you'll permit an old soldier?'

He grasped the flesh of Hagley's nose between his thumb and forefinger and tweaked vigorously.

'How do you know my name?' the injured man said, tears of pain starting in his eyes.

'What Christian has not heard of it? In St Cuthbert's-by-the-Wall, we speak of little else. Percy Quigley, sir, sexton. Up you get now and let us navigate our way home.'

'Is there blood on my face?'

'Somewhat.'

He passed Hagley a snuff handkerchief which the cleric had the speed of thought to refuse.

'You are a sexton?'

'That is my honour.'

'You said you were a soldier.'

'A veteran of Balaclava. And now sexton to Mr Pons.'

'What name is that?'

'The Reverend George Pons. Him of the silver hair and wooden leg.'

And this, Quigley thought, is as good as any Margam novel. Hagley threw off his helping hand.

'I can find my own way,' he said.

'Quigley begs to differ. The young fellow that gave you one up the hooter had indignation writ all over his countenance. I left him looking for a constable.'

'What?' Hagley cried.

'Our passage home should be by indirection, I fancy. What's more, I believe we should leg it.'

Seizing his man just under the elbow, he ran him down Merton Street into the High. Just as they were about to cross the road into Longwall, he had a bright idea, or perhaps a rush of blood to the brain, and threw his free hand up in a dramatic gesture.

'Why, if that is not Lord Bolsover!'

'Where?' Hagley yelped.

'I could swear. Shall I run after him, Mr Hagley?'

'I have no idea what you're talking about.'

'Yes, you do,' the Captain leered.

He cupped both hands to his mouth and bellowed Bolsover's name. Hagley took his chance and bolted.

'In short, he knows we're on to him,' Quigley smirked at the end of his report. 'Called at the Hall the following morning, Principal unable to receive me. Was penning an urgent note which he sent out by my old pal Blossom. Contents of which you have in front of you now.'

'Pons?' Bella wanted to know first. 'Mr Pons of St Cuthbert's-by-the-Wall?'

'A mere flourish.'

'And the gentleman's wooden leg?'

'The same.'

'I thought it rather a good touch,' Urmiston said loyally.

There was time to discuss these details because Hagley's letter was brief. *There is mischief in Oxford*, it said. *Meet Thurs.* The note was written on Bolsover Hall paper but unsigned. The addressee was Colonel Walter von Vircow-Ucquart. Bella examined the envelope.

'Who is this?'

'My dear lady,' Quigley smiled indulgently. 'Is that a real name? I think not. What you got there is an alias. Such as to disguise this Lord Bolsover as keeps cropping up. All plain as a pikestaff to me. Mr Hagley wishes to confer with his old pal.'

'If this *is* Bolsover in disguise, he has the cheek of the devil to put up at Claridge's,' Urmiston observed.

'Black eyepatch,' Quigley suggested. 'Empty sleeve.'

'I don't believe that for all his boldness he is walking around London as Lord Nelson,' Bella snapped.

'I have seen wonders done with an empty sleeve.'

'You say you have never met Bolsover, Charles?' she asked, ignoring the Captain.

'That is so.'

'Then we shall go to tea at Claridge's.'

Urmiston brushed the lapels to his new suit with something like real pleasure. His linen was crisp and only that morning Mrs Bardsoe had tied his stock just so, saying in addition that he looked a fine, well-set-up gentleman, though perhaps in need of a haircut.

'Who do you go as?' Quigley asked of Bella.

'Albert Edward Pons, brother to the one-legged George,' she replied with a flashing look. 'Is anyone watching the hotel?'

'Murch,' the Captain said, deflated.

Vircow-Ucquart walked with the aid of a stick. His huge lump of a head was shaven and blue glasses were looped over his ears. Bella and Urmiston alighted from a cab just as he entered Claridge's. Murch, who was lounging nearby, indicated his identity by laying a hand across his chest, his index finger extended. For good measure, he semaphored with his eyebrows.

'It is not Bolsover, of course,' Bella said in an undertone.

'I am very relieved to hear it. An ugly-looking brute.'

'The question is, who is he?'

'Here, my good fellow,' Urmiston said, palming Murch the letter from Hagley. 'Put this to good use. You'll know what to do.'

He took Bella's arm and they smiled their way past the doorman. Vircow-Ucquart was on his way in to tea. When seen closer to, the greatest surprise was the left side to the man's face. Fire had pulled down one cheek and emptied the eye to the socket. What had once been jowly flesh was replaced by a glistening white scar, wrinkled like boiling milk. Bella exchanged glances with Urmiston.

They took a table facing the Colonel and watched him order tea and sandwiches. His English, though murmured, was curt and guttural in tone. The waiter nodded and left at once to do his bidding. Bella bit her lip.

'Let us see how he reacts to the letter,' Urmiston whispered.

This had been hand-delivered by Murch to the doorman, who gave it to a page, who gave it to the reception desk. In time it was brought in on a small silver tray by a frail old messenger with snow-white hair. Vircow-Ucquart merely glanced at the envelope and laid it down by his napkin. Then he resumed his expressionless inspection of the room. His head turned in Bella's direction, paused a moment, and then swung back. His tea arrived and he waited patiently for the waiter to arrange everything to a nicety.

'Do you speak any German?' Bella asked with sudden inspiration. Urmiston patted her sleeve. He rose and walked over to Vircow-Ucquart's table.

'You will forgive me for disturbing you, Excellencz,' he said in schoolboy German. 'But do I have the honour of addressing one of the Crown Prince's most able lieutenants?'

'And who are you?'

'Medley, of *The Times.*'

'I have never heard of you,' Vircow-Ucquart replied with the greatest possible nonchalance.

'Then it was not you that I spoke with at Metz; and later outside the walls of Paris in 1870?'

'I do not speak to the press, in France or anywhere else.'

'Then I must apologize for the intrusion. Would you pass my kindest regards to the Reverend Mr Hagley when next you see him?'

This got Vircow-Ucquart's attention. He removed his glasses and gave Urmiston a dreadful Cyclops stare. A little tear ran from the corner of the empty eyesocket.

'Tell me again your name?'

'Henry Medley, Oslo correspondent of *The Times.*'

'Oslo!' the German boomed. He had very few facial expressions left, one of which was intended to indicate mirth. It involved a baring of his teeth, such as might be needed to eat a still-living fish or tear flesh from a particularly acidic orange. Urmiston bowed and retreated.

'Well done,' Bella said when he returned to their table. 'Where did you learn your German?'

'Charlotte Street,' he replied obscurely. 'What do we do now?'

To his great surprise, Bella laughed a deep-throated laugh, enough to turn heads at the adjoining tables.

'Do you know, that's a question I can't answer. Hagley and this fellow know each other, obviously. The mischief referred to in the letter would seem to make him complicit in the general scheme of things. I liked it when you mentioned Hagley's name: he seemed to react positively. But where they are to meet on Thursday is still unknown.'

'In Oxford, perhaps?'

'That would suit Captain Quigley very well. But I think not. Perhaps here.'

Urmiston touched her wrist. Vircow-Ucquart was at last opening the letter. He read it through at a glance and then threw it down. In place of a guilty start or smothered oath, he piled gâteau on to his fork and masticated it with awful thoroughness. Bella studied him.

'He is a mere go-between,' she concluded. 'Rather a forbidding one at that. You mentioned Charlotte Street earlier.'

'I was a waiter at Sieghardt's for two years when my financial situation was at its most pressing,' Urmiston said, blushing.

'Did you wear one of their long white aprons? I should like to have seen you.'

'You probably did. Waiters are indistinguishable one from another to most diners.'

Bella rapped the table with her teaspoon.

'What nonsense you do talk from time to time. You are a very handsome man, Charles. Look! Our gallant Colonel has become bored with cake.'

Vircow-Ucquart was indeed scraping back his chair. At the last moment he remembered the letter and stuffed it anyhow into his trouser pocket.

'Note how he does not look at you as he leaves,' Bella whispered. 'This must mean that he has no intention of killing you in the immediate future.'

'You relieve me greatly.'

'Unless,' she teased, 'he has gone upstairs to fetch his pistol.'

'As to that,' Urmiston said thoughtfully, 'does it not strike you that we have somewhat overplayed our hand? All three of us are now known to Hagley and the German. And thus to Bolsover, too.'

'Yes, but we are not investigating a crime, though one has certainly been committed. We must not be distracted by Quigley, who sees it all in his own too lurid light. We are not policemen, or avenging angels. We are simply students of human nature, which is mystery enough. We are looking for the one unburned stick in the bonfire's ashes.'

'And is this how books are written?'

'It is my method,' Bella retorted cheerfully. 'This German – and even Hagley – are minor characters. Lord Bolsover is our villain. I am increasingly sure that he is.'

'But why would he so lightly kill a girl in Covent Garden? And how, if at all, is he connected to this German?'

'We say in novels: the plot thickens.'

'In novels! Then I have it,' Urmiston mocked. 'We are actually following Bolsover's half-brother here, the one that was locked in the east tower since birth, to be fed and raised by a blind mulatto woman. The real Bolsover, discovering the existence of a twin, blinded by rage at the realization that the half-brother has a greater claim on the estate and having in his possession some loose sticks of gelignite –'

'I do hope you are not about to descend into mere facetiousness,' Bella snapped. A red flush was creeping up her neck. Urmiston was alarmed to find her very angry indeed.

When they came out of Claridge's and he found her a cab, she went straight home to Orange Street with barely more than a nod. Murch was waiting and watching from across the road and the two men walked out of the West End together, wrapped in companionable silence.

Vircow-Ucquart followed them at a convenient distance, clearing the Oxford Street pavements of mere Englishmen who strayed across his path with slashing strokes of his cane.

In Orange Street, Bella was still smarting from Urmiston's mockery. She attempted to calm herself with a third glass of Pouilly, through it was hardly yet six o'clock. Useless to acknowledge that Urmiston was as baffled as she with the addition of Vircow-Ucquart to the plot, and that he might have spoken out of exasperation. She had shown him anger and that was an emotion Bella prided herself on keeping in check. The true culprit, she thought with a fine irrationality, was Henry Ellis Margam. Even the six syllables of his ridiculous name annoyed her.

Vircow-Ucquart was the stuff of sensationalist fiction all right, belonging to that ruined world of death by fire, death by water, the innocent dragged down with the guilty, the stench of sulphur rising through otherwise unexceptional city pavements. But Bella's purpose in writing novels was, she hoped, more sophisticated. If she created monsters, she preferred them to be home-grown, although (and it shamed her to remember this) the plot of *Deveril's Disgrace* hinged on a babblingly mad octoroon girl with blue eyes.

For something to do to vent her ill-temper, she kicked her shoes up and down the drawing room. Had Urmiston been there, she would have kicked him, too. As for Hagley, who was beginning to elbow aside Bolsover in her anxious thoughts, had he been present she would have torn his ears off, the way epaulettes are stripped from a dishonoured soldier.

At this unfortunate moment, Marie Claude came in from a visit with Miss Titcombe to the National Gallery. She hesitated in the doorway, recognized Bella's mood, thought about saying something but settled instead for rolling her eyes.

'*What?*' Bella shouted.

'Nothing.'

'Are you coming into the room or are you going to hover there like a moth? Or a fruit bat or something?'

Marie Claude fled. Bella pursued her as far as the foot of the staircase.

'I am *not* merely some foolish woman with a talent for scribbling!' she bellowed. 'And if you dare to utter one word more to suggest that I am, I will lock you in your room until you starve to death, you ungrateful child.'

'I have said nothing!' Marie Claude yelped.

'No, you haven't. But don't you *ever* roll your eyes at me again!'

'Will you please stop shouting?'

Bella found she had a shoe in her hand. She threw it at the landing and watched it bounce off the banisters and fall back at her feet. Marie Claude ran screaming to her room. Bella retrieved the shoe and went back to look for its partner. Under the sofa.

As always happened when in this frantic mood, she thought of her husband, Garnett. The memory of him only came to her when she was truly angry. It was a realization that made her blush. She sat down, defeated.

Garnett Wallis had gone out early one morning from their home in Hertfordshire, riding across the fields to join the local hunt. It was three days before Christmas and the mantelpiece was littered with invitation cards sent from five or even ten miles away.

The ground was frozen, a perfectly unremarkable circumstance, given the season. Garnett's horse slipped on an ice pond at the bottom of a neighbour's meadow, breaking its leg and pinning the rider down with a broken pelvis. And even then Garnett might have survived the accident but for the pure ordinariness of a sudden but prolonged snowfall. He was found a little after two in the afternoon and carried home on a hurdle. Doctors were summoned, telegrams sent. It was all to no purpose. Pneumonia, that unfailing friend to old people, took the ebullient and adored Garnett Wallis off in his thirty-sixth year.

In his pocket, intended for the postbox outside the inn where the hunt was to meet, was a letter to a mistress Bella had not known existed. Six days after the funeral, she found the woman's letters to him. She thought the whole morning about reading them and then burned them one by one in the drawing-room grate. Watching them curl and blacken was a greater horror than closing Garnett's eyes with the stroke of her thumb.

She looked up from this reverie as Marie Claude entered the room.

'The Captain Quigley has sent a message by a child. You are to go at once to Shelton Street.'

It took Bella a moment or two to clear her mind and remember that was where Charles Urmiston lodged. Then she jumped up, her face white.

'A cab, Marie Claude. As fast as ever you like. Run into Leicester Square if you must. But find me a man who will drive like the devil. Say it is life or death.'

The cabbie was young and superlatively cocky. When he heard where he was to take his fare he pointed out that a one-legged chicken could walk there in five minutes. Bella flung two florins full into his chest and that, along with the terrible expression on her face, closed his mouth. The crack of his whip rang like a pistol shot down Orange Street.

She was met at the little shop by Mrs Bardsoe, a mixture of blunt common sense and quivering outrage.

'The foreign brute followed Mr Charles into the parlour here, swept me right out the road and straightways began belabouring the gentleman with his stick, his cane. Not a word said, no sign of a prologue, that poor brave man defending himself as best he could. Bottles smashed, that picture there knocked clean off the wall.'

'He truly said nothing?'

'Not a word. I took him to be a robber of some sort, was slow to get a picture of it in my mind. But then I ups and hits him to the side of the head with that stone mortar of mine on the table there. He went down like a sack of taters. So now I'm out in the street shouting blue murder. I find Ma Rawnsley's boy, a bright enough spark, and has him run to Captain Quigley's double-quick smart.'

'You knocked the German unconscious?'

'German, was he? I laid him out like a corpse, ma'am. So anyway, there I am wringing me hands when who should pitch up but Billy Murch? As soon as he sees the state I'm in, he breaks into a run and we go in to see to Mr Urmiston. Billy gives him the fireman's lift up to his rooms and I'm to wait behind locked doors until the Captain shows.'

Simply by reciting the story, Mrs Bardsoe's composure was beginning to crack. Bella opened her arms and the plump little body melted against her.

'Not a strong man, Mrs Wallis,' she wailed, 'never a one for the rough-and-tumble of life. But game as you like.'

'Where is the German now?'

'Why, the Captain and Billy are seeing to him. Murch fetches his cart round, the animal is rolled into my parlour carpet, and off they go.'

'Do you know where, Mrs Bardsoe?'

'Well, not to no hospital, I'll swear to that.'

'And Mr Urmiston? Has a doctor been called?'

'Bless you, Hannah Bardsoe can set him to rights faster than any doctor you'll find round here. Come.'

Urmiston lay on his bed, naked to the belly. When he saw the women he made a shamefaced attempt to cover his paper-white ribs and chest, crisscrossed with ugly red weals. Bella ran to him and knelt by his head.

'Never mind that for a moment, Charles,' she whispered, her breath fanning his cheek. 'It is a ridiculous question, but are you all right?'

'Nothing is broken. I have that from Mrs B,' he smiled. 'Though I feel like a spring-cleaned carpet. This is what they mean by being given a dusting, I believe.'

'We'll have you up on your feet in no time at all, sir,' Mrs Bardsoe said from the shadows. 'Think of it as nothing more serious than falling out this here window.'

Urmiston tried to laugh, but a huge wince pinched the sound in his chest. Bella turned to the landlady.

'There is truly nothing broken?'

'I'll wager my life on it. Two dislocated fingers what I have pulled straight. A powerful bruised left hip. The rest is what you see.'

'Where is Vircow-Ucquart?' Urmiston whispered.

'Quigley and Mr Murch have him.'

'Poor devil,' he replied. 'I would like you to know, Bella, it was Mrs B that saved me from being thrashed to death. She is a very brave woman.'

'Stone me, Mr Charles,' she cried. 'It was my furniture he was knocking about. But you're right – I fetched him one the side of the head he won't forget in a hurry.'

Bella smoothed the hair from Urmiston's brow.

'Listen, my dear. Mrs Bardsoe and I are going downstairs to make all well in her parlour and I hope take a little restorative together. Shall you manage here for a while? Is there anything you need?'

Blushing, Charles Urmiston beckoned her closer. But Mrs Bardsoe easily guessed what he was saying.

'Now do you find your way down those awful old stairs, Mrs Wallis, and I shall just tidy him up, the same as I have done enough times before. I mean with other invalids,' she added hastily.

'Perhaps, though –' the patient mewed.

'Now, now, Mr Urmiston. Don't come it the green girl with Hannah Bardsoe. We'll attend to what's needed and then I will knock you up a salve that would inspire a dead horse. I have it all in mind what's needed. And then, when you're plumped up on more pillows than what you have now, you shall have a poached egg or a bit of herring roe, whichever you choose.'

Down in the parlour, Bella was sweeping up broken glass with a battered brush and pan. The man she most wanted to meet on earth was the Reverend Anthony Hagley. From a shard of glass picked up from under the table, she recognized one of Mrs Bardsoe's treasures, a memorial mug issued for the funeral of the Iron Duke. Completely unbidden, she burst into tears.

'Why!' Hannah Bardsoe cried, bustling in on her. 'This won't do, my dear. This won't do at all. What's a few knick-knacks, compared to the saving of that good man upstairs? Though a glass of rum with you, Mrs Wallis, by all means.'

'Now then, Fritzi,' Captain Quigley whispered, patting Vircow-Ucquart on his good cheek. 'Can you smell the river? Because that's where you are. This gentleman here is for gutting you with a rusty bale hook, ain't that right, Billy?'

'That, or reach down his throat and pull his liver out with my bare hands,' Murch suggested by way of alternative.

The German licked his lips. He sat tied to a chair in his shirt and trousers, a lump above his ear the size of a teacup.

'This is kidnap,' he muttered. 'My government shall be informed.'

'You're talking through the cheeks of your arse now, Fritz. Moored up outside, waiting on the tide, is a brick wherry going round the Naze to Ipswich. The boys have promised to give you a lift halfway home. The Goodwin Sands is where they'll drop you off. Wasn't that it, Billy?'

'The same.'

Vircow-Ucquart squinted furiously.

'This you cannot do. I am a German officer. I am a *gentleman*.'

'You are a murdering bastard.'

The captive laughed, in spite of the peril he was in.

'That weakling? I give him only a good thrashing, that is all. For his impertinence.'

'I am talking about Welsh Alice,' Murch said, his cross eyes terrible to behold.

Vircow-Ucquart looked genuinely at a loss.

'What person is this?'

'Slashed to death in Maiden Lane.'

'Where is such a place?'

'At the bottom of Covent Garden.'

Quigley was watching carefully: he saw a very slight compression of the German's lips.

'I know only Hyde Park. I have not been in this garden.'

'Welsh Alice. Young girl, china-doll face. Police looking for you. This here boat trip I'm talking about is to save you from the gallows. You and the chair both, over the side, kaboosh. Like a Viking funeral sort of thing.'

Murch suddenly pushed the Captain out of the way and put his face within an inch of the German's.

'You killed her, you wicked basket. And I shall have you for it. Before you drown, you'll suffer, so help me.'

'I did not kill this girl!'

'No?'

'That is not my way,' he yelped.

'Captain,' Murch growled, 'let me at him with the tin-snips.'

'Shears,' Quigley explained. Turning back to Murch he asked, 'And for why do we need those tin-snips, Billy boy?'

'I'm going to trim off his murdering fingers for starters. And then –'

'Not his todger, Bill, for all love! Leave him his todger.'

'It was not me!' Vircow-Ucquart roared. 'I was not even there any longer. It was Freddie!'

'Freddie,' Quigley scoffed.

'Lord Bolsover!'

'Oh, very rich. A made-up name if ever I heard one.'

'Ask your friend Medley. Medley of *The Times.*'

The Captain sighed. 'Do you know what he's talking about?'

'That's where you found me! In Medley's lodgings! You are all of the same gang in some way. But I have money. Whatever it is you need, you say. Say now! And then all is forgotten.'

'I'll look them shears out, Bill. The old tin-snips.'

He wandered away in the gloom at the back of the go-down, his boots crunching on little drifts of grain.

'Listen to me,' the German said urgently to Murch. 'You must believe me. I was not there. I don't play games with women. You have got the wrong man. Lord Bolsover –'

'Not one word more,' Murch commanded. 'Take your punishment like a man. Toes and fingers first and then a trip down the Thames. But better you go with empty pockets.'

He reached into the German's trousers and found the letter from Oxford.

'What's this?'

'It's not important.'

'*Meet Thursday*? And where is that to be? Captain!' he called. 'This here gentleman is to meet someone on Thursday.'

'What's that to us, Bill?' Quigley responded from the back of the empty warehouse. His position now was betrayed by the clash and clank of metal and some vile curses.

'Can I lay my hands on those old snips?' he shouted. 'I cannot. And there's rats here as big as armadillios. I seen nothing like it since Dick's day.'

A claw-hammer skittered out of the gloom. Vircow-Ucquart flinched.

'My friend,' he whispered to Murch. 'The money, we were talking about some money. Gold sovereigns –'

'Hold your horses,' Quigley cried in triumph. 'Here we are.'

'Very well!' their victim cried hastily. 'We meet on Thursday and I take you to him.'

'What's he saying now, Bill?' Quigley called.

'He's on about this Bolsover again, I don't doubt.'

'Pay him no mind, Bill. Never was such a person.'

'I take you to him,' the German bellowed at parade-ground volume. 'In Paris! He is in Paris! The Hotel Louvois maybe.'

'Which they are rusty,' Quigley said quietly, standing directly behind Vircow-Ucquart's chair.

'Pass them here.'

There really was a pair of tin shears. Without the least hesitation, Murch opened the blades wide under the screaming man's nostrils and cut off the tip of his nose. Then they opened the door at the end of the shed and ran the chair and its occupant across the plank flooring and, taking a side each, pitched it out into the Thames.

There was no brick barge; and far from filling, the tide had yet to reach its ebb. Vircow-Ucquart fell into three feet of grey-black ooze. They watched for a few moments while the German thrashed about, trying to avoid being buried alive. His roaring attracted three naked urchins a hundred yards off, panning the river bed for treasure. One by one they shaded their eyes with their forearms.

A thought occurred to Captain Quigley.

'How did you know about them tin shears, Bill?'

'I never expected you to find none,' Murch protested mildly. 'Once found, it would have been a crime not to use 'em. Give me a hand to sweep up some of this here corn for my old horse.'

ELEVEN

Murch went back to Rotherhithe next day to spy out the lay of the land from his acquaintance the thoroughly evil M'Gurk but refused his offer of a drink, pleading an engagement later that morning. Accordingly the two men leaned on a cranky wooden fence overlooking the Thames, a short way from where Vircow-Ucquart had been flung from the grain loft. The river was busy. They watched a grimy paddle steamer running downstream. M'Gurk pointed.

'You want to keep your eye on that. There's boilers there that'll blow any day soon.'

'You don't say?'

'The wife's brother has the care of them,' M'Gurk explained.

'You paint a picture. What does she carry, the old tub?'

'Enough,' the Wapping man said shortly.

There was a properly businesslike pause before Murch broached the next topic.

'You haven't come across a Fritzi by any chance? Fell out the sky, seemingly, along with his chair?'

'I knew it had to be you,' M'Gurk rumbled.

'How is he today?'

'He has mentioned money.'

'Listen, Ollie,' Murch said suddenly, 'is it right that your Liza should wade about with the boys in her birthday suit? And her no more than a maid?'

'Been having a gander, have you? She ain't got nothing they don't already know about. So mind your own bleedin' business,' her father added. He leaned over the fence and spat into the lap of the tide. Then, for good measure, he eased himself with a foghorn fart.

'He done you some wrong, the foreign bloke,' he suggested.

'Got on my wick,' Murch confirmed.

'How much d'you want for your part in it?'

'He's all yours,' Murch said. 'God help him.'

'Slow to rile, that Billy, but once he gets his dander up there is no stopping him. My late husband was the same.'

Mrs Bardsoe was helping Charles Urmiston to his first faltering steps since the beating, his arm round her neck and shoulders, hers encircling his waist. The salve she had prepared for his wounds smelled very agreeably of wet summer meadows. Urmiston tottered about in his nightshirt, unable to prevent himself easing his ribs against his landlady's pillowy bosom. The sensation was disturbing.

'You don't think cutting the man's nose off was a step too far, Mrs B?' he asked, to cover the first faint prod of arousal.

'I do not. Whatever was he thinking of, coming over here and interfering with the rights of true-born Englishmen? And him with only one eye in his head.'

'He survived, though?'

'Bless you, sir, the M'Gurks have him safe. Though I wouldn't like to say when he'll see the West End again.

And as for blowing his nose, well, he won't need no wipes no more!'

Her laughter jiggled her breasts and set Urmiston's pulse racing all over again. He reached out with his hands and balanced himself against the bedroom wall.

'Do I detect a healthsome little show of sweat?' Mrs Bardsoe asked, not without a secret smile. 'Shall I fetch up the tin bath and a pail of hot water?'

'I believe I shall manage without,' Urmiston said. 'Let your healing balm have its full effect. But I tell you what it is, Mrs B, I must get down to Fleur de Lys Court today.'

'Ho!' Mrs Bardsoe cried. 'Never think of it! There's a bruise on your hip as big as a cowpat. No, no, the others must come to you. Go to Fleur de Lys Court, forsooth! If that don't beat all.'

'Well then,' Urmiston said uncertainly, 'at the very least I must send them a letter.'

He managed to shoo her out long enough to find his trousers, which he put on as if for the first time in his life, his fingers extremely slow in the matter of buttons. Socks and boots defeated him utterly.

'Now,' his landlady said, coming in with a kettle of hot water. 'What a sorry sight we have here. No ducking nor schoolgirl blushing, I'm going give you a general once-over and spruce-up before your friends arrive – I have sent an intelligent boy to fetch them. A shave and a clean shirt will set you to rights. And after that a nettle tea.'

'Could I not have coffee?' Urmiston remonstrated weakly. Mrs Bardsoe smiled.

'Go on then,' she relented. 'And I suppose a cigar would be to your taste as well? Men! Now hold your head very still while I have this here razor in my hand. And for why, Mr Urmiston, dear? In case I cuts your blessed nose off, that's for why!'

This witty sally sent her into peals of laughter. There was something irrepressible about her that gladdened Urmiston's creaking gate of a heart. When she had finished shaving him, he reached impulsively for her warm, moist hand. Her eyes widened.

'Whatever next?' she wondered in the least chiding way possible. They were both blushing. But Urmiston had a ready change of subject, bringing forward something that had been on his mind all night.

'I have to ask you, Mrs B. This cutting-off of noses. Is that really the way things are settled in the real world?'

'Ho! What does a quiet body like me know of the real world? If by those words you mean *your* world? All I know is that we are forced to look after our own in this station of life. I know the policeman Higgins, the local bobby, for he comes in here for salve to his piles, which he has something crucial. But I would no more ask him his opinion on how to go on in life than I would one of them china dogs you see downstairs in my parlour.'

'He is unreliable?' Urmiston suggested stupidly. Mrs Bardsoe smiled.

'He is a copper,' she explained gently, as if talking to a visiting Trobriand Islander. 'He joined for the boots and his brains are right there in his feet. A nice enough cove and his wife is a pleasant body. But oh dear me, if we had to depend on the coppers for our justice, the world would come to a stop by next Friday teatime.'

'I hadn't realized.'

'That's because you're made of better stuff than us.'

'If there is better stuff than you, Mrs B, I hope to meet it before I die.'

'Go on out of it,' she squealed, delighted.

But there was a problem with these hints and glances, as there almost always is. Urmiston had loved his wife after his own fashion, making loyalty and a great deal of patience his way of showing it. Towards the end Marguerite – more and more so after his dismissal by the Great Western – had grown fractious and weepy. Tears he could cope with, for he very often felt like crying himself, trudging home to Lambeth from his waitering job at Sieghardt's and realizing he would never again buy new shoes or own decent linen. But then came silence between them, a long and bitter silence that lasted until her death.

Lodging with Mrs Bardsoe had already shown him some of what he had missed in his own life – earthiness, a careless physicality, delight in the small pleasures of the day and (like the conversation he had just had about the policeman) a brutal realism. The widower in Urmiston liked Hannah Bardsoe far too much. Aroused, as he was now, he felt guilty. And she, intelligent soul, sensed it.

Captain Quigley was the first to arrive, his fist filled, preposterously, with a nosegay of violets. They were made of cloth.

'Care of patient exemplary,' he noted. 'Lady of the house preparing coffee. And at my suggestion, a thimbleful of rum.'

'I am in your debt once again, Captain. The villain found more than his match in you, I believe.'

'What is that smell?' Quigley asked.

'Mrs Bardsoe's balm. Er, goose fat and other ingredients.'

'Is it red, the mixture?'

'Green.'

'A red ointment the only thing. Chilli pepper. Camphor. Maybe a pinch or so of gunpowder. Strong salts various.'

'Mrs B tells me Vircow-Ucquart is captured by the mudlarks.'

'The M'Gurk family. Which is terrible for him.'

'Has he talked?'

'Before he lost his bugle, he did say this Bolsover character was jaunting off to Paris.'

'You think Mr Hagley plans to meet him there? It seems unlikely.'

'Ah, now, as to that –'

He was about to review the whole campaign when Bella appeared, bearing a tray of coffee. She kissed Urmiston lightly on the cheek.

'You are looking more human this morning, Charles.'

'I expect to be fighting fit by tomorrow.'

'We shall see. Captain Quigley has told you about Paris, I don't doubt.'

'The Hotel Louvois,' Quigley supplied helpfully.

'I'm assured by the Captain that in his extensive military experience, time spent on reconnaissance is seldom wasted. All the same, we stay where we are. And *that*,' she added, turning to Quigley, 'is my final word on the matter.'

Urmiston thought for a moment or two and then nodded his agreement.

'We have perhaps been fishing in too deep waters,' he said.

'Vircow-Ucquart would have killed you if he could. Or would not have shown a moment's remorse had you died under his hands. It has made me think. What is it that they don't want us to find out about them?'

Captain Quigley blew out his cheeks and absent-mindedly drank the medicinal rum he had prescribed for the patient.

'What else, if not blue bloody murder?'

Urmiston shifted uncomfortably inside his shirt. The broken skin on his ribs and back was itching and his head throbbed.

'We don't know,' he said. The words came out far too bluntly.

'Steady the front rank,' Quigley muttered.

'I realize I am a tyro when it comes to situations like this. My opinion counts for very little. But nothing sharpens the mind better than a good drubbing. With your permission, I would like to put forward a theory.'

'Please,' Bella encouraged.

'I start by making a very large assumption, that it was Bolsover who killed the girl in Maiden Lane.'

'You can be sure of it,' Quigley cried.

'No, Captain,' Urmiston said quietly. 'We can't, not entirely.'

'What is your theory?' Bella asked.

'It came to me last night that we could divide the story –' he nodded to her politely at the use of the term – 'into two quite separate moments. The first is when his lordship, for whatever reason, uses a part of his capital to endow a missionary enterprise in Oxford and install his particular friend as Warden, or Principal. At the very least, Bolsover bought a house for Hagley. A very large and commodious house.'

'Go on.'

'We don't know and it hardly matters how it benefits them both – I'm sorry if I am coming it the lawyer somewhat.'

Bella studied him calmly, her grey eyes searching his face for the last scrap of meaning.

'Is it your point that he was perfectly free to do whatever he liked with his own money?' she asked.

'There is no crime in being philanthropic.'

The three of them sat digesting this for a moment or two. Captain Quigley clog-danced briefly on the bare boards, coughed, smoothed his moustache.

'But a rum do, all the same.'

'Yes. Given Bolsover's moral character, as far I have understood it, very strange.'

Quigley leered hideously.

'Perhaps it was done for love.'

'Would that be so wrong either? Then again perhaps he was tricked into it, blackmailed even. Anything's possible. But the outcome was a good one and I think what the Captain has discovered in Oxford stands apart from all the rest of it.'

'You say so,' Quigley protested. 'But there's a lot we don't yet know about what goes on there.'

'The second part of your theory?' Bella prompted with the same attempted calm.

'Concerns the murder of Welsh Alice. We can say three, possibly more, people were present but almost certainly

Bolsover, Hagley, and now, according to the most recent evidence, this German fellow. They make a most ill-assorted trio on the face of it.'

'And?'

I think we must assume they know each other well, perhaps very well, but I do not think it feasible that three friends, after a supper somewhere, decide to go out – in *harness* – to find and murder a young girl. And certainly not behind some scaffolding in a residential street within cry of two popular pubs.

'And if one of them – or all of them – hated women enough,' Urmiston blushed, 'Well, I know little of the subject but I believe there are houses to accommodate that particular kind of lust.'

Bella turned to the Captain, who shrugged. 'The point is that we must believe one of these men – and we really can't say which one – killed Welsh Alice.'

Urmiston gave way to impulse and scratched the wounds on his chest. Little flowers of blood appeared on his linen almost at once. 'The poor creature died of a sudden, irrational, ungovernable impulse on the part of one of these men. The three of them were walking together somewhere, we can't say where, with nothing more on their minds than commonplaces. They are interrupted – let's say they are propositioned – and within seconds a woman has fallen to the pavement with her throat slashed. And then they walk on.'

Captain Quigley marched to the window and opened it a crack. Urmiston was at a loss for a moment to know why, until he realized that what had begun as the scent of summer meadows in the room was changing now to a more foetid stink. It was the smell that comes from river weeds stirred by a stick, or oar.

'Mrs Bardsoe swears by this concoction,' he apologized faintly. 'It did wonders for Penny. Mr Murch's horse.'

'Linseed the only remedy for a horse,' Quigley corrected. 'I suggest we fumigate quarters with a cheroot each.'

'That would be agreeable,' Bella said. 'But not one word to Mrs Bardsoe about linseed, horses, or any other medical topic, understood?'

For a while they smoked in silence. Urmiston concentrated all his attention on not setting fire to the sheets. Quigley sat with one leg cocked up on the other, gazing judiciously at the ceiling and giving the company his impersonation of a man in deep thought. Bella mused.

'Very well,' she said at last. 'Among those three men, the one most capable of a sudden irrational act is Bolsover. Is that what you're saying?'

'That is my theory,' Urmiston murmured. 'We know what Vircow-Ucquart is capable of with a cane, in a Prussian sort of way; but it is hard to suppose that Hagley carries a knife or razor with him when he goes to supper. That only leaves his lordship.'

'Does your theory support any further conclusions?'

'Only that we don't know half enough about Lord Bolsover.'

'Suppose,' Quigley proposed quietly, 'suppose he has done this sort of thing before?'

'We don't know and we can't say,' Urmiston said.

'Because, my dears, if he has,' the Captain continued, unabashed, 'wouldn't that explain a bit why Mr Hagley and the Fritz were with him? To keep him on the leash, as it were.'

'Too fanciful,' Bella objected.

'You don't slash a girl the way he did in Maiden Lane just because she says the wrong thing to you,' the Captain persisted. 'If you're a belted earl, you don't go out to dinner with a razor in your pocket.'

'Was it a razor?'

'That's what the police doctor thinks.'

Bella jumped up and walked to the window. She pushed the sash up as far as it would go and perched uncomfortably on the sill. Three floors below, the citizens of Shelton Street bickered and called to each other, or rummaged in the vegetable and old-clothes stalls. There were patterns in the way people moved and interacted, much clearer to the eye than ever they would be at street level. Because, she thought ruefully, in the gutter the observer was part of the story.

Urmiston and Quigley watched and waited.

'If all this is so,' she asked almost absently, her eyes still on the scene below, 'why does Hagley wish to meet him now?'

'You are forgetting,' Urmiston reminded her gently. 'As it turned out, he wished only to meet Vircow-Ucquart.'

'All right, but why?'

'Because,' Quigley suggested with telling simplicity, 'they are his lordship's minders. Bolsover a gentleman who likes the smell of blood. Same as he likes bully lads and fine wines.'

'If I had a friend as combustible as Lord Bolsover,' Urmiston agreed gloomily, 'I would not let him out of my sight. They have no idea whether the police have discovered witnesses, nor whether there is some other trail of evidence that might lead to them. They know we know something. Hagley in particular realizes he left his cigar case at the scene.'

'That ties him nicely to Bolsover in any court of law,' the Captain added.

'What do the police say about Alice's murder?' Bella asked.

'Nothing so fanciful,' Quigley grunted. 'A tart with no drawers has her throat cut behind some scaffolding. Not much of a story there.'

Bella turned away from the window with a set expression, picked up her gloves and quitted the sickroom without another word. Her cheroot was left smouldering in a saucer, the smoke drawn to the open window in an undulating blue-grey wave.

Steyne, Bolsover's house in Berkshire, looked well enough in sunshine but on an overcast day, such as this was, its yellowy stones darkened and – the thought flew into Hagley's mind by association – sulked. That morning, to the consternation of his servants, his lordship had ordered fires lit in every room. No sooner done than he further commanded all the windows to be opened. Hagley was received in a gale of woodsmoke, attended by rushing maids and footmen.

'There is some reason for all this, is there?' he enquired too jovially.

Bolsover stared at him. 'It is what I want,' he said.

'Yes, but the reason –'

'I have given you the reason. You have come from Oxford?'

'From London. We are in trouble, Freddie.'

'I am not in the least trouble, unless it is that the house will shortly burn down. And if it does, what's that to you?'

Hagley walked to each mullion window in turn and drew it close. Bolsover had flung himself on to a huge couch and resumed his glass of claret. He looked tired and drawn.

'You are beginning to creep about, Anthony, my dear,' he scoffed. 'Too much holy Moses, or whatever it is you do. Too much snuffling round your young gentlemen. Do you kiss them all goodnight? Is that what has induced the bent back and the tiptoe steps?'

'Vircow-Ucquart has disappeared.'

'How I wish that were true. I favoured him at first because of his appalling ugliness – you can have no idea of the horror that face inspires in others. It was thrilling for a while. But I am tired of it now. He is the bad penny that one throws into the gutter, only to see it back in your pocket the next day.'

Hagley poured himself a brandy, pleased to find his hands were shaking only very gently.

'This room was once precious to us both,' he observed.

'That was in the days when you were more impressionable. And far more reckless. I have largely forgotten those times.'

The sheer impudence of the remark made Hagley want to go over and slap his face. Instead, he controlled his voice.

'Vircow-Ucquart is a loyal friend. As am I, still. I tell you now, there is trouble for all three of us. A rogue of some kind has been asking questions in Oxford. Two other people, unknown to me, were spying on Vircow-Ucquart at Claridge's, one of them claiming to be a *Times* reporter. The other was a woman. The Prussian scribbled me a note and set off after them. He has not been seen since.'

'And what did they want to know, these people?'

'There are things about a recent event in Covent Garden that would be better kept secret.'

Bolsover yawned.

'A shilling whore who joined the choir invisible a few years earlier than she expected? How many times does that happen a week? Ring for Maudsley.'

When he came, the butler was ordered to find someone called Jean and bring her to the drawing room. Maudsley was not the usual image of a senior servant. He was broad and clumsy, with thick wrists and huge square hands. He hesitated for a mere fraction of a second and then nodded.

'You don't bow, Maudsley?'

'I have trouble remembering that,' the man said with equal insolence.

Jean, when she came, was a girl of about twenty. Hagley's presence startled her for a moment, but she made him a bob and then stood with her hands folded in front of her.

'This is Jean,' Bolsover drawled. 'Tell Mr Hagley your duties, Jean.'

'Well,' she said uncertainly, 'I am your lordship's maid.'

'As you might be to the lady of the house in a different circumstance?'

'I have never worked nowhere else,' she said cautiously.

'Mr Hagley and I have been discussing aspects of the Bible just now and in particular the role of the handmaiden. It is Mr Hagley's contention that I do not like women enough to grasp the concept.'

'Sir?'

'This is quite enough,' Hagley said, feeling the blood run to his cheeks.

'Have I ever frightened you, Jean?'

'No, sir.'

'Threatened you?'

'No, sir.'

'Do you like being my handmaiden?'

'As far as I understand it, yes.'

Her eyes flicked to Hagley, who stood. He reached and took both her hands in his. They were moist with sweat and, close to, he could see her burning face.

'This has been most useful testimony, my child,' he said with all the clerical unction he could muster. 'We need not detain you further.'

'Have I ever seen you naked, Jean?' Bolsover interrupted. She bit her lip.

'I believe you have, sir,' she said in a tiny voice.

'And were you afraid then?'

'Never in life,' she whispered.

After she had gone, Hagley wiped his hands on a handkerchief before rounding on his host and former lover.

'Are you quite mad? Do you think this extenuates in any way what I came here to talk about? I am trying to tell you, Freddie, we are in very great trouble.'

'You know,' Bolsover said dreamily, 'you can get people to do anything you want with money. Last night I entertained your successor at Brailston, a very different sort of parson. A hearty innocent. He plays village cricket and botanizes. I told him I wished to make him a generous donation to the fabric of the church.'

'That was decent of you,' Hagley said carefully.

'It was. He turned up on the dot of eight, and we dined *à deux*. I thought it would be amusing to have the food served him by naked servants. He managed not to blink an eye. I can do that sort of thing. I can do anything.'

'Your servants agreed to all this?'

'For a consideration. I chose only the ugliest, the grossest among them. We were given our soup by a venerable kitchenmaid almost too old to see. Other dishes were brought in by my groom and a simpleton boy from the gardener's staff.'

'Freddie,' Hagley whispered helplessly, 'I am only here to save you.'

'You are here because if I go down, you will go with me.'

And that, Hagley thought, was the beginning, middle and end of it. The death of the Covent Garden drab brought their whole relationship into sharper focus. More than that, it opened a box of similar nightmares better left untouched.

'You are thinking of crossing into the Continent, I believe?'

Bolsover laughed. 'You walk like a parson and damn me if you don't begin to talk like one. I am going to Paris for a few days or a week. I buy my shirts there. Are you going to advise against it?'

'I was hoping to accompany you,' Hagley protested gently.

'Well, well, this is a romantic gesture indeed. I stay at the Louvois.'

He said this with some considerable spin and laughed at Hagley's reaction.

'A good-class family hotel, as the manager has insisted more than once in the past. That is, when attempting to explain certain house rules that appeared to have been broken by the distinguished English milord and his clerical friend.'

'Do you not think,' Hagley asked with as much innocence as he could muster for the question, 'we might go to Rheims instead?'

'Generally speaking, I detest champagne. And I certainly detest provincial cities. No, Paris suits very well.'

'But not the Louvois.'

'We shall see,' Bolsover said, laughing.

And how I hope you fall overboard and drown before you get anywhere near France, was the Reverend Mr Hagley's most unchristian thought. His smile was as flimsy as tissue paper.

'Then Paris it is,' he said.

Marie Claude had taken Bella at her word. That evening the two women went to the Aquarium, a place of such moral squalor, as it seemed to Bella, that she was alarmed for her companion. Perhaps Marie Claude liked the place for its faint echo of café life, the buzzing of waiters and the sauntering crowds that passed, seemingly at ease but as nervously alert as any fish. Bella was not so entranced.

'Hello, ma,' a pimply young clerk addressed her cheekily. 'Out for a spin with your daughter, is it?'

'Will you be a good little boy and go away?'

But he took this as an invitation to banter further.

'May I?' he asked, scraping back a chair. 'How about a nice ice or another cup of coffee?'

'Go away,' Marie Claude said.

'Ah, a French miss! Albert Judd. Firm of Minshall and Greaves. Man about town, bong viveur. I know France. I had a day trip to Zeebrugge just this last May.'

'Albert,' Bella began. But at that moment an altogether different kind of man stood over them.

'Is this little bag of wind troubling you, madam?'

Judd jumped up at once.

'Never argue with the navy, that's always been my motto.'

'Good lad. Now hop off.'

The sailor was a far more respectable proposition. His face was seriously whiskered and his hands blunt. His eyes were a startling blue. On an impulse, Bella asked him to join them.

'Well,' he said uncertainly.

'We are perfectly respectable,' she said, laughing.

His name was Bolt and he was in London on the last day of shore leave. He joined his ship next morning in Portsmouth.

'And where do you go?' Marie Claude asked.

'Channel Squadron,' he said, smiling. 'No palm trees, miss, nor no other exotic climes neither.'

'But you have been to such places?'

'I have seen Japan in '63, serving in the *Havoc*, a little wooden tub you would not cross the Channel in. Though we had our say, when the time came. Brisk work at Kagosima Harbour.'

'Was there a war there at that time, Mr Bolt?'

'There was shot and shell to be sure.'

'What are they like, the Japanese?'

'I would say bloody-minded little chaps.'

Bella warmed to him.

'Would you take a glass of brandy with us?'

'No to the brandy, with grateful thanks. But I will smoke a pipe if you permit.'

'Are you married?' Marie Claude wanted to know.

'Bless you, miss – yes, and with a daughter I hope turns out half as pretty as you.'

'Oh how I have always longed to be a sailor!' she cried. Bolt was amused.

'And many a jack would be happy to serve with you, I can swear to that! But it is not all glory, miss, not by a long shot. Some of it is a very dirty business.'

'Were you born within sight of the sea, Mr Bolt?' Marie Claude wanted to know. 'Is that what drew you to faraway places?'

He laughed indulgently, forgetting himself so far as to pat her hand.

'I am from Berkshire, my dear. My old father had the Feathers on the road to Wallingford. I knew nothing of the sea until I was fourteen.'

'You said Wallingford?' Bella asked.

'Do you know that lovely old place?'

In novels – like the one she was carrying around in her head – such a coincidence would lead to a revelation and the plot would bound forward; and it did occur to Bella that she had only to ask the right question to have Bolsover rise as if from the pages of a pop-up book. Bolt studied her attentively, waiting for her reply. It was a dramatic moment: the noise, the crush, the question left hanging in the air, Bolt as the innocent messenger of some crucial piece of intelligence. Bella smiled.

'I had an aunt who lived there once,' she improvised.

Bolt nodded. He tucked his pipe away inside his breast and reached for his uniform cap.

'That's how it is – one thing leads to another. We are all connected in some small way. 'Tis but all one story, however big the book may be. Every life touches every other. And if that is not the good Lord's purpose, then I'd like to know what is.'

He stood, and in his frank seaman-like way, touched his cap to them.

'You will not take coffee or a plate of cakes?'

'I will not. I bid you goodnight, ladies.'

That night Bella and Marie Claude slept together in the same bed, something that did not happen often. Marie Claude's neediness was hardly ever carnal. She liked to be admired for her almost cat-like beauty, that concealed a hidden truculence none but another woman could understand or tolerate. And Bella did so admire her, marvelling at her narrow hips, the extraordinary delicacy of her wrists and ankles. It was a body born for white shell beaches or the greenest tropical forests and not London's reckless vulgarities. For her, Marie Claude was like a picture in an exhibition, beckoning but at the same time unknowable. The burden of her pillow talk was how happy she had been in Paris and how miserable she was in London. Neither statement was true. Naked and sleeping, as she was now, one arm flung across her face, the other folded on her gently fluttering stomach, she was, Bella considered, a creature from some other dimension altogether. I am, she thought, merely her curator.

And a bulky one at that. She nudged the sheets away with her feet and let the night air flow over her body, suddenly as glum as Marie Claude was silent. She thought of her fellow novelist, Mrs Toaze-Bonnett, tucked up in Pinner under far more chaste arrangements, her hair doubtless under a little linen cap and not clinging to shoulders slick with sweat. Mrs Toaze-Bonnett (like Bella, a widow) wrote five hundred words a day, pruned roses, sang in the parish church choir and forgave the rest of the world its sins. By any standards, she was the most thumping bore in Christendom. But, Bella reflected bitterly, she had grasped one essential truth about life: that happiness was the greatest fiction of them all.

It was said that the sage old fool Sheriff Jinks, the hero of her novels, was based on her late husband, a shipping agent for Pierotti & Clunes. Nobody could remember a thing about this unhappy man, unless it was his eccentric habit of walking each year from Pinner to Ramsgate, the town of his birth. 'I use the pistol but sparingly,' Sheriff Jinks confided in *Handiman's Revenge*, 'but trust rather in the word of God and a rough-hewn wit. I believe in tall trees and plain speaking.'

Bella slipped out of bed, found her nightgown and patted down her body with it. Moving with excessive caution she opened the door to the bedroom and crept downstairs, where the scent of beeswax mingled with tobacco and that faintly sulphurous smell that even a summer's day delivered from the streets outside.

She walked about the drawing room, thinking over the novel that might come from all these recent alarms and revelations. Bolsover was the villain of the piece; but who was the hero? Urmiston it could not be. He was too gentle and compliant, too self-effacing. Murch (she smiled to herself) was the physical type, crossed eyes and all – there was something glamorous in his bony self-containment and want of a smile. Suppose, for example, that Murch was not just another ruined Londoner but the greatest fencing master in all Europe? She found him a place to live – the royal mews in Stuttgart – and changed his unfortunate eyes to – yes! a vow of silence he had undertaken the day he accidentally killed his brother in a duel with sabres.

But then again, why do stories need heroes? It seemed to Bella that what the world wanted was innocence – to read of young men and women polished like wineglasses, reflecting back not the world as it was, but mere sunlight. Murch would not do, after all. She liked him for the very things wineglasses were designed not to be – an awful matter-of-factness, the absence in him of promise and celebration.

She fell into her spoonback chair and thought of Mr Bolt and his beefy sailor's figure, sitting with the mail-bags, waiting for the first train down to Portsmouth. A little of the desolation in that imagined scene crept into her heart.

When she went back to bed, she folded Marie Claude into her arms without waking her and lay waiting for the first light of the day to march bit by bit across the ceiling. If there was a satisfaction in being Mr Henry Ellis Margam that morning, she was as far from it as Kagosima Harbour lay from Leicester Square.

TWELVE

The next day turned out to be sultry and overcast. The hazy cloud that obscured London raised the temperature and thickened the air. In the mid-morning, feeling tetchy and ill-tempered, Bella had a sudden recuperative idea. She asked Charles Urmiston to dinner that night, promising a cab at the door of Shelton Street for seven. He was on no account to accept the invitation out of duty. If he felt too battered to attend, then he must refuse. But she knew he would not. Nor did he – the boy that took round her note returned it with 'At Seven' scrawled across the bottom. Those additional stains were not from tears of gratitude – the invitation had caught Urmiston in the tin bath, wearing a helmet of suds.

Bella spent a happy half-hour in the principal cellar of the house in Orange Street, choosing wine. In the afternoon she walked out into Leicester Square to buy flowers. These exceptional preparations astonished Marie Claude.

'Does the Prince of Wales come tonight?'

'Don't be impertinent.'

'If it is Lord Broxtowe I am going out.'

'When has Lord Broxtowe ever dined with us? And if he ever did, don't you suppose I would pack you off with the blessed Lydia Titcombe for the evening?'

For answer, Marie Claude burst into tears. It seemed that two nights ago Miss Titcombe had been shown the door. She had lately inherited a cottage on the Kent coast from her aged grandmother and there she planned to set up house with her beloved, keeping chickens and growing vegetables. There were other romantic inducements. The property had a well from which to draw water and from her early childhood visits Lydia remembered bacon hanging on hooks. Rare orchids hid in the fields roundabout and any amount of wading birds decorated the mud flats. Bella was stunned.

'She has no idea who you are,' she observed incautiously.

'Oh yes!' Marie Claude shouted. 'Do find it funny, why not!'

'I find it sad. Poor Miss Titcombe. Who will she ever find as beautiful as you?'

'I hate you both! I wish I were dead!'

'No you don't. Or not more than usual.' She embraced the sobbing girl. 'You will live a very long time and see miracles,' Bella promised.

'I don't want to see miracles.'

'Twentieth-century miracles.'

Marie Claude howled. By the time Urmiston arrived, Bella was emotionally exhausted.

'This is kind of you,' he said shyly.

'It is something I have wanted to do. I entertain very seldom.'

Marie Claude came to table in a surly and jealous mood but found their guest to have impeccable manners, which was to say French manners. He knew Paris; and of course, Boulogne. Without revealing the reason for his journey, he gave a pleasant and witty account of travelling by train to Mentone and the people he had met along the way.

'This *comtesse*, the mystery woman, offered you a job?' she asked incredulously.

'As tutor to her daughter.'

'Was she beautiful, the girl?'

'I was shown a daguerrotype.'

'The picture bewitched you?'

'I am slow to bewitch,' Urmiston smiled.

'But about that you can't say. No one can say.'

'Well, let's say it has happened to me very seldom in a long, long life. And it did not happen that afternoon.'

'Tcchh!' Marie Claude scolded.

After taking coffee and cognac with them in the sitting room, she excused herself and Bella was at last free to lay out what she wished to say. During the day something had happened, the way things do happen – tiny vexations, unbidden thoughts. When she finally came to the point, it was this: she did not wish to continue any further along the path that led to Bolsover.

Urmiston listened with grave attention.

'I take it you mean that you have uncovered enough about this monster to write your next book,' he murmured. 'And that anything else – any further twist or turn – would not further your interest.'

'Could you make the writing of a book sound a little less effete? A novel is an exercise in imagination, Charles. How it all comes out in the end, I mean in real life, is none of my business. You look shocked.'

He steepled his fingers, gazing at the carpet. When he looked up again, his smile was tentative.

'I must ask you: have you come all this way simply out of literary curiosity? You don't care at all for the outcome?'

'I am struggling to find the outcome.'

'I mean in what you term real life, Bella.'

'I already see one obvious possibility. We give the cigar case to the police. Quigley deposes a statement saying how he came by it and the thing is out of our hands. The three villains we have identified are brought to justice.'

'Or not.'

'Yes!' Bella exclaimed, niggled. 'Brought to justice or not. But can't we rely on the police to do their duty?'

'I have no idea. I have never spoken to one, other than to ask directions.'

She found herself losing her temper. Pouring another cognac for them both, a little of it splashed over her wrist. She sucked at her skin, not without failing to notice his tiny wince of dismay.

'You are disappointed in me.'

'I am surprised.'

'You think we should go to Paris, as Quigley wants?'

'I shall go,' he said simply.

'Oh, Charles,' she cried. 'Are you going to be my hero?'

Charles Urmiston was in no way Philip Westland when it came to pleasantries. Instead of batting the shuttlecock back over the net, he fell to examining the carpet again. She waited. At last he rose and carefully set down his glass.

'I understand what you have said but find I cannot leave things at that. Bolsover wronged me. Without his essential viciousness my dear wife might have lived a little longer – or at the very least ended her days in comfort and not squalor. Moreover, the evidence has convinced me that he murdered that poor Welsh drab and for that too I shall hunt him down. To the ends of the earth, if necessary.'

'As a form of adventure?'

'As a means of exacting justice,' Urmiston corrected, perhaps a little too sharply. 'I thought we had just agreed that romance was your department.'

'This is very cool, Charles.'

'Perhaps. I must thank you for an excellent meal.'

'We are to part on such stiff terms?'

Urmiston hesitated.

'I am much more the coward than I should like to have people believe,' he said. 'You can see that in me, I am sure. But somehow, with all this, I have crossed over into a different country.'

'Then beware,' Bella cried. 'Percy Quigley can be no guide at all to you in this new place.'

His smile was very faint.

'The Captain? I have met his kind before, though in a very adulterated form. He is the dog who runs after a thrown stick and cannot always find it. Who peers pitifully from the bushes. No, the man who has stiffened my backbone is Billy Murch.'

'*This* is your new friend?'

'I have hardly exchanged a dozen words with him. But there is something implacable in him that I have never met with before.'

He tried to continue the thought and then shrugged.

'My wife used to ask when we would go back to Campden Hill, to things as they had been. She thought – well, it doesn't matter what she thought. I promised her that we would. And even half-believed it myself. I know now I can never go back to who I once was. I will help kill Bolsover for that one realization alone.'

'But your fortunes might change,' she cried.

'It is not about money, Bella. It never was about money. Billy Murch has somehow shown me that, without asking a single question of me.'

Quigley knew a man who lived close by Victoria Station in Gillingham Mews. Mr Cumberledge's hobby was to file and cross-reference newspapers, a work he had started with his daughter, and after her death, his granddaughter. William Cumberledge would have done this work for love, for he was in character a saintly fool with something of the common squirrel about him. The newspapers he had hoarded over fifty years filled the basement from floor to ceiling, the earliest editions several inches deep in water. The all-important abstracts were cut and pasted into folios that were shelved in his living quarters, where he received from time to time lawyers' clerks, amateur will hunters, incurably inquisitive local historians and members of the criminal classes.

'You have,' he explained to Quigley, 'deaths by fire, by shipwreck, avalanche, by balloon, railway – this last subdivided into collision, explosion, runaway trains, stationary trains, bridge disaster, signal failure –'

'Has there ever been death by disappearance on the railways?' Quigley asked with his usual whimsy.

'Of the entire train, do you mean?' Cumberledge responded. 'In 1861, yes. The Bombay Express left Poona at seven in the evening and was never seen again.'

'What happened to it?' Quigley asked, squelched.

'History offers nothing but wild conjecture. But it carried 127 officers and men of the Warwickshire Regiment and any number of Hindus. Plus, of course, Lady Bantling, her children and their paternal uncle, Colonel Horace Bantling of the 15th Hussars.'

'Never seen again?'

'I thought everybody knew the story,' old Cumberledge murmured peaceably. Behind his chair, his granddaughter Amy put her thumbs to her temple and wiggled her fingers. She was a child of extraordinary beauty, even seen in the half-light of what would have been the sitting room in any other circumstances. Quigley admired her firm young bosom, surely not got from mixing flour-and-water paste for her grandfather? He dragged his mind to the matter in hand.

'For a consideration, my clients are interested in murders, unsolved, involving young women, perhaps in a country setting.'

'By gunshot, stabbing, strangulation or poison?' Cumberledge asked at once. 'If poison, by rare agents or household products? Presenting symptoms of wasting illness or sudden and convulsive disorder?'

'Probably not poison. Strangulation the most likely.'

'Ah yes. By cord or rope, scarf, stocking or other underclothes; or manually? By day, at night, in public or domestically –?'

'In the Wallingford area.'

Cumberledge sat back with disappointment written all over his face.

'My dear Captain Quigley. You have made it too easy for me. Amy, would you reach down Murders, Unsolved, Berkshire?'

Quigley gazed appreciatively as the little minx fetched a library step and strained to reach the topmost shelf, on which were ranged the most recent files. He saw by what means her girlish bust had been developed. Cumberledge sat with his head in his hands, genuinely dashed.

'From memory, in recent years there have been eleven recorded cases of unsolved murders in Berkshire and adjoining parishes of Oxfordshire, of which seven were probably instances of domestic violence.'

'Wifey bashed over the head with the garden spade,' Quigley suggested. 'Husband does a bunk, never seen again. Lodging with relatives in Norfolk.'

Cumberledge stirred slightly in his chair, taken by these imaginary details.

'Norfolk?' he mused.

Amy dropped a folio into her grandfather's lap and announced that she must go out and buy a bit of fish for their supper that night. Quigley was sorry to see her leave, enough to give her the old lascivious wink, getting in return the tip of her tongue pushed between cherry red lips. Oblivious, Cumberledge searched the ledger.

'Ah! A person that might interest you is a Miss Jane Dorriman of Laburnum Lodge, Newbury. Not Wallingford, of course, but not entirely unadjacent. Daughter to the locomotive engineer and designer Negley Dorriman.'

'There are people in the world called Negley?' Quigley wondered.

'Now – it says here – residing at Portland Place. Can that be right? It must be a very lucrative business designing steam engines. Is the family armigerous at all?'

He stood, looking distracted.

'I have here somewhere a file of prominent persons from the world of industry presently resident in London, cross-indexed by length of residence.'

'Do not trouble yourself, old cock.'

'But I think I must.'

While he squirrelled, Captain Quigley read an inch or so of yellowing newsprint. Jane Dorriman was nineteen years old at the time of her death. Her character was described as unblemished. She lived a quiet childhood in Newbury until brought to London by her widower father for a medical consultation about her asthma. She was found in Hyde Park with her clothing disarranged and her throat cut. Quigley came upon what he was looking for in the last two sentences of the Reuters report, touching on the bereaved father's anguish. Negley Dorriman was a director of the Great Western Railway.

Urmiston went to Portland Place later that day. He was shown by a butler into a high-ceilinged room where a plumply nondescript kind of man sat with a shawl round his knees, hands clenched in his lap. The furniture and decorations were in impeccable taste but it was plain to see that Mr Dorriman took no pleasure in them. At the side of his chair was an occasional table crammed with medicines.

Even after Urmiston had completed his introduction, the engineer sat as if mute, his eyes blank.

'I know who you are, Mr Urmiston,' he said after a long pause.

'We met socially once, sir, at the time I was employed by the company.'

'I remember that. And the case that provoked your dismissal.'

'Mr Dorriman –'

'I have not left this house for nearly three years. I think you know the cause. At first I thought I could control my grief. I toured the world – can you picture that to yourself, Mr Urmiston? I taught myself to hunt and shoot. For a while I had with me a girl I represented to the greater world as my daughter. I took her to places Jane had always wanted to see.' He glanced. 'I was of course quite deranged. I don't suppose I exchanged more than half an hour's conversation with the poor creature in all that time.'

'What happened to her?'

'We parted in Calcutta. More specifically, she ran away.'

They sat in silence for a while. A servant came in, bearing a bottle of wine and one glass. Dorriman indicated by a wave of his hand that Urmiston alone should drink.

'Jane was my only child. You must not think of her as a simpering miss. Sparks flew from her. She was the flint. Bolsover was the powder.'

The shock of hearing this name so casually introduced brought Urmiston bolt upright. He so far forgot himself as to jump up and walk the room. Dorriman watched, dabbing at his mouth with a cambric handkerchief.

'If I had not recognized your name, I would not have had you admitted, Mr Urmiston. You can say if you like that I have been waiting for you. We are two ruined men, destroyed by the same villain. There may be others like us. Are you going to patrol the carpet or will you sit down again?'

'I beg your pardon.'

He sat, his emotions churning. Again, Dorriman waited.

'You met Lord Bolsover?' Urmiston asked at length.

'He was her murderer, there can be no doubt. Yes, we met at dinner in the Café Royal. He said something insulting to Jane and she replied, with more than a little force.'

'Is it possible to ask what was the nature of the insult?'

'It was a remark of such indecency that I took him to be drunk. There was a scene such as happens when one meets boorish people and we left the restaurant without completing our meal. Twenty-four hours later, my daughter was dead.'

'You say there can be no doubt as to Lord Bolsover's guilt.'

'I have none in my own mind. It happened that the Prince of Wales was dining at a nearby table that night. He sent a note to our hotel reprehending Bolsover's words and actions and saying he had made known his displeasure to the author of them. The next morning, when walking in Burlington Arcade, Bolsover accosted us and called us upstart swine. A better man than I would have struck him. I should have knocked him to the ground. Or at the very least slashed my cane across his face.'

'Your daughter was found in Hyde Park?'

'Not very far in. It was thought she had been dragged from the pavement in the Bayswater Road.'

'And had she a reason for being in that vicinity?'

'She was walking back to our hotel.'

Dorriman broke his composure long enough to touch his cheek. There were tears running into the lined and weary face. Urmiston bit his lip.

'Forgive me, sir. These are shocking stories yet they do not constitute proof of who killed your daughter.'

'What has made me rich, Mr Urmiston, has been the twenty-seven patents held on engines designed by me. I have seen the product of my inventions at work in nine different countries. I am in every other respect an unimaginative man. I cannot prove but I *know* Bolsover is guilty of that crime.'

'When Jane was discovered, you of course at once alerted the authorities. You made known to them the story you have just told me?'

'I went to the police, yes. You have to imagine willing but not very intelligent men. I urged them at the very least to take a statement from Lord Bolsover. This they were very loath to do. In the end it did not matter. Bolsover had fled to France that very morning.'

Dorriman smiled wanly.

'The verb is mine. It was explained to me with great patience that he had gone to Paris to attend a reception at the British Embassy. He travelled over with the Foreign Secretary. This made a great impression on the investigating officers. That, and the singular fact that a month later, he used some of his wealth to endow a missionary charity in Oxford.'

He wet his lips with the tip of his tongue.

'I received a letter about this great example of Christian philanthropy from William Ewart Gladstone. It seemed to him inconceivable that the man I was pursuing so relentlessly could be what I said he was. Mr Gladstone had prayed hard and long for guidance on the matter. He could not rid his mind of the idea that I was very close to a charge of criminal slander made against a true-blue Englishman.'

'How could he make such a reckless assertion?'

'He and the Second Earl were at Christ Church together. Bolsover's father, you understand.'

'But how does that alter cases?'

'According to Gladstone, never was a more pious man. There was in time a coroner's inquest at which a verdict of murder by a person or persons unknown was returned.'

'Forgive me, but you never thought to take the law into your own hands?'

'It happens in novels,' Dorriman admitted, brushing feebly at the rug over his knees. He turned his head away towards the window and, after a few moments, Urmiston realized that the interview was at an end.

Walking back down Oxford Street, he thought of going to see Bella and laying before her this latest crumb of the story but the noise and the crowds worked on him like an opium dream. Here were hundreds of men who were not Hagley or Bolsover; and as many women who were not Jane Dorriman. They streamed towards him, their minds on hats and shoes, toffee apples, schooners of sherry, wedding veils and feather beds. They were the innocents.

Literature could not make heroes or heroines of them, any more than Urmiston could stop one in his tracks and tell him about a man with a rug over his knees whose daughter was so casually murdered in the Bayswater Road by a peer of the realm.

THIRTEEN

For a third morning running, the sky was overcast. An intolerable night of damp sweats gave way to daylight streaked with brown. The house stank and opening all the windows made things, if anything, worse.

Bella lay in the bath, reading and smoking her first cheroot of the day. The water was unheated but she had forced herself to make this her summer practice. For Marie Claude (who appeared briefly to snatch a kimono from the chair) cold baths were an infallible sign of Anglo-Saxon stupidity. As for reading in the bath, that was, in her opinion, simply trying to appear clever.

'You would not read in the sea.'

'But I did. Last year, in Etretat.'

'You must always have the last word,' she shouted, before flouncing out. Bella threw her book at the door and clambered out after it. Her skin was reddened, her heels an alarming blue. She wrapped herself in a towel and padded back to her bedroom goose-pimpled and contrite.

In all the earlier Margam novels she had found a plot that borrowed from the world she knew best, of garden parties and musical evenings, gossip and intrigue. The books were popular because the violence was largely sexual.

Pistols were brandished to intimidate weepingly indecisive women and girls too young to realize the effect they were having on out-and-out villains invited the kind of frenzy that had them locked in steamer trunks or tied hand and foot in railway carriages careering down the track to Carlisle.

Naked, she studied herself in the pier glass, seeing a healthy woman with much more of the peasant about her than she would care to admit. Her hips were broadening and there was a roundness to her belly she deplored but could do nothing about. Without shoes to pitch her forward a little, she appeared a very solid figure indeed. Moreover, she reflected gloomily, one more than usually anxious, a new thing for her.

Still naked, she marched to Marie Claude's room. Dressed in the silk kimono, the Frenchwoman had returned to bed, her arm dramatically flung over her brow.

'It is disgusting, what you do,' she complained. 'To walk about without a robe.'

'I wanted to ask you about Mr Urmiston.'

Marie Claude's shrug sent the kimono up round her ears.

'I have no opinion.'

'He has an enemy, a bad man. He wants to kill him.'

'Men always want to kill each other. It's very childish. To kill, you need big hands and that big jaw, like an ape. Not little hands and a long nose.'

'Do you still love me?' Bella demanded suddenly. The question astonished her more than Marie Claude.

'Mrs Venn is bringing me some coffee,' the young girl warned in a small voice.

'Could the question be any simpler?'

Like a mouse diving behind the curtains, Marie Claude burrowed into the bedsheets, shrieking.

'I cannot bear to live like this another hour!' Bella said.

She turned and fled, meeting the housekeeper at the top of the stairs.

'If not with her, then without her,' Captain Quigley repeated.

He and Urmiston were sitting in the snug of the Six Bells, where the Captain liked to sup and meditate his next moves. His manner was unusually quiet, not because of any special burden of thought, but rather that he had in the past waged a campaign to empty the pub of its rowdier and more jocular elements, either by sarcasms or fisticuffs. He liked the present arrangements better. Where market porters had once drunk themselves into a stupor there now sat meek little tally clerks and the better sort of cabmen. In this new calm, Quigley had installed himself as the equivalent of President of the Mess. The booth they sat in was reserved exclusively for him. It was known as Quigley's Corner.

The two men were of course talking about Bella. As if to signal that the leadership of the group must change, Quigley was wearing the kind of braided cap favoured by park-keepers and missionary explorers. It was also a day for medals. The Captain had four, all got from a junk dealer in Old Compton Street. One was English, one French and two Turkish. The ribbons to all of them had been refurbished from the same bit of scarlet silk found in the gutter outside this very pub.

'I think she has gone as far as she wishes to go,' Urmiston agreed.

'I don't say as how I'm surprised. What's left of this is men's work.'

'As to that, it may be too early to praise God,' his companion warned, speaking as much to himself as to anyone else.

In front of them was a page torn from a child's atlas, depicting a political map of Western Europe. Britain was coloured pink, France an unusually pale green. Prussia spread like an emerging purple bruise. The Captain smoothed the sheet with a none-too-clean hand and blew a little smoke across the Channel.

'France,' he observed. 'Paris. The Hotel Louvois.'

Urmiston felt dismay sweeping over him. He did not like to dampen Quigley's enthusiasm, nor to throw obstacles in his path, but the thought of the two of them wandering the Left Bank together left him horribly underwhelmed.

'Lucky for us you speak the lingo,' Quigley continued, very blithe. 'Though we might consider taking old Solomon with us as a sort of local guide. Comes from Trier. Father a distinguished rabbi in those parts. Dead now, at a guess. Pushing up the German daisies.'

He peered at the map.

'Paris a different kettle of fish,' he admitted. 'Can you think up some wheeze to fetch his lordship back to London – some guise or pretext, as they say?'

'I cannot.'

Though it was hardly past ten in the morning the Captain was on his third brandy and water. It was abundantly clear to everyone except himself that he did not have a huge appetite for the descent on Paris. He drummed absent-mindedly with a box of matches.

'Bring Billy Murch in, possibly,' he said. 'Maybe this sailor I was telling you about – Stoker Miller. Good man in a tight corner. Four of us. Travel light, live off the land if necessary. Weapons? Pistols, I think.'

Urmiston cut him off before he could go any further.

'I am going back to Shelton Street, Captain. I suggest we both give this more thought before we involve anyone else.'

'Ha! Cold feet, is it?'

'As you yourself have observed on more than one occasion,' Urmiston snapped testily, 'time spent on reconnaissance is seldom wasted. Or, as my grandfather was fond of saying, measure twice, cut once.'

'You had a grandfather, did you?'

Urmiston rose and walked out on stiff legs. By a huge effort of will he managed to control his irritation and crossed Covent Garden looking much less like a stalking pigeon. By the time he got to Mrs Bardsoe's, he was in a cheerful, even a skittish frame of mind.

Waiting for him in Mrs Bardsoe's downstairs parlour was the man Urmiston least expected to see.

The Reverend Anthony Hagley did not trouble himself by rising but sat very much at his ease in a red plush chair, reading his Bible. When he raised his eyes from the page, they were the colour of flint. The two men examined each other, much in the manner of a *Punch* cartoon for which the caption had yet to be written.

'Vircow-Ucquart told you where to find me,' Urmiston guessed.

'He is in hospital. The German Embassy has been informed and is considering its position. There may be diplomatic consequences.'

'I can quite believe he is in hospital. The rest I do not credit.'

Hannah Bardsoe came in with coffee, her lips set in a straight line. The clerical visitor had left her distinctly unimpressed and some of her black mood seemed to be directed at Urmiston also. In the middle of her ministrations the shop bell went.

'Leave that tray to me, Mrs B,' Urmiston said, springing up.

'Which there is very little milk and none at all of cake or biscuit,' she said sourly. 'On account of we are not a hotel.'

Hagley ignored the rebuke, save for a faint lifting of the eyebrows and the smallest of smiles. Urmiston trembled. The hand that poured the coffee shook.

'Such is domestic bliss,' Hagley suggested with a smirk.

'I wonder why you are here to witness it.'

'I can hardly claim I was in the neighbourhood. I am in London to attend a meeting at Exeter Hall. Your situation has changed a little since we last met, Mr Urmiston.'

'And yours too, I understand. You are now at Oxford, I believe?'

Hagley brushed away the remark.

'Let us come to cases. You and your confederates – one of them a ruffian calling himself Quigley – will cease this foolishness forthwith. If you don't, I shall take steps to see that you do.'

'Very little of threat in that. Were you present at the murder of a poor Welsh girl, not half a mile from here?

Did you help in getting the killer away? Or was that Vircow-Ucquart's job?'

'A Welsh girl?'

'Don't play with me, Mr Hagley. You are aiding and abetting a murderer.'

Hagley seemed startled, not so much at the accusation as the tone of voice Urmiston employed.

'These allegations are all very heated. I wonder at you, Mr Urmiston.'

'Nevertheless –'

'Ah, there is more to be said, is there?'

'This one last question, yes. Were you also present in London the night Miss Jane Dorriman had her throat slit?'

Hagley brushed the front of his coat with two or three passes of his hand, a sign to those who knew him well that he was very angry indeed.

'I don't know how you came to fall in with the man Quigley but you would be well advised to break off the connection.'

The two men sat staring at each other while Mrs Bardsoe's clock ticked on the mantelpiece and the boards of the shop creaked as she moved about on the other side of the door. Hagley had learned the knack of dominating an awkward moment – he sat as still as a china cat. It was Urmiston's heart that was going like a trip-hammer. More extraneous sounds: a handcart passing in the street outside, its iron rims ching-chinging on the cobbles. A child's voice screeching. A dog yelping. Still Hagley did not move a muscle. Urmiston wetted his lips.

'Miss Dorriman's father is neither a thug nor a bully. I have found him a most responsible witness.'

'What airs you give yourself, Mr Urmiston.'

'His daughter was murdered in the most foul way imaginable, some would say by the hand of a madman.'

For a moment it seemed as though Hagley was going to let that go by. But then he reached for his coffee cup with the greatest possible display of negligence and managed a mild laugh.

'You have conjured a deal of moral indignation since your dismissal from the Great Western, Mr Urmiston. You are harbouring a grudge the size of Gibraltar, my dear fellow. Lord Bolsover is no more capable of murder than I am. And, just to be clear about it, no madman either.'

'I have yet to mention that gentleman's name,' Urmiston pointed out in a quiet and trembling voice. 'I am grateful to you, therefore, for confirming it to me in such a frank and open way.'

In the deathly silence that followed, Hagley's cheeks flushed and he seemed to find difficulty in controlling his hands. Urmiston watched, his chest pounding. But the Reverend Hagley had been this way before. The fight for his self-possession finally subsided. He pulled out a silver hunter from his fob and managed a theatrically elaborate sigh.

'Ask the person who works in the shop to send out for a cab, will you? I am a little pushed for time.'

'You may find your way to Cambridge Circus and search for one there. I should tell you, Mr Hagley, your friend will be hunted down and destroyed, like a mad dog. He will end up in a ditch with holes in his waistcoat, whether here or in France, it makes no matter.'

A muscle jumped in Hagley's cheek.

'You ridiculous little understrapper,' he exclaimed. 'You think you can speak to me in this way? You think you can utter any threat you like against a gentleman of irreproachable character? I shall have you taken up in charge for it.'

'There is a police station in St Martin's Lane. Let us walk down there together. I shall welcome the chance to make a statement.'

'And what will that amount to? The testimony of a man who was dismissed his post, presently living in a slum hovel? Against the word of a gentleman? You are forgetting yourself.'

'The night before Lord Bolsover killed Miss Dorriman, he excited the indignation of the Prince of Wales who was dining at the same restaurant and overheard some of what was being said. According to today's Court Circular, the Prince returns from Aldershot this morning. Tomorrow I intend to lay the facts as I know them before him and ask his advice about what to do next.'

Hagley's contempt was bottomless.

'And where will that interview take place? At his club?'

'Wherever His Royal Highness is gracious enough to receive me.'

'You poor devil. I really fear for your mental condition.'

'But I don't think it is *my* mental condition that has brought you to London this morning.'

Hagley flushed and slapped the table with his Bible, enough to make the cups rattle.

'Damn your impertinence, Urmiston.'

He looked up as Mrs Bardsoe entered.

'The Reverend had best be off, oaths and all,' she said. 'For I have took the trouble to send for Billy Murch who I know would like to debate him on several points.'

'Murch?' Hagley asked, bewildered.

'Concerning the German gentleman who lost his nose recent.'

Hagley turned back to Urmiston.

'You are swimming in very deep and treacherous waters. I will not be threatened.'

'If you walk to the top of the street and turn left, you will come eventually into Cambridge Circus,' Urmiston murmured. 'Good day to you, Mr Hagley.'

'You are a fool, Urmiston. You always were a weakling but I had not realized the extent of your naïveté. Someone is behind this – not you, not your ugly friends, Quigley and this other fellow just mentioned –'

'I wouldn't call Murch ugly, sir, not to his face, oh no, not for a thousand pounds,' Mrs Bardsoe warned, her face brick red.

Hagley flapped his hand as if batting away a housefly.

'This has nothing to do with you, madam. You will oblige me by holding your tongue.'

'And in my own parlour!' Mrs Bardsoe exclaimed wonderingly.

'I came here to warn you,' Hagley said to Urmiston. 'There will be no more criminal interference in my affairs. Whoever is pulling the strings in this sorry Punch and Judy show had better beware. They are out of their depth.'

After he had left, hardly before the shop bell had ceased vibrating, Mrs Bardsoe turned to her lodger. She took his hands and bounced them against her chest, her eyes dark with apprehension.

'I don't know what all that was about but you saw him off. My word, you gave him what for.'

'I am terrified,' Urmiston muttered.

'Of him? Some jumped-up parson?'

'I am fearful of what I have brought to this house.'

'Well,' Mrs Bardsoe allowed, 'there's never been a dull moment since you first hung your hat on the peg, that much I grant you.'

Impulsively, Urmiston took hold of her soft and doughy upper arms and kissed her. He was aiming for her cheek but she turned her head expertly and their lips touched, hers fragranced by liquorice, from a twig of the same she used to clean her teeth in the mornings. The kiss became an embrace.

'Now!' she said, pretending to be shocked. 'Here's a nice thing to come out of a few harmless remarks, I must say.'

'How lucky I am to have met you, Hannah,' Urmiston whispered.

'That's still to find out,' she said, her voice muffled by his shoulder. 'But I should take it kindly if you was not to get your head blowed off before we go any further down this particular road. I aren't altogether stupid, my dear. You are up to something.'

'There are vile people in this world, Hannah.'

'And don't I know it. The less we have to do with them, the better I shall like it.'

He smiled and kissed her again, more lingeringly.

'Is Mr Murch truly coming here?'

'If I am not mistook, that is him coming through the shop at this very instant,' she said, disengaging herself with a final peck on Urmiston's chin.

It was not Murch, but Bella. One glance was enough for her to realize what she had interrupted. Hannah Bardsoe's distracted laugh and Urmiston's burning face told the story.

'Which I shall just run round to the Welshman for a can of milk and a bag of buns,' Mrs Bardsoe cried, sweeping her forearm over her hair.

'I have come to apologize for how I spoke to you recently,' Bella began. 'I know Quigley is representing it as desertion. But I am a writer, Charles, not a warrior. And neither are you. I beg you to let it go.'

'Which is the greater enormity? To kill him or to let him go scot-free? It's a moot point, don't you think? Hagley –'

'Yes, what of him?'

'He was here. You missed him by two minutes.'

'He was *here*?'

'He came to warn me off.'

Bella searched his face with her fine grey eyes.

'This is bringing things very close to home.'

'I think I realize that.'

'All right,' she said. 'I admit it: I am happy not to have met him. What is he like?'

And at once snapped one hand into the palm of the other, annoyed with herself for providing Urmiston with proof that she was living this crisis at second hand.

'Not one word spoken of Marguerite, not one recognition of my widowerhood. But cheap jibes directed at Mrs Bardsoe and this house, that he is pleased to call a slum.'

'And how did you answer him on that?'

Urmiston flushed. His silence touched Bella to her heart.

'It is not in your nature to play the avenging angel,' she said. 'You are too kind, too gentle. We – all of us – would do better to draw a line and let it all go hang. I am appalled at what you are planning.'

'I take it you have been speaking to the Captain.'

'Not half an hour since. He is for setting out today or tomorrow, crossing by the Folkestone boat. I came straight round to warn you.'

'It is my day for warnings,' Urmiston said in too light a tone. 'I am scarcely enthusiastic about the idea, Bella, as I think you realize. And it has occurred to me more than once that your novel will do for Bolsover what I may fail to do in life. I mean, destroy him. But I cannot leave it as it is. I cannot.'

'You mean three decent and generally harmless men will go to kill a fourth, upon the mere suspicion of murder? I could not write such a plot, not even I. Are you really such a man of action?'

'You are right, I am not, not in the least. But I shudder to admit that I am a man capable of this one isolated action. Yes.'

'Then I must come with you,' Bella declared.

'The Captain has described our expedition as man's work,' Urmiston pointed out.

'I am not coming to load your pistols for you. It is to save you from the consequences of knowing Captain Quigley. And to bring you home safe to those who love you.'

At which, though it was a most general remark, Charles Urmiston blushed. Pat upon her cue, the shop bell rang and Mrs Bardsoe bustled in, talking, as was her habit, the moment she crossed the threshold. Before Urmiston became her lodger her remarks were addressed to the empty air. But now, as Bella had divined only too well, she had an audience only dreamed of since the death of her husband.

'And I suppose you have been gassing about the reverend gentleman's visit,' she said, dumping her bag of buns on the table.

'We have been talking about sandcastles,' Urmiston said. 'And how it is wise never to build them too close to the tide.'

'I have seen many a child's heart broke for that reason. What a fund of common sense you have.'

Bella laughed delightedly and kissed her on the cheek.

'We do not needs buns, we need a good bit of halibut. If Syrett's is still in business round the corner, let us sit down together at one of his little tables and do justice to his fish.'

'And if you don't have a memory like an elephant!' Hannah Bardsoe cried admiringly. 'Syrett's! I haven't been there in many a moon.'

They crossed to France the following morning in flat calm. Though there was fog in the Channel, Bella and Urmiston sat in deckchairs abaft the saloon. Quigley and Murch were inside. It was the Captain's fond belief that the smoky and fussy little steamer carried what he called Ship's Bitter, an almost fabled restorative, best drunk with a mutton chop and a plate of mashed potatoes.

'And if that's not available, a glass or two of the India Pale Ale, Billy. And for ballast, a Melton Mowbray and some pickled red cabbage. Maybe a plate of ham on the side.'

'That purser,' Murch observed idly, 'is none other than Walter Neary, that used to have the Rose in Coleman Street.'

Quigley peered.

'Buggered if you're not right. It's a small world and no mistake.'

The thought cheered him through half a dozen bottles of Ind Coope.

Mr Neary's duties took him to pass the time of day with the deck passengers and in this way he happened on Bella and Charles Urmiston. They agreed it was a disappointing morning for telescope work, more was the pity, for the purser had it of the first mate, who had it of the captain, that Admiral Sir Geoffrey Thomas Phillips Hornby was in passage that morning with the battleship *Alexandra*.

'A rare sight, madam. A passing rare sight.'

'You are a long-serving sea-officer yourself, Mr Neary?' Bella enquired.

'Bless you, madam, I should say so,' Mr Neary lied amiably, who came from Hoxton and until this present service had never been nearer the sea than Margate, where his sister-in-law kept a brothel. He saluted and paced slowly away, his hands clasped behind his back.

'What a staunch-looking fellow,' Urmiston murmurred, causing Bella quite visibly to wince. By a slight diminution of the thrumming noise made by the deck plates, she divined that Calais was in the offing. There was a piercing shriek from the ship's siren as the vessel cut like a blunt knife through the becalmed French herring fleet. Quigley appeared at the saloon door, wiping froth from his whiskers. His face could not conceal a certain unease, not to say outright anxiety.

'It is like watching a child hesitating to jump into a river,' Bella sighed. 'I wonder I have put with him all these years.'

'Mr Murch looks the part, however.'

And this was true. The lanky Murch had the knack of posing, one shin crossed over the other, his battered top hat tipped at a jaunty angle. People excused themselves to him as they streamed from the saloon to catch their first whiff of France. The Captain they simply pushed aside by the small of his back, cigar or no cigar. Quigley had left behind his peaked cap and was sporting a wide-brimmed straw. He resembled the French painter Courbet, had Courbet legs no longer than a Shetland pony.

Bella asserted her authority on the train to Paris by taking this ludicrous headgear and skimming it out of the window, where it sailed into a glassy river covered in harvest dust.

'Sunstroke to follow,' Quigley lamented.

'We are not travelling in the deserts of Mexico,' she retorted. 'Nor is it necessary to shout when addressing the natives. Nor to examine the contents of a sandwich before eating it. What Mr Murch calls meat paste the French call *rillette*, which is delicious.'

'Handsome,' Murch admitted. 'If a trifle salted.'

The sandwich had been offered by an elderly woman whose piglet was peering morosely out of a jute sack. She was, she explained to Urmiston, on her way to see her daughter in Ménilmontant, she who had so recklessly married the first man she met. This had taken place on market day in Rouen, not bad weather, raining a little but what can you expect of March? Who could have foreseen it? No sooner had the old lady turned her back to buy a yard or two of embroidered tape – for the chairs, you understand, that her own dear mother had bequeathed and were now most cruelly in want of repair (for which she blamed the cat – not a bad cat, in fact a furious mouser, though like all cats of an independent turn of mind – and blind in one eye), anyway, no sooner had she turned her back but what Suzette was snaffled by a discharged soldier with one arm. Worse than that, a Parisian.

'*Et maintentant*,' the old countrywoman added triumphantly, making a pun of how she had been snaffled, '*elle est fauchée comme les blés*.'

'Stony broke,' Bella supplied.

They took a cab to the Hotel Louvois on the Left Bank. It was not, as Urmiston had guessed, of the first rank, but neither could it be said that it was modest. Its keynote was a seedy flamboyance. The five-step marble staircase was attended by two doormen in ankle-length green overcoats, their top hats buffed to a shiny gleam and finished off by broad white satin bands from which the ends hung loose. What looked like an elegant clientele could be seen taking lunch in a yellow-and-gilt salon and the sound of a string ensemble floated out across the pavements.

At the Captain's suggestion, the English party made a pretence of peering into the Seine for a few minutes, the better to inspect comings and goings on the opposite side of the road.

'So, can you picture our man staying at a gaff like this?' Captain Quigley asked Urmiston.

'Very easily. The three girls going in now do not have entirely the appearance of innocence, for example.'

'Professionals, you'd say. And the old cove with them in the top hat –'

Bella started forward.

The man entering the hotel was Lord Broxtowe.

FOURTEEN

'I am here for a funeral,' Lord Broxtowe explained with sly good humour. 'My cousin Ferrensby. Nice man. Lived here for more than forty years. Married a dancer in his youth, exquisite chit of a girl. She died in '62. They were very much in love, you understand. Ferrensby the most enormously fat man with as much wit as a cabbage. But kind.'

He smiled at Bella.

'Did you perhaps harbour some other, darker explanation for my presence?'

'I was amazed to see you, was all.'

'I used to come to Paris for venial pleasures quite often as a younger man. But in the end – have I mentioned this before? – everything palls. I am in the hotel here with Dr Duddington, the fellow you met at Goodwood once. The good Bishop Duddington. A person of irreproachable morals, Bella.'

She remembered a man half Broxtowe's age, as plump as his friend was gaunt and blessed with a truly beautiful shy smile.

'Has the funeral taken place?'

'Yesterday,' Lord Broxtowe confirmed. 'Duddington did the honours. Damn good turn-out and in addition a very decent class of people. The Ambassador's wife came to the service and I gather the Mayor of Paris was there too. It seems that Ferrensby endowed not one but two ballet schools and a dogs' hospital. The French like that sort of thing in an Englishman.'

Lord Broxtowe's suite overlooked the river and he asked Bella to drag a small couch to where they might sit side by side and watch the barges fuss past. In one, perhaps a hundred cattle were standing patient and unmoving, their heads held low, as if listening to the river chuckling under their hooves.

'Little do they know what awaits them,' Broxtowe said. 'Though I'm told that when they smell the blood of the abattoir they can get fractious. As I think I shall, when the time comes.'

As was his way, he held Bella's hand lightly in his and for a long time he seemed to be dreaming, his pale lips moving in the unconscious manner of a very old man. When he spoke again, she was startled.

'I am very disappointed to find you here.'

'Why should you say that?' she asked uneasily.

'I am guessing at your reasons. You will end as a corpse in one of your own stories before you have finished.'

'I am in Paris very unwillingly,' she allowed. 'In one sense, to protect a friend.'

'Not that ghastly fellow Quigley, I hope.'

'Hardly, though he is of our party.'

Lord Broxtowe nodded. For a while his eyes returned to the river, where the water was broken up into silver streamers by the passage of another barge, this one with washing strung from the wheelhouse to the forward hatch.

A bold woman stood at the prow, arms akimbo. Bella was taken unawares when he gently disengaged his hand from hers.

'Mark me, Bella: you will do better with a pen than a dagger when it comes to someone like Bolsover. I take it that's your purpose in being here?'

'Yes.'

'You should go home. I only wish I had the power to make you.'

There was a knock at the door and the silver-haired Duddington drifted in. Over his clerical vest he wore a linen jacket of the kind worn by some gardeners. Pickwickian glasses hung from the sagging top pocket.

'My dear Mrs Wallis,' he said at once. 'What a pleasant surprise.'

'I'm astonished you remember me, my lord,' Bella exclaimed.

'We met at Goodwood. You wore the most wonderful hat that day. I will not attempt to describe it but it – and the wearer –' he added gallantly – 'have long stuck in my mind.'

'Duddington's good at this sort of thing,' Lord Broxtowe muttered.

The bishop smiled his angelic smile.

'I think I was offered champagne half an hour since.'

'Then be a good fellow and give a tug to the sash thing over there. Our friend Marcel will oblige us.'

Henry Treloar Duddington was as well connected a bishop as any who sat in the House of Lords. His wife was a lady-in-waiting to the Queen when she was at Windsor and a rich woman in her own right. The two were devoted to each other.

'We were discussing earlier,' he explained to Bella, 'whether there is ever a wrong hour for champagne. My wife, for example, takes half a pint at breakfast in a silver mug. That is a very appealing sight. Your friend Broxtowe here is of a more sentimental nature. Or perhaps the better word for it is traditional. For him champagne goes with red plush and candlelight, face powder and pier glasses. Garters, even.'

'That is true,' Lord Broxtowe grumbled. 'But since you are exhibiting your worldly side, Duddington, I will tell you straight that Mrs Wallis is here to meet that infernal swine Bolsover. Not to meet – meet is quite the wrong word. To confront.'

Duddington made her a polite but noncommittal nod.

'Well,' his friend complained tetchily, 'you might say more.'

'I take it you already know the nature of the man. I have met him twice, once as it happens here in Paris. Indeed, in this very hotel. A dissolute, Mrs Wallis. I would say a woeful desperado. You would do well to steer clear.'

'Thank you for that,' Lord Broxtowe muttered.

'Have you heard he is in Paris?'

'I cannot be sure,' Bella said.

'Then –?'

Duddington's glance was quizzical, in the warm manner of a clever fellow with all the answers. Bella bridled.

'I have reason to believe he has killed at least two young women,' she said. 'In the most hideous way.'

Duddington blinked. He was saved from replying by the knock and entry of a hotel servant, bearing a silver ice-bucket of champagne. Marcel was one of those grave and unsmiling servants who manage to convey the manners of the better sort of undertaker. He bowed courteously but briefly to Bella.

'Marcel, would you be so kind as to fetch another glass for our guest? And perhaps a plate of those little cakes, tiny little cakes, that look like rosebuds?'

'*Avec plaisir*, milord.'

Duddington waited until the door closed.

'Let us come to cases, Mrs Wallis. Do you have proof of these accusations?'

Bella hesitated. She saw that Duddington was capable of more expressions than a winning smile. His face was now composed into an attentive seriousness and his whole demeanour was no longer that of a chubby and gently-mannered angel. While he waited for her answer he took the spectacles from his breast pocket and polished them slowly on the hem of his jacket. His eyes never left hers.

'A street girl was murdered in London a fortnight ago,' Bella said. 'Her throat was slashed with a razor. I will not trouble you with the details but I am at least certain that Bolsover was in London that night and at the scene of the crime. I have no direct proof that he was the killer.'

'Then – forgive me – are you wise to take him on?'

'Bella would like to settle his hash,' Lord Broxtowe observed testily. 'At the very least, push him down a long flight of stairs or something of the kind.'

'I must tell you both, I have friends who have come here prepared to kill him.'

'Well,' Duddington responded, 'I hope they will attempt nothing of the kind. There is a Christian text to hand –'

'– Vengeance is mine and so forth –' his friend supplied.

'Exactly. You would expect me to say as much, I am sure.' His tone was very sombre. Bella gave him a polite nod, realizing what a faintly ridiculous figure she must cut. She could see that the bishop enjoyed the company of women quite as much as his friend Broxtowe but never perhaps as an unwilling accomplice to murder. She cast about for a change of direction.

'May I ask how and where else you came to meet Lord Bolsover?' she asked Duddington.

'At Windsor. He recently gave over a part of his fortune to found a missionary enterprise in Oxford – but I see that you know about this. The Queen was interested in him – there are many bees in that poor sad woman's bonnet – and he was to have been presented to Her Majesty. However, her secretary Ponsonby is far too nimble a fellow to encourage any such thing and he was shown the door. The man who took his place was an insufferable little squit called Hagley. Or as he styles himself, Principal Hagley.'

'Duddington won't at all mind if you do for him,' Lord Broxtowe chuckled.

'It *is* jolly, I suppose,' the bishop chided, 'in the way that all evil is if you stand far enough back. But of course I have a professional duty to go down to the ringside, as it were. There it is not so pretty. I will tell you what you may already know, Mrs Wallis. Hagley is here in Paris. He had the vile impudence to attend the service for poor Ferrensby yesterday morning and to my utter amazement actually tried to engage in conversation with me.'

'Did he know Lord Ferrensby in life?' Bella asked.

'So he claimed. I doubt it very much.'

She was agitated enough to rise from the couch and walk about the room. Through the window she could see Billy Murch lounging against a parapet, hands plunged into his pockets. Even in such an indolent posture, there was enough about Murch to make those who strolled past give him a wide berth. There was danger in him and the idea of that gave Bella strength.

'I am hoping Mr Hagley will lead me to his friend.'

'You must forgive me: but is that really your concern?'

'He kills women, my lord. He has not yet killed a bishop.'

'Withdraw that remark,' Broxtowe snapped, red spots in his cheeks. Bella blushed.

'I apologize.'

Duddington smiled. 'My intention was never to patronise you. But I was once told – by no less an authority than Darwin – that you can never outrun an enraged bear.'

He glanced at his friend and Broxtowe nodded.

'I cannot tell you where Mr Hagley is today but I know how he can be found. When Marcel comes back in, we shall put the problem to him. I do not like what you are attempting – indeed I heartily deprecate it. But I see you cannot be altered in your course.'

'Far better you were put over someone's knee, given six on your bottom and sent home,' Lord Broxtowe exclaimed absent-mindedly.

Duddington's blush was a wonder to behold, rising from his neck into his cheeks in a single instant. Bella anchored her lower lip between her teeth to prevent making matters worse.

'No, but seriously, Bella, you are standing in the anteroom to hell,' her old friend ruminated. 'Leave it be, while you still have chance.'

She was to remember this remark a very long time.

It was not Marcel that they met later in a café in Rue de la Huchette but his nephew Jojo. He was a grave and courteous boy with a shortened right leg and a convict's haircut. His linen was clean and though his suit was threadbare, it was well-brushed.

'I will make enquiries,' he said to Bella in a voice that was barely more than a whisper.

'I must tell you, M'sieu Jojo, this is a gentleman – how shall I put it? – of a certain disposition. We may say having unusual interests and desires.'

Jojo smiled faintly. Bella was about to say more when Urmiston laid his hand on her wrist. The boy made an almost imperceptible nod of gratitude.

'We are who we are, madame,' he murmured, causing Bella to blush in furious shame. 'Do you have a hotel in this quarter?'

'The Dacia. Quite close by.'

The Frenchman nodded.

'Give me four hours,' he said, rising and shaking hands with all of them in turn.

'Well,' Captain Quigley blustered, when Jojo had limped out, 'he don't exactly get my vote.'

'A civil enough cove, though,' Murch objected.

'We should eat,' Urmiston said. 'Here is as good as any place and our friend will come back before midnight.'

'Run after him, Charles. Run after him now and give him my apology,' Bella said, flushed.

'And what apology's that?' Quigley wanted to know.

But Urmiston was gone.

He caught up with Jojo quite easily, crossing the Seine by the Petit Pont. Urmiston proposed a further glass of red and they walked into the Ile de la Cité to a small corner bar, kept by a man who nodded amiably to them both.

'Is Marcel truly your uncle?' Urmiston asked in the most conversational tone he could find. The question still sounded horribly obvious. Jojo smiled.

'He is my mother's brother. We come originally from Boissy-Saint-Léger. His kind – our kind – are not easily tolerated there. You realize of course that he recognized at once the man you are searching for. But he has to be discreet. It is also in his nature,' he added.

'Has your uncle ever mentioned another Englishman, a milord? Who has also stayed at the Hotel Louvois in past times?'

A faint wince of irritation crossed Jojo's face.

'I am not a police spy, m'sieu. I do you this small service tonight as a mark of respect for Marcel. Whom I admire. Tremendously. And that is all I will say.'

'Forgive me, but I must ask –'

'You want to know how I will recognize M'sieu Hagley. We are not engaged in a wild goose chase, I promise you,' the boy whispered drily. 'I do not promise what I cannot deliver. But now I must ask you a question. Has the gentleman met you? Will he recognize you?'

'We are old enemies.'

'Then you must surely return to your companions. Tell me what you want to know about him.'

'Where he stays, at what hotel. And most importantly, what he is doing here in Paris. And where he plans to go next.'

The boy opened his hands briefly and then with a sigh let them fall back to the table.

'What you really want to know is whether Freddie is in Paris with him.'

It took Urmiston a moment to recognize the name but then he nodded.

'At this moment, I cannot say. And now, I think, you should rejoin your friends. Where I go next you would not wish to follow. And in any case –'

Jojo pointed with his chin through the window of the café. The man perched on a stone hitching post, smoking peaceably, was Murch.

'Just keeping an eye on things,' he explained when Urmiston joined him. 'This here church behind us. Would that be the Notre-Dame at all?'

'Does Mrs Wallis not trust me one jot? Am I to be forever followed about like a child in need of a nanny?' Urmiston cried.

'She loves you better'n a brother,' Murch said gently. 'Come away and watch Quigley eat his pigeon, which he has ordered. It will be a sight for sore eyes.'

He took Urmiston by the crook of his elbow and so they retraced their steps. Halfway across the Petit Pont, Murch laughed.

'I forgot to tell you. Hannah Bardsoe reminds you to lay off the garlic, which she considers the devil's work.'

Urmiston experienced a sudden flood of yearning for his landlady. At this hour, when dusk was falling over London like purple soot, she would be grappling with the written word. She was a devoted fan of Mrs Ioaze-Bonnett's works and was halfway through *Jake Masterman, River Pilot*, a story she followed with moving lips, her hand inside her blouse, spectacles balanced on the pudge of her nose.

'Are we wasting our time, Billy?' he found himself asking, slowing to a halt and staring into his companion's face.

'Don't you know how very matter-of-fact these things are, Mr Urmiston? As we might say, simple to grasp and understand? I have not come here to look at churches. When the time comes it will be better that you are off to one side, so to speak. Stay a step or two behind the game. The same goes for the lady and Captain Quigley. But I have the stomach for it.'

Shockingly, he held his bony hands in front of him, unmistakably miming a stranglehold. His crossed eyes held Urmiston's.

'Little Alice Tarrant – Welsh Alice as we called her – was never close, as you might say. But I knew her since a babby. Among our class of people, we know what to do. It's not pretty, always, but we look after our own. You will see.'

Quigley managed his pigeon, Bella and Urmiston ate veal, and Murch investigated an omelette Savoyarde, a dish that so utterly delighted him that he rose and shook the patron's hand, mumbling cockney thanks.

'*Un vrai type*,' the burly M. Texier commented, though secretly pleased, enough to present a *digestif* to the whole table.

'Now this is more like it,' Captain Quigley opined. 'For want of a pack of cards, I say we wait the evening out with a round of ghost stories. Mrs Wallis to be handicapped by the stewards as follows: that she does not speak for more than two minutes by this old watch.'

This was agreed. The most interesting of the four tales that resulted was Murch's. In his days as a fencing master, he was walking home one night when he chanced upon a man with a naked sabre tucked under his arm.

'Make that a dark and stormy night, Billy,' Quigley suggested.

'It happened to be as calm and starlit as you like. There never was a quieter sky. I first came across him in Lamb's Conduit Street –'

'Now why on earth was you up there? You said you was on your way home –'

'Will you *please* shut up!' Bella exclaimed. 'Go on, Mr Murch.'

The fencing master was intrigued enough by the man with the sabre to follow him across Theobald's Road and into Holborn, so to the top of Drury Lane. He took him to be an actor in costume and was on the point of catching up and explaining that to carry a sabre about without its sheath was asking for trouble, the police being what they were. But before he can say a kindly word, the gentleman turns in at the White Hart. Murch paused for effect.

'The Captain can confirm that is a very ancient pub indeed.'

'I can, I do. So, to make no bones, when you gets inside, he is not there, the cove.'

Murch stared at Quigley for a full half-minute.

'He was not there. But on the floor was a woman, hacked to pieces most dreadful. I know the sabre, do you see, and these were sabre cuts. Her blood was running out of her in rivers and her eyes already glassy.'

Murch looked at them each in turn.

'The only problem was nobody but me took a blind bit of notice. It was busy enough, I'd say very busy. I said to myself, never having been to this particular house before, I said, what kind of people are these?'

Urmiston stirred uneasily.

'You were transfixed, I imagine, Mr Murch.'

'I would say more outraged. More – I have heard the word used – incensed. I take one pace inside the place and –'

The door to the café opened and Jojo staggered in, his shirt red with blood. He fell to the floor, taking a chair and table with him.

The café's patron, Texier, was quicker than any of them, rushing from behind the bar and kneeling beside the boy, Jojo's lolling head cradled on his knee. He bent his head to the dying youth's lips and listened as the blood bubbled. At last he looked up.

'Hotel Malines, Rue des Pommiers,' he said.

'Is he dead?' Bella whispered, distraught. 'This wasn't Hagley. It can't have been Hagley.'

'One of you must find Marcel,' Texier ordered. 'Bring him here.'

'Did he say the word Hagley to you?'

'Madame, pay me the courtesy of doing as I ask. Run and fetch Marcel. I have something else to do.'

'I'm coming with you,' Murch said.

'I will come too,' Urmiston said, rising.

Murch pushed him back down into his seat. Texier walked behind his counter and produced a short axe. Though he spoke no English, he could read ice-cold anger when he saw it in another's face and passed Murch a wooden billet, painted black.

'Have a care, Billy,' Quigley muttered.

'Mrs Wallis to find Marcel and bring him here. You and Mr Urmiston to tidy up. Take the boy into the back and have him laid out proper. Then go back to our hotel. You understand? Go back and wait. Let there be no ifs and buts about any of this.'

Texier said something that Bella translated.

'He says that it is not strictly our quarrel.'

'Tell him Murch begs to differ.'

He nodded to Texier and they left.

The Malines was a homosexual brothel from its front step to its fifth floor. Texier announced his intentions in the lobby by swinging the axe and decapitating a plaster statue of a naked shepherd boy. Two youths sitting on a red velvet couch fled, one directly into the street, his peignoir flying.

'Armand,' the manager remonstrated in an agitated voice, his hands fluttering. 'Did any of us know this was going to happen?'

'The boy bled to death on the floor of my café.'

'Mon Dieu!'

'We shall speak later, Albert. Where is he?'

When he got no answer he swung the axe again and buried it deep into the *comptoir*. Murch, who spoke no French at all, could understand well enough the burden of what was being said. He reached across and plucked the man clean out of his cubbyhole, sending him sprawling on to the marble floor. Before Armand could stop him, he brought his billet down on to both exposed shins. There was a spurt of blood: the manager had half bitten off his own tongue.

'I will ask you again,' Armand murmured.

They ran up the stairs, pushing aside tiny shoals of boys who screamed at their approach. On the third floor there was a suite. Texier spat on the palm that was to hold the axe. Murch pushed him gently aside. He raised his boot and kicked in the door.

Inside was not Principal Hagley, but Vircow-Ucquart. He sat at a table, drinking with his companion, who jumped up as soon as he recognized Armand, his hands folded over his bare chest.

'It has nothing to do with me,' he screamed. 'I only came in ten minutes ago! Armand, you must believe me!'

Vircow-Ucquart sat stock-still, a gauze veil over the lower half of his face, his one good eye unblinkingly calm.

'What he says is true,' he grunted. 'You have come for me. Make it quick.' He spoke in English.

'Where is Hagley?'

'Would I tell you?'

Later that night, when the story of the Englishman and the German was told in the café, Armand supposed Murch to have been a butcher by trade. Using only the black truncheon, Murch reduced Vircow-Ucquart's body to a set of broken bones, first the major skeleton and then the fingers, wrists, ankles, knees.

'You and I would have slashed in fury,' the patron said in an incredulous whisper, '*mais*, *mon Dieu*, with him I saw something completely different. The German bore the first two or three blows in silence – oh, a brave enough man, yes – but then he seemed to realize what was befalling him. Crack! Another bone shattered. He began to cry.'

'He sobbed for mercy,' someone suggested.

'No,' Armand corrected. 'He cried, like a child. He gave up his soul, like a child.'

'The Englishman killed him.'

Armand shook his head and poured another Armagnac with meticulous attention. The company watched him uneasily. A passer-by entered the café, caught the mood at once and retreated. The silence was unbearable.

'He died,' he said at last. 'When we left, he was still breathing. But there was nothing left in him that was human. Please God I never see such a thing again.'

The dining room of the Hotel Dacia was unlit and had already been set for breakfast but the proprietor, a woman, cleared away a table and provided what she thought of as appropriate to the occasion: a piercingly dry Muscadet and some thirty-year-old cognac, almost as thick and smooth as honey. Marcel sat and sipped, his hand shaking only very slightly, his expression inalterably grave.

'He was an excellent boy. His mother had him late, you understand, and died of the fever in bringing him into the world. He was raised by my second sister as her own, a little runabout child with a fistful of flowers in his hand as often as not. There are a few good souls in Boissy who remember him with affection and that's where he'll be laid to rest.'

Bella gently placed her hand over his and after a moment or so, he sighed out a smile.

'I am perfectly calm, I think. Mr Hagley and the German were, as you suspected, guardians to the mad one, Lord Bolsover. I do not think he is here in Paris. The German, we know about. His body is being taken by barge to a certain location beyond the limits of the Prefecture; it travels in a sack of cobbles and one supposes will resurface in the fullness of time. Months, maybe.'

'And Mr Hagley?' Urmiston asked in a low voice.

'Has fled. I imagine back to London. I can find out if you wish. It was probably the German who killed Jojo. But Monsieur Hagley was there, we can be certain.'

Urmiston shook his head.

'I think Bolsover was also there. I think he killed the boy.'

'If he did, he is a dead man.'

'Marcel, we all of us feel a great guilt for the grief we have visited on you,' Bella said, tears in her eyes. Marcel smiled.

'About grief, madame, we can say that it is like love, a cake that cannot be cut more than two ways.'

Quigley, who had said nothing for a quarter of an hour, scraped back his chair and offered Marcel his hand. The eloquent simplicity of the gesture caught the Frenchman off guard for a moment but then, as his nephew had done only a few hours earlier, he shook hands with each of them in turn.

The person missing from this midnight meeting was Billy Murch. He stood in the shadows of the Gare du Nord, arms folded, his back against a grimy brick column, seemingly half-asleep. Once or twice whores accosted him. He pushed them away gently with the flat of his hand. A drunken soldier came to harangue him. After a few moments of trying to waken a response in coal-dark eyes, the man saw the danger he was in and weaved away. Not until three in the morning did Murch give up his vigil – and then only because he was moved on by a caped gendarme with the same flinty expression as his own.

'Why the Gare du Nord?' Quigley whispered when he finally arrived back at the Hotel Dacia.

'I had the idea they would try to flit.'

'What, at this hour of the morning?'

'I would, if I were them.'

'Marcel says the bloke that runs the brothel knows nothing about no Lord Bolsover.'

'That's what he said to me,' Murch said calmly. 'To begin with.'

Quigley was not a Catholic and barely a churchgoer in any sense of the word at all, but when he heard this last remark of Billy Murch's, he did as he had seen done from time to time, and crossed himself vigorously.

FIFTEEN

Immediately after jojo's stabbing, Hagley had the presence of mind to dress Bolsover and himself and run downstairs. As in a fairy story, their way was signposted by little rivers of blood. They picked up a cab up in the Boulevard Raspail, two drunken and dishevelled figures who might just conceivably have been to dinner with friends. Bolsover, quite horribly, was laughing. Hooligans in opera capes.

'*Eh bien?*' the cabbie asked.

Hagley's thoughts were wild as unbroken horses.

'A St Denis,' he commanded.

'Rue St Denis?'

'*Non. La ville mê me.*'

It was ten kilometres distant. To make his meaning clear, Hagley opened his pocketbook and thrust a handful of banknotes at the man.

They travelled with the blinds down and Hagley absolutely forbade his companion to speak a word during the journey, which seemed to last for ever. From time to time on the road out of Paris he peeked into the dark that was the real France, as contrasted with the naphtha flares and electric light strings they had so recently left behind. Bolsover lounged in a corner of the carriage, drinking brandy from the neck of the bottle.

The cabman was frail and grandfatherly but not stupid. He could recognize disaster when he saw it. To the huge fare was added as much again to stop the man's mouth and more yet to have him find them a crabby hotel behind a brickworks. The windows were shuttered and not a light showed anywhere. As Hagley banged on the door for attention, the cabbie slapped the reins over his horse's rump and neck and disappeared into the dark. Bolsover, released from the injunction to remain silent, bellowed after him like an enraged ox.

The unshaven brute who finally admitted them was in his nightshirt and reeked of alcohol. There was a ridiculous scuffling as the three men negotiated a short passage side by side and tumbled into a bleak reception area. Bolsover at once ordered champagne. The man leaned past him to spit on the floor.

'Wine,' he corrected. 'Or nothing at all.'

'We require rooms,' Hagley said in a shaky voice.

'I am sure you do. You will of course be gone by seven in the morning.'

'What kind of a hotel is this?' Bolsover asked.

'One known to the police,' the man said meaningfully. He tossed a key on to the desk. 'I have one room vacant. There is a bed and a couch of sorts. You will find nails on which to hang your fine clothes. Sleep well.'

'The wine,' Bolsover reminded him.

'But of course. The finest our cellars can provide.'

The room stank of cheap perfume and the bed was unmade, the bottom sheet rucked up and stained. Hagley opened the window and unhinged the shutters. There was a view of a hundred yards or so of ruined meadow, beyond which the brick ovens roared. Bolsover threw himself on to the bed and began to laugh.

'Is this really so funny?' Hagley scowled.

'Why stop here? Why not press on to the Marne? Or further still? There must be a deserted mineshaft somewhere where we can eat mice and grow our beards for a year or two.'

'Would you prefer prison?'

'I have heard such very dull reports of it. They say the room service is abominable. How lovely you are when indignant, incidentally.'

Hagley sat on the filthy couch and stood up again immediately. The pain of being sober was as terrible as toothache.

'You killed that boy,' he yelled.

'He was annoying me. And who is to say he is dead?'

'Of course he is dead. How much spilt blood does there have to be?'

'Do I need a sermon at this hour of the night? I think not. Where is this place?'

'We are in St Denis.'

'Really? The Duchess of Berthon-Gaultier has a villa here, did you know? We went in a party to lay flowers at the statue of Marie Antoinette. Another cheap whore.'

'You have just murdered someone,' Hagley shouted.

'And what if I have? Vircow-Ucquart will sort things out. He loves playing nanny.'

There was a knock and the patron entered with a bottle and two water glasses pinched between his fingers.

'You can be heard downstairs,' he growled. 'Drink your wine, sleep it off and then sling your hook. There is a train back to Paris at five past the hour, every hour. I will wake you at six.'

'Do you offer weekly rates?' Bolsover enquired. 'This is such a fine hotel, I can't imagine why people would ever wish to stay at the Ritz.'

The man hitched his nightshirt and scratched his groin. He addressed himself to Hagley.

'Make it clear to your nancy friend that I was a guest at Vincennes before I took this place. If he says anything amusing I promise to laugh. Right now I am debating whether to throw him through the window there.'

'He is tired and the medicine he is prescribed has mixed badly with an evening's drinking.'

'Is that so? I don't really give a shit but if you value your freedom, keep your voices down.'

'Spoken like a gentleman,' Bolsover said. 'Stay and have a drink with us. And do carry on scratching your balls. It's charming.'

'You don't listen,' the patron decided. He took an easy step forward and punched the Third Earl of Bolsover to the carpet. Blood spurted from his nose and he began a choking fit. 'Both of you can clear off right now.'

'There will be no more trouble,' Hagley promised in an agonized whisper.

The hotelier held out his hand for money, and yet more money.

'Everything's fine,' Hagley said. 'You haven't seen us, we were never here.'

'My lips are sealed,' the man said sarcastically.

After he had gone, Hagley helped Bolsover to the bed and washed his face with water from the jug and ewer.

Loosened his tie and waistband, removed his shoes. Opened the shutters wide and peered out into the night. Lit by the red glow from the brickworks, an emaciated pony cantered around, sometimes silhouetted, sometimes moving like smoke.

'What a strange evening,' Bolsover said absently, a handkerchief to his swollen nose.

'This is the last time I try to save you from yourself,' Hagley replied bitterly.

'I think that's wise. You have no great aptitude for the task.'

'Has he broken your nose?'

'I don't think so. I found it arousing.'

'You don't know what you're saying any longer, Freddie.'

For the rest of the night, Hagley sat over his friend like an anxious nanny, listening to the caa-caa of his snore. His eyes ached and thoughts darted like bullets through the fog of what had happened to them. It grew light shortly after four and when he saw what desolation they were in, he put his head in his hands and prayed. And, like a man suddenly flung furthest from God, wept.

True to his word, the patron of the hotel woke them at six. It amused him to see them in evening clothes, drinking a bowl each of foul coffee, their bread rolls untouched on the pine refectory table at which his guests took all their meals. An army of flies swarmed.

'The station?'

The patron pointed laconically. 'That way the brickworks. That way the station.'

The train they took back to Paris was filled with commuting workers, some of them with sacks of tools between their boots but some quite clearly waiters and bar staff. From these they attracted very sharp glances, all the more because Bolsover, in the ruins of his evening dress, cadged cigarettes and kept up an inane monologue about Marie Antoinette.

They dived into a Turkish bath next door to the terminus station. Were shaved by an attentive Algerian, had their clothes sent out to be sponged and cleaned. Lay in the steam room, surrounded by walrus like figures. Hagley, but not Bolsover, staggered to a tiled alcove where he was hosed down by a naked attendant. He asked the time. It was barely nine o'clock. While he cowered under the hose, he heard a loud and imperious voice ordering champagne.

A contrite Bolsover was far worse than the same man drunk. He cried, he flung his arms round Hagley. His naked flesh wobbled and the sweat that ran from it was an ugly grey.

Because they had once been lovers, Hagley submitted to the tears and the distracted gestures. He knew he should send to the brothel and find out what had happened after they left. Then he must track down Vircow-Ucquart and make him get Bolsover away, maybe into Germany for a while. He should *act.* Instead, Bolsover clung and blubbered, not letting him move an inch. Their naked skin slid and skidded.

'Nobody has loved me as you do, not since the day I was born.'

'That isn't true, is it?' Hagley said, bitter. 'Tomorrow you will feel quite differently. You will forget the pain you are feeling now.'

Bolsover looked at him, his eyes very dark. Hagley knew what he had just said was the truth. Tomorrow, in clean linen and with his hair re-curled, his former lover would revert to playing the fallen angel. The clock would run backwards to the time when his theatrical beauty was at its most irresistible. He would be a different kind of child altogether. It was a shock to realize that he hated Bolsover, loathed him to the roots of his being.

'I have to return to England,' he heard himself saying.

'A feeling that has swept over you very suddenly, I take it?'

'Perhaps I am trying to distinguish between work and leisure.'

'Work?'

'I am the Principal of a missionary college.'

'How you have learned to prate since your elevation. We shall have you writing pamphlets soon. A bishopric beckons. In New Zealand, possibly. Would that be far enough away?'

'Be sensible, Freddie. I am only thinking of our safety.'

'You are thinking of your own skin.'

'Yes,' Hagley said.

'Then go.' Bolsover sulked, searching for his towel.

'You should do the same.'

Bolsover stood, flecks of spit in the corners of his mouth.

'I will not be betrayed, d'you understand?'

Hagley felt a terror rise in him.

'This is not the time to speak so wildly.'

'It is a solemn warning. You and I will come to a reckoning one day,' Bolsover promised.

It was not the threat contained in these words but the utter impossibility of dealing rationally with him that sent Hagley away to dress. Locked inside a mahogany cubicle, his hands trembling, he said his goodbyes to the man who had seduced him from being a licentious parson to an accessory to murder. In other circumstances he would have tried one last reconcilation. But this was a day for finalities. It was, he reflected ruefully, a day for betrayal.

He made no attempt to search for Bolsover in the bowels of the premises but stepped out into classic Parisian sunshine. For some reason he thought it better to find his way to the Rue des Pommiers on foot and so it was that he went, about as conspicuous in the streets as a sailor wading ashore from a shipwreck. His whole body trembled and only with great effort could he prevent his teeth from chattering.

When he came to the brothel, he found that during the night the place had burned down. All the pretty boys had escaped unharmed, a vicious old concierge from across the street reported; but M. Albert, who came originally from Marseilles and whose house it was, was taken away by ambulance minus his front teeth and with both arms broken.

'And as I explained to M. le Commissaire Garnier, that doesn't happen just by falling downstairs,' the woman concluded comfortably, at the same time eyeing Hagley with the sort of close attention that policemen love. He raised his hat to her and walked back out into the Boulevard Raspail, his linen wet with sweat. His whole being had the effect of floating. He had read somewhere there were spiders that travelled hundreds of miles across the Pacific

Ocean, borne along by their own gossamer. Whether they ever found dry land again was a matter of chance. That was exactly his case.

It occurred to him too late that he had gone to the Rue des Pommiers to ask after Vircow-Ucquart. It caused him to falter in his step only for a second. Wherever he was, the German was on his own. As for the once-bewitching Freddie, for all Anthony Hagley cared, he could stay in the Turkish bath until he died. The thing now was to get away. To flee. There was common sense in that useful word. Whatever the future risk, he should run, and keep running. He should teach himself to believe that what had happened was a specially hideous nightmare.

SIXTEEN

Urmiston had barely slept, tossing and turning on a mattress that sagged with the imprint of a hundred other bodies, the oval mirror by the washstand thickened by flitting ghosts of men and women he would never meet. Twice in the night he got up to push open the shutters and lean on the sill of the open window, staring out at the dark, his body trembling.

On the second occasion – or had he dreamed this? – there was the faintest knock at the door. When he opened it, Bella stood there in a crushed and damp nightgown, straight from bed. Her expression was blank enough to suggest sleepwalking but then she lifted her arm and brushed her hair away from her brow and her eyes came into focus. He found he could not speak to her. The two figures stood either side of the threshold for a full minute before Bella turned and floated away down the hotel corridor. Her bare feet made not the smallest sound.

When he came down to breakfast he was revolted by the faintly caramel stink of the unaired rooms. It was as though yesterday, like a recalcitrant guest, had refused to leave. Bella sat with him, mute and grey-faced. They passed toast and coffee to each other without making a single eye contact. Murch and Captain Quigley sat apart, at a table on the far side of the room. It filled Urmiston with a thick rage that they seemed to be acting and talking normally, as though the previous night they had done nothing more dangerous than smoke one cigar too many.

'Murch has to go,' he heard himself saying.

Bella looked up.

'You have changed your tune, I think.'

'I thought I had the guts for this but I see now that I don't. There's nothing wrong with Billy – he's a brave and resourceful man. But I want no more of it. If you like, a little late common sense has surfaced.'

'Perhaps you are saying it is you who must go.'

'I think that must be it,' he said stiffly. When she stared him down, he added, 'We have killed someone, Bella.'

'I have killed nobody.'

'Because we came to Paris two people are dead. You don't see that? Are we merely characters in some book by Margam? Two people who were alive yesterday are dead today.'

'You might wish to keep your voice down.'

'None of this is worth one line of literature.'

She half rose in her seat and slapped him hard against his cheek, her eyes blazing. A dozen heads turned.

'I think three days ago in London you were lecturing me on the moral obligations you felt that I, apparently, did not. How dare you speak to me in this way?'

She pushed back her chair and left the breakfast room, walking fast and soon enough breaking into a run. Bewildered waiters stepped aside to let her pass.

Murch – brisk, close shaven, his wiry hair flattened with water – quitted his conversation with Quigley to join

Urmiston. He had left the hotel earlier and bought a single rose from an old lady humping a wicker basket of them down the Boulevard St-Michel. It was intended for Bella. He laid it on the table in front of her empty place.

'Want to say what that was about?' Murch enquired in his calm and steady way.

'You might make a guess.'

'Won't say? We came to do a job, I suppose?'

'I can go no further,' Urmiston heard himself saying. 'In any case, I think we have all come too far. The question is, whether we lay what we know before the police.'

Murch rapped his nails sharply on the lid of the coffee pot.

'There will be no talk of the police. Where has she gone?'

Urmiston shrugged. When he finally left the table, he forgot to bring the rose with him.

Half an hour later, the four of them found each other again in the foyer of the hotel. Fellow guests were assembling, studying maps and flyers from restaurants and bars, sharing information with their neighbours about museums, churches or simply the best way to Montmartre. In this timid but noisy gathering was a pale man with blond hair, carrying an easel and a case of tubes and brushes. Seeing a quartet apparently undecided how to spend their day, and very much wanting to advertise his own reason for being in Paris, he hovered nearby, smiling shyly. When he finally plucked up the courage to speak, his greeting was in German.

'Just what we need,' Quigley muttered.

Only Urmiston could face talking to him.

Dressed in corduroys, his neck decorated by a faded square of red silk, the slender Herr Mueller wore a leather harness, on the back of which was a beech frame supporting several canvases.

'You see at once my purpose in being here,' he explained happily, turning so that his work could be inspected. 'I have never before painted this way, never with such blue in the palette. Can you see? It is almost a spiritual quest. At home –'

'Yes, where is home?'

'In Münster. We are farmers there, shopkeepers. Churchgoers. Here it is a little like looking into heaven.'

'I do not paint,' Urmiston muttered lamely.

'No, but come with me! I show you where I set my easel! It is not far. I beg of you, sir.'

Urmiston would gladly have followed him all the way home to Münster. He felt as light as thistledown. But immediately he stepped outside the frowst of the hotel, he felt better. The staff were hosing down the pavements in front of the building with silvery ropes of water and a stirring breeze pointed to a cloudless sky. Mueller waited with his ridiculous wooden harness, like a milkman who has lost his churn.

When they reached the Seine, he indicated some steps leading down to the river, as if welcoming Urmiston to his studio. The painting he was making of Notre-Dame, when reverentially unwrapped from its cloths and set up on its easel, was – to Urmiston's untutored eye – very good indeed.

'You have some genuine ability, I would say.'

'You are kind. But oh, if only I had words to describe what is in my heart!'

'You have the painting.'

'Yes,' the artist replied after a moment, deeply gratified. 'You are in Paris long? May we meet later and talk?'

'Alas, I go home today.'

'Such a pity. You are a man who understands life. I can see that. I myself must return home soon. And then the dream will fade.'

'Is that all this is? A dream?'

The German's face fell. 'Maybe I don't express myself so good. At home, yes, I have all that a man might wish – wife, children, pupils, patrons. In my garden find an apple tree, under which I may sit –'

Out of the corner of his eye Urmiston noticed Captain Quigley and Billy Murch, waiting for him on the opposite pavement. He excused himself and crossed the road.

'The Captain and me are staying on for a few days,' Murch said in a low voice. 'We will see the boy buried in his home village.'

'You don't think it wiser to make yourself scarce?'

'We'll come to no harm. We'll be back in London the end of the week, beginning of the next.'

'Billy –'

The Captain squared himself up, looking up and down the street with what he hoped might seem a keen eye.

'All discussed with the lady of the party, deployment of forces agreed.'

'Maybe I should come with you to Boissy. Indeed, I think it my duty.'

Murch shook his head.

'Mrs Wallis is very low. She will need someone to see her home. I don't say this to cause offence, but you too are in no state to hang on here a moment longer than is necessary. With the Captain and me, things is different.'

'How, different?'

'Look here, Charlie,' Quigley interrupted them in a kindly voice. 'The boy is dead. We can't put that right but me and Billy have been this way before. We know what has to be done.'

'I can't discuss this on the street,' Urmiston said, far more shakily than he intended. 'Come back to the hotel.'

'It's all decided,' Murch contradicted gently. 'You should go home and forget the whole thing.'

'Forget! Do you think I shall ever forget last night?'

'I don't lose my temper with you, Mr Urmiston, but put it this way. Just do as you're told.'

'Let us at least go to where that poor boy was murdered and see what else we can find out.'

'Nothing much left to look at.'

His expression was completely neutral but Quigley understood at once. He knew what smoke smelt like when it penetrated wool and serge. The bedroom he had shared with Murch stank like Paddington Station, a simile he had employed when they rose to shave. Only now did it make sense.

'Wake up to it, Charlie,' he said. 'These are marching orders he's giving you.'

With that, the two friends set off for Armand's café, Quigley stepping straight off the pavement and walking across the Boulevard St-Michel in an unwavering straight line, as though the morning traffic did not exist.

Down by the Seine the painter had removed his jacket and jammed a straw hat on his sparse blond hair. Watched with envy by Urmiston, he lit the first pipe of the day and gazed in rapture at a Paris innocent of all nightmares. Under the wide brim of his hat, he further shaded his eyes with his hand, like a child looking into a sun-filled bay.

Urmiston walked slowly back into the hotel.

Halfway home across the Channel, the ferry gave a single blast on the ship's whistle, slowed and hove to. Those in the saloon, seeing the sailors' dark blue guernseys running past the windows, joined the deck passengers crowding the starboard rail. There was a faint edge of panic flooding over the ship, not made any the less by the stentorian boom of a bosun telling everyone to keep calm. A foolish woman screamed: the mob of people swayed as if struck. Against her will, Bella set down her coffee cup and followed outside.

In the lee of the ferry, two men were clinging to a greasy yellow spar. A third body bobbed in the chop of the waves. It was the corpse of a shoeless child, his shirt inverted over his head, his arms outstretched.

Once the ferry passengers realized they were not themselves in any danger, there was a ghoulish interest in watching the rescue of the survivors. A deckhand jumped over the forepeak to secure a line to the dead boy. Horribly, he was cheered. Even more horribly, he waved his appreciation.

Bella forced herself to watch, though with only half her mind on the scene. She had gone to France to protect Charles Urmiston and in that she had failed catastrophically. At this moment, he sat on a slatted bench, his back to all the commotion. Although things between them could not be made any clearer, there was enough of the slighted woman in Bella to be huffed. Not for the first time since she began writing the Margam novels, someone had taken her to be far stronger than she actually was.

'A mere child,' a woman passenger observed, indicating the tarpaulin under which the dead boy lay. 'Were they all drunk, do you think, to be smashed into like that by some other vessel?'

'Is that how it pleases you to think?' Bella asked.

'Well, I don't know!' the woman exclaimed wonderingly. 'I was only asking a civil question, I'm sure. I beg your pardon for speaking at all.'

Bella pushed her gently aside and walked to where Urmiston sat.

'Are we to carry on like this indefinitely?'

He looked up at her with empty eyes.

'What has happened?' he asked.

'A fishing smack was run down in the night. But I asked you a question, Charles.'

'I cannot answer. I cannot think.'

'That is sentimental nonsense.'

'I am not the person I thought I was,' he whispered.

'And if I say I need you?'

He looked up, shaking his head.

'And that others may need you even more?'

When he did not reply, she walked back into the saloon. There, a florid man was passing around his billycock hat, soliciting donations to the welfare of the fishing-smack survivors. A little silver and a single banknote lay in the bottom.

'They're from Ramsgate, the lads. Never stood a chance. Two others, one of them the boy's father, gone to the bottom.'

And, she thought bitterly, how well you shape the story, how complete the dotting of the i's. How simple it all is.

'Do you know the name of the sailor who jumped into the sea to save them?'

The florid man stared at her.

'Devil I do. It ain't hardly about him. He was doing his duty, brave lad that he is. This is about widows, missus.'

The deck plates began to thrum and the ferry came round by its head. Bella opened her purse.

'Your husband out there has took it bad,' the man said, nodding to the figure of Urmiston. She glanced. He sat with his head in his hands, cloaked in misery.

'What is it?' Hannah Bardsoe wanted to know.

'I think we can call it Street Scene with Tabac,' Urmiston said, his voice trembling. 'Those blue tables are where the local people sit to gossip.'

'And did you sit there in your turn?' she asked carefully. 'And are those tables really blue, I mean in life?'

She propped the little canvas against the teapot and stood back, lips pursed.

'You took a fancy to it,' she decided.

'I bought it for you, Hannah, if you will accept it.'

'For me!' she cried.

'I thought we might go there one day. Sit down at an empty table – see, there is one, next to the red door –'

'You bought me a painting?' she asked, unsteady.

Urmiston sat down in her spoonback chair and, putting his head into his hands, burst into tears. He did more: he began howling like a dog. Nothing would comfort him, not a word, not her warm arm around his shoulders.

'My dear, my dear,' Hannah cried, terrified out of her wits. He disengaged her arm and flung himself out of the room, running upstairs, his howling turned to urgent barks of despair.

'Whatever have you done?' she screamed after him.

In the picture, a kind of soporific calm prevailed. Herr Mueller, the innocent from Münster, had painted the little bar in the Rue de la Huchette as though it were a way station on the road to paradise. A figure – maybe Jojo, maybe a girl, but anyway represented by a single stroke of red – walked away into the rapturous blue fog Mueller had discovered while smoking his pipe and trembling for joy at the glorious abundance of the material world.

SEVENTEEN

At orange street, there was a note from Marie Claude. She had accepted an invitation from Fern Jellicott to go painting and sketching in Cromer. If Bella could remove herself to Paris at only a few hours' notice, then why couldn't she, Marie Claude, do as she wished? They were hardly married, she added spitefully, and it was her own money she was spending. Mrs Venn confirmed: the mam'selle had set off with four pieces of luggage – dear Lord, enough for a visit to the ends of the earth. She was wearing the steel-grey dress Mrs Wallis had bought her in the spring, and had sent to the Burlington Arcade for a box of watercolours. It arrived soon after she left.

Bella was too tired to be angry. She went to Marie Claude's room. In the pages of fiction it would have been in wild disarray, with discarded scarves and scattered shoes everywhere. But the Frenchwoman had habits of tidiness that would not have disgraced royalty. The bed slept soundly under its silk cover, the little green chair dozed by the empty hearth, the studio photograph of Bella (from Mr Debenham in Regent Street) was centred exactly on the mantelpiece. It was as though Marie Claude had not left the previous day, but some months ago.

While she was still poking about – the sponge as big as a cat had gone from the bathroom, along with the blue-and-white kimono – there was a distant knock at the front door and Mrs Venn dragged herself upstairs to announce that she had shown a gentleman into the drawing room.

'A Mr Philip Westland, who has called on the offchance of seeing you and so forth.'

Bella ran downstairs at the risk of killing herself.

'I got as far as Cairo,' Westland explained. 'Hated the people on the boat, set up at Shepheard's, fed the gazelle they have wandering about in the gardens there and just could not bring myself to rejoin the party. They sailed without me.'

'Oh fie,' Bella said. To Westland's amazement she burst into tears.

'I half hoped you might be pleased,' he muttered, greatly embarrassed. She flung herself into his arms.

'Have you ever read a work of fiction?' she howled.

'*Pickwick Papers.* Does that count?'

'Philip, you are come like a knight in shining armour, just when I need you most. I can't tell you how unhappy I am.'

'How happy I am to hear it,' he said drolly, kissing her first on the forehead and then on her lips. 'Should we sit down, or should we go out somewhere? Would the Café de Paris suit?'

'No, it would not. Would you consider taking me away out of London altogether? I mean for a day or two? I can't think where, but far, far away. And not Cromer.'

Westland studied her. His gaze was so intense that she could not meet it and dropped her chin to her chest.

'For a day or two, I think you said.'

'I cannot deceive you with the promise of anything else.'

'Has it occurred to you that I might have jumped ship at Cairo for a reason?'

'It has,' she admitted, blushing. He smiled.

'You are too honest, Bella. But I will tell you this. My cousin has a cottage he keeps for me at his place in Shropshire.'

'You would take me there on such meagre terms? A chance to run away for a few days in the company of a bad-tempered woman?'

'I should of course say no. And thrice no.'

At last she looked up.

'And what do you say?'

'First, we will sit down and you will tell me why you are so unhappy. Omitting nothing, Bella. I have not come home to be beguiled by mysteries. You must speak frankly, the way they do in bad plays.'

'I cannot tell you everything.'

'Then tell me nothing at all and I will be on my way.'

She pulled him to her side and told him everything. He listened; in places he laughed. When she came to what had happened in Paris his eyes darkened and he took her hand in his.

'This fellow Urmiston. You say you went there to look after him? Is he some kind of special ninny, then?'

'You and he would get on well, the way men do. But I am not his nurse, no. And acting jealous doesn't suit you, Westland.'

'I suppose I am jealous, a little. I feel the need to invent some rival personalities, like the flame-haired Mrs McCorquadale, or Aaisa, the Berber temptress. But what it is truthfully, Bella, I care even less for this fellow Margam, who has led you into such reckless danger.'

'I said I was unhappy earlier. I should have said I was miserable. I am trying to get you to see me as I am. Margam is part of it but nothing like as dangerous a companion as you wish to make out. He puts the bread on my table.'

She put up her face to be kissed.

'Nothing and no one stands between us,' she whispered.

'Except Miss d'Anville perhaps.'

The unexpectedness of this remark and the flatness in his tone jolted her upright. She had described her relationship with Marie Claude in completely honest terms, something she had never before attempted to do before another living soul.

'Think about it, Philip. She is very young. One day – it might be tomorrow – she will take wing and fly.'

'In the present circumstances, doesn't that come a little too pat?'

'Have you been listening at all? I returned from Paris in turmoil I could never have imagined. Until you came, I was at my wits' end. And then this, something wonderful. Could I care less what happens with Marie Claude?'

'I don't know,' he said with dreadful heaviness.

She rose and walked the room, very shaken by the turn the conversation had taken. Westland's eyes followed her.

'I held you to be the person most likely to understand who I am, who I really am. As you demanded of me, I have told you everything. If everything is not enough, then let us part now.'

For a moment she thought she had lost him but then he sighed hugely and asked if she had a Bradshaw's in the house.

'If ever I were to give myself over to another man for the rest of my life, it would be you, Westland,' she said, standing with her naked feet in the dew, watching the early-morning sun diffuse light down the valley. He stood behind her, his arms round her waist.

'That must be my fate, then. To wait for you.'

'No,' she said. 'I mustn't be selfish. But you are the kindest and gentlest man in the world.'

He kissed the nape of her neck.

'Did I tell you I had my fortune told in Cairo? An ancient crone dashed the coffee from my cup and read the grounds. She saw me living on an island – but not, she warned, these islands. After the exchange of some geographical possibilities, I took her to mean Cuba.'

'That was romantic.'

'Well, it was more kindly than romantic. After all, if you looked into the bottom of a cup and saw a poor naked wretch eating shellfish with nothing but a goatskin umbrella to keep the sun off him, you would want to improve his fortunes a little, I should think.'

'Did she mention me?'

'No, she did not.'

She turned and kissed him lingeringly. For a single beat in history she considered how happy she might be with him. But telling him about Marie Claude had been a mistake. In all other respects so quick and generous, he failed to understand. Quite accidentally, she had provided the excuse he needed not to pursue her any further. He felt he was betraying an existing relationship.

'If Garnett were still alive and thus you found yourself in love with a married woman, would it make a difference?'

'Listen, Bella. I am a rather nondescript sort of fellow who has taken great pains never to be hurt by life. You have not hurt me now. I am perplexed, is all. I shall go away at the end of what is for you a holiday and find somewhere I can wait things out. I think Cuba is a bit extreme. The Scillies, possibly.'

'You have a very exalted idea of honour.'

'Of love,' he said.

They walked, because that is what one does on holidays of this kind. Seeing a church tower a country mile or so distant, they walked there, making their way along the edges of fields, jumping ditches. Westland, just as she had imagined, was a clumsy explorer. His shoes found mud, the elbows to his linen suit were greened. He had nothing to say about the church when they found it but sat on a bank outside the lych-gate, fanning himself with the straw hat he had plucked from its peg in the cottage. There was a public house nearby: they drank lemonade served to them by a young girl in a faded dress and bare feet.

'You are townspeople,' she suggested.

'From London,' Bella confirmed.

'I heard tell of it often,' the girl said, not to be outfaced.

'You think you might go there one day?'

'And for what reason? There's nothing there for me, I shouldn't think.'

'You are right,' Westland said. 'You can do better.'

'I never said that,' the girl muttered, aggrieved. She felt she was being patronized. The gentle Westland saw it at once.

'I was meaning to say that here is better,' he explained softly. 'Else, why would we be here?'

'Ho!' the girl said knowingly.

They followed the river down to a bridge, exchanged pleasantries with the parson who was fishing there, crossed over to the other bank and waded through chest-high mallows to find their bearings.

'There is never a policeman about when one wants them,' Westland said, peering doubtfully at the landscape.

'Touching what I told you about Paris, you have not said a single word, I notice.'

'No. I don't say I understand half of it either. To be completely frank, if it *is* this fellow Margam who is leading you about by the nose, then you should brain him with one of his own books. Put his eyes out with a steel nib. He isn't you, Bella.'

'I have made him me.'

'What rot. In life you would kick him downstairs without a second thought. Is he here now, for example?'

'Of course not.'

'He won't jump out of that blackthorn with a thrilling piece of plot?'

'It seems unlikely.'

'Thank God for that. Needlework or petit point is the only consolation a lady needs.'

They lay down at the edge of a cornfield and he submitted to being kissed on the eyes and lips, the weight of Bella's body across his. Larks floated far above their heads. For ten sublime minutes Bella lay listening to his heart.

'Of course,' Westland said, almost to himself, 'it is Margam that is my real rival and not some ethereal French beauty.'

The remark lasted out the whole of their stay.

'Where will you go next?' Bella asked on their last night together.

'Not far,' he answered. 'A man at my club has offered a berth on his yacht. Norway and so forth. The salmon there are as big as women and twice as willing. This is the promise he has made anyway.'

'Won't you fall in and drown?'

'No,' Westland said. 'I shall save myself for other battles. Considering the mortal sin into which you have plunged me, I think it permissible to say that I love you, Bella. I shall fight. In my own way, I shall persevere.'

'I can promise you nothing,' she warned.

It was dusk and they had been in bed since late afternoon. He got up and, stark naked, began lighting the fire inside a cranky and rusting stove.

'I don't know whether you like stew,' he said. 'But that is what you're getting.'

'Where did you learn to cook at all?'

'In a tent, at the bottom of the garden. Quite a long time ago.'

She jumped up and – also naked – hugged him.

'What if I say I love you?'

'It is what I came home to hear.'

'And will you truly wait for me?'

'Oh, I should think so,' Westland said.

EIGHTEEN

The rest of that summer passed with its usual calendar of triumphs and reversals. A Scotsman called Coffey drove a thousand geese from Norfolk to London without losing a single one. As widely reported, they followed the sound of his bagpipes. In Ireland, Lady Keniry was discovered in bed with a foot servant by her husband: the aggrieved party shot her and eight of the nine house servants, including a fourteen-year-old girl, before turning the gun on himself. A two-headed lamb was born in Dorset; in Ayr a man fell a hundred feet from a church tower and survived without a scratch on him. A horse called Moncur won a two-mile handicap at Doncaster by the biggest margin ever recorded.

There was a letter from Oslo. The writer had not fallen overboard once but had contrived to be left behind on a tiny island in Norway's greenest fiord. This had not been planned but was a consequence of his friend's absent-mindedness. (And a ridiculous dalliance with an Italian lady they had picked up along the way.) The island showed some promise but was smaller than the one illustrated at the bottom of a Cairene coffee cup. The Italian lady resembled a wardrobe to be found in the Army & Navy Stores, Victoria. The letter was signed by a single initial.

In September, Bella's publisher, Mr Frean, wrote her a note expressing the hope that the new work was progressing well, that the London autumn was not too melancholy (though he had heard from sources that the first of the fogs had created three days of havoc by water and on land) and that she continued in good health, as ever. Never one to interrupt an author in mid-stream, he hoped nevertheless he was free to mention a curious case reported in *The Times:* the mysterious disappearance of a noted Oxford divine, the Reverend Mr Hagley. How strange the world wagged, he concluded cheerfully, when a clergyman should vanish completely in a city filled with such notorious gossips. Finally, he himself was well, indeed blooming, having been introduced to sea-bathing by a charming boy with one blue eye and one brown.

Three months had passed since Paris and Frean's news of Hagley was itself a fortnight old. He had not been seen since the afternoon of 3 September, when he left Bolsover Hall to call on the Dean of Balliol.

'Which my old pal Blossom says was to have been tea and toast, along with remarks pertinent to the Gospel, et cetera.'

Quigley had returned to Oxford on his own initiative. He and Blossom were reunited in the Eagle and Child and spent two happy evenings on the ale, returning to a deserted Bolsover Hall for generous measures of the Principal's whisky. Only a fallout over the monarchy had brought this idyll to its close.

'Who was it, I wonder, who offered the fateful insult?' Bella asked lazily.

The finished pages to her work lay lodged in a small leather suitcase at her feet. In the late summer, she had taken Marie Claude away to Devon for a week, so that the office could be re-whitewashed and given what Quigley called a general tarting-up. This was the prelude to making the final copy of the new novel, as yet untitled.

For once the Captain had made no mistakes over his commission and the place looked cheerful and in its own small way, homely. The only false note struck was the presence of a clothes mangle, promised to a neighbour, acquired in the Quigley way of things, but never collected. Bella actually enjoyed its presence. Often, she paused to search for a word and found herself studying the mangle as if the answer was to be found within its bleached rollers and the heavy seriousness of the cast-iron frame.

'I may have said something untoward about the Royals,' Quigley admitted. 'But Blossom will hear no ill about any of them. A man who has shaken hands with the Prince of Wales, d'you see?'

'And where was this?'

'On the up platform of Oxford Station. Both of them half-cut, of course.'

Bella grimaced, enough for Quigley to change tack. He pointed to the suitcase.

'I see you have finally managed to cobble together something.'

'We call the process literature,' Bella responded, tart.

'You got a story out of old Bolsover in the end.'

'Yes,' she said. 'I got a story out of him.'

'And who,' the Captain wondered, 'was the damsel in distress?'

'I beg your pardon?'

'Doesn't there always have to be a damsel in distress?'

He waggled his eyebrows, driving Bella to snatch up her bonnet and depart for lunch.

The thing that was missing was not the identity of the lady in distress, for such women hung on racks like clothes in a wardrobe. Walking down the Strand, Bella could see any of half a dozen likely candidates, pale girls with their tippets drawn up around their necks, their gloved hands joined, their little narrow feet as delicate as foxes'. Hadn't Marie Claude fallen in love with one such, the vapid Jellicott? Miss Jellicott lived in Barnes and barely had the strength to lift her arms to unpin her hair.

'She is a lost soul,' Marie Claude explained. 'She goes for help to séances in Camberwell.'

'Never the ideal place to find yourself.'

Fern Jellicott, with her milk-white body and childlike breasts, her elaborated habits of indecision, the trembling lower lip that began the moment she was asked even the simplest question, was now immortalized in the pages of fiction. She was – although the thought made Bella uncomfortable – Bolsover's last victim, to be snatched from death at the very last moment by Billy Murch, or the version of Murch that appeared in the story. It was the Murch-like Willem Meinherzen's shadow that flitted over the tumbling fury of a hundred-foot waterfall in Bohemia, marking his prodigious leap to pluck the girl to safety. Bolsover – Bella had not yet decided on his fictional name – stumbled, slipped on a wet rock and plunged to his ghastly death in the pool the locals called the Cauldron.

Such is literature. In life, Bella would cheerfully have pitched Fern Jellicott over a gloomy Bohemian cliff, along with her cloaks and capes, her watercolour boxes and diary written in purple ink. It annoyed her that Murch, now transfigured as Meinherzen, international fencing master, should have to dart through the air like a swallow to save such a puling ninny.

For two days past, she had been trying to think up a more spectacular end for Bolsover. It did not make much of a story that he brought about his own death by the accident of wearing the wrong shoes in a rural setting. Bella had killed him several different ways, most dramatically by having him pierced by a lifeboat rocket in a catastrophic explosion of magenta and white smoke. But in the end art imitated life, with the usual unsatisfactory consequences. Bolsover departed the novel with a sneer on his lips, a monster never brought to justice. In one version of his demise, he had not fallen into the Cauldron, but seeing the end was at hand, evaded his pursuers by executing the perfect swallow dive.

'Sometimes it is better this way,' Murch-Meinherzen declared, his slim bare arms around the hideous Jellicott, as the rescue party, led by a man very like Urmiston, announced itself with hunting horns. The rain lashed down on a Bohemia that had some striking resemblances to Dartmoor.

Murch had become Meinherzen so comfortably because little had been seen of him since what Quigley persisted in calling the Paris jaunt. When they came back from seeing Jojo properly buried, Murch, as if sensing that the mood was against him, drifted away from the group. Mrs Bardsoe had heard that he had sold his cart and sent Penny into retirement in Kent. Quigley believed him to be still in London, though untraceable. He had gone to ground, some said on the south bank of the river, some as far north as Edmonton.

That suited Bella very well. What he had to offer her in the pages of a novel was a character that she found both repellent and attractive. His calm and unblinking ruthlessness fascinated her: tricked out with a new accent and a more acceptable social background, he was a hero such as she had never before attempted. Meinherzen spoke seldom, moved with stunning economy, fenced, shot, tracked a human trace with the cunning of a stag-hunter. He spoke five languages but only those closest to him knew that he was born an Englishman. (This was another inspired inversion of reality. That year's Derby-winner was called Galopin: his owner was Prince Gustavus Batthyany, a Hungarian who but for his name many would have supposed an English aristocrat of the first water. Bella was introduced to him at the Goodwood meeting and the germ of a better idea was born.)

Meinherzen had the aristocratic trick of never explaining himself. In the drawing rooms of the rich, no one could remember him entering the room or leaving it: he was talking to his hostess one moment and then, when she looked round, he was gone. His evening clothes were of impeccable cut, his linen whiter than snow. Where he lodged in London, how he came to know Prague so well, or Nice, who gave him the scar that ran from his brow to his jaw – none of these things were known.

He travelled alone. Lady Troughton quizzed him extensively at a ball in the Paris Embassy about his taste in women, by which she meant their absence in his life. Meinherzen was saved from replying by the intervention of the

Foreign Secretary, who drew him away into the library to discuss highly secret matters of state. When her ladyship next asked after Meinherzen, he had gone. Two days later, a peasant girl of the Jura, attracted by a riderless horse cropping the lush grass in some out-of-the-way valley, had caught him bathing naked, his body backlit by the sun. From the dusty clothes scattered about, she took him to be the servant of a rich master. Thinking to steal from his saddlebag, her hands had closed on a pistol. When she turned round, Meinherzen was levelling its twin at her breast.

Bella could not have written so effectively about this mystery man without creating someone who in turn was hunting him. The foil to Meinherzen's cruel implacability was a bumbling and soft-edged Englishman with weak eyes. He too was a driven man, tempered by a conscience that had him wake up sweating. Meinherzen flew like an arrow, his pursuer with the erratic zigzag of a butterfly.

For a time during the summer, the Reverend Anthony Hagley acted like the man who believes that by not mentioning a problem it will go away of its own accord – dwindle to a point somehow and disappear.

There were other things to occupy him. True to Blossom's prediction, the three missionaries sent to the Zambezi did indeed perish. One – perhaps the luckiest of them in the circumstances – was drowned trying to land in an open boat at the mouth of the river. The huge surf that ran across the sandbars plucked him into the life eternal before he had set foot in Africa. His patented oilskin valise (to which was bound an enormous white sun umbrella) was discovered a week or so later; but the body of Mr Wilson

Priddie, late of Magdalen College, Oxford, was never found.

The anxious and unimaginative Hainsworth died of the bloody flux a month after landing. The missionary Hagley thought about most was the man with whom Captain Quigley had enjoyed a brief conversation in the Eagle and Child. Immune to the portfolio of killing diseases that seemed spilt so carelessly along the river, Tobias Ross-Whymper swiftly became the admiration of all who met him. He was calm, he was energetic, above all ceaselessly devoted to the service of God. And then, one afternoon, he walked out from a camp among some native grass huts with nothing in his hand but a canvas bucket – and was never seen again.

Hagley could not rid his mind of this mystery.

'We cannot believe he is dead,' the father explained over dinner in the Randolph Hotel. 'The boy was intended for the diplomatic service, as you know. Then God chose him for this other purpose and it seems inconceivable that He should not have guided his steps accordingly.'

Hagley inclined his head. The grim old stick in unfashionable evening clothes pushed away his plate.

'I know it is none of your business directly how these ventures are organized –'

'In this particular case you will recall that Bishop Colenso –'

'Yes, yes,' Ross-Whymper's father said testily. He seemed to want to say more but instead pulled a letter from his jacket.

'You had better read this,' he said.

Hagley recognized the handwriting at once. He scanned the contents with mounting dismay and then laid it by his plate, his face crimson.

'Do you have the honour of knowing Lord Bolsover?' he asked.

'You stand accused by him of incompetence and gross dereliction of your duty as moral guardian to my boy.'

'During his time at the Hall, your son had nothing but kind words for me,' Hagley objected, his voice wobbling.

'This fellow Bolsover endowed your charitable enterprise?'

'That is widely known. He himself is esteemed as a Christian patriot. Mr Gladstone—'

'Goddammit, sir, do not talk to me of Gladstone. Is any of this true? That you have acted carelessly and – Bolsover's word for it – viciously in the execution of your duties?'

'I cannot imagine what his lordship means by that passage in his letter,' Hagley said, his head swimming.

'You have a servant, Blossom?' Ross-Whymper asked.

'I recently turned him off, for drunkenness. An utterly unreliable witness.'

'I have met Blossom,' the old man said with glittering eyes. 'I do not like you, Mr Hagley. Do not like you and cannot trust you. I have laid a complaint against you with the Charity Commissioners.'

'And will that bring back your son?'

Ross-Whymper stared at him, his eyes popping.

'You are, as others have said of you, a cad. And don't talk to me of the dignity of your cloth. You are not fit to wear it.'

*

And then the worst news of all, all the more painful for being so predictable. On a blustery day in late September, Bella turned in at Fracatelli's, where the tablecloths glowed like snow and the chandeliers chattered. It was Signor Fracatelli's whim to have his waiters reach on tiptoe and flick them as they passed, giving a pleasant impression of secret tinkling conversations going on above the diners' heads.

She was ushered towards a particular table by Fracatelli himself. The man who rose to greet her was Bishop Duddington.

'Mrs Wallis, how delighted I am to see you.'

Fracatelli beamed, saw to it that Bella was seated just so, and fawning over the bishop, snapped his fingers for his most amiable waiter. Duddington smiled.

'Everybody likes a uniform,' he murmured, indicating his purple vest, his britches and clerical gaiters. 'I go to the House this afternoon. We are debating amendments to a bill on a subject of such high importance that I cannot disclose its contents, even if I could remember them. This lunch is my reward.'

'You have dined here before?'

'Oh, as to that, we are here because Broxtowe told me it would please you.'

'Was his death peaceful?' Bella asked in far too casual a tone. Duddington at once tempered his expression. His smile became more grave

'I saw him ten days since. He was frail. No less genial, I should add, but quieter. Have you ever been to his house in Yorkshire?'

She shook her head. When he saw the tiny tears clinging to her eyelashes, Duddington nodded sympathetically.

'It is sad,' he agreed, 'but what he faced was something we all must come to. And I believe with all my heart that God was waiting to welcome him.'

'You were speaking about his house,' Bella said in a choked voice. Duddington searched her eyes with his.

'There never was a more devoted staff. The draughts from the doors and windows could dry a prodigious amount of corn, it is true, but nobody except me seemed to notice. Broxtowe has always engaged his servants together with their families, so that the place is more akin to a village green than a private home. The children played at cricket in the long gallery. There were of course any number of exceeding pretty girls about.'

Bella smiled dutifully, though the tears were still there.

'I must thank you for the tact you have employed.'

He reached for a bottle cooling in its bucket.

'We agreed this particular conversation was a job calling for champagne. He even specified the year.'

Bella could hold herself in no longer. Her sob could be heard the length of the restaurant. It had been on Duddington's mind to invite Urmiston to this same lunch; and now he wished he had. Luckily for him he stayed silent. Had he mentioned the name, Bella would almost certainly have fled back out into the Strand. He fished for the handkerchief in the sleeve of his coat and passed it across.

'My dear Mrs Wallis, I am most awfully sorry. I had no wish to upset you.'

He raised his glass. After a moment or so, Bella joined him.

'To a dear friend,' Duddington proposed.

'And to friendship,' she replied, pleasing him greatly, even though she spoke in such a tiny voice.

'Will you go to the funeral?' he asked. 'I shall be happy to accompany you.'

'I cannot,' she said. 'I hope it is not unchristian of me, but I cannot.'

Duddington nodded and with his trademark elegance changed the subject, launching out into more anecdotes of Broxtowe's servants, including an account of his hermit, a draper from Leeds who lived in a limestone cave on a remote part of the estate.

Above their heads, the chandeliers tinkled prettily.

NINETEEN

'Nothing?' Captain Quigley asked, accepting a plate of ham and some cold pease.'Not a word,' Hannah Bardsoe confirmed in a beaten-down tone of voice. The Captain poured her a pale ale. When, on an impulse, he reached and held her clenched hand in his, she smiled weakly.

'Oh, I have no call on him, I know that. But a line or two to say he's safe would be gratifying to a body.'

'How long has it been now, ma?'

'Nine weeks and two days,' Hannah Bardsoe said instantly. 'He walks out that door, six in the morning, wearing his suit with the little check, a nice grey stock I bought him and that silly old hat he sometimes wears and pfffft! Neither hide nor hair has been seen of him since.'

'Don't you worry.'

'Easy for you to say, Quigley. I *do* worry. I know you and Billy done your best to find him but –' she hesitated a moment – 'well, it's not in his nature to hurt a person, not a man to give heedless offence. The gentlest of gentle souls. And it seems to me,' she added, her eyes filling with tears, 'what as how I am the only one now who give a brass farthing as to his well-being and present whereabouts. It seems to me his other friends have forgot him.'

'Blimey, ma,' Quigley protested with a full mouth.

'Eat your ham, you fat-arsed chancer,' Mrs Bardsoe said, wiping the tears from her cheeks.

In Cornwall, it was a day of scudding clouds and brief intervals of watery sunshine. Urmiston had taken to regular walks along the cliff path after lunch, more often than not, even in the sunniest weather, plucked at by the steady and uproarious westerlies that seemed to blow over the Lizard peninsula. The sea – which he feared with a townsman's dread – crashed on to brown and black rocks and though his way took him more than a hundred feet above the turmoil of it, at night he tasted salt on his lips and smelled it on his clothes.

Seldom a day passed without him witnessing what he took to be maritime disasters, some of them an ignorant misreading of the price of fish but every so often a genuine calamity. In the late August gales a waterlogged and dismasted barque ran aground on the Manacles. Five of the crew survived. They were Frenchmen, short, ugly men with something of the character of pencil stubs, blunt and well-used. Offered brandy, they sat in the gorse with their heads between their knees, as though disgraced in love.

Lucette Landrieux was also French, a tall woman, taller than Urmiston himself. Her cottage was in a sunken lane, gable end to the sea, about a mile from the cliffs. A painter, her studio was a cow byre. Unlike Urmiston, she seldom walked further than the lane end, where a Mrs Howard furnished milk and home-made bread.

'My poor Charles,' she smiled, softening his name to the French pronunciation. 'I think you go out along the cliffs to feed the terror inside you. And in those boots it is only a matter of time before something terrible will happen.'

She had the pleasing habit of drinking tea in the Cornish manner, from handle-less mugs as big as flower vases. And, scandalously, she smoked cigarettes one after another, sometimes lighting the next before the first was out. Her wiry grey hair flew from her head like a tangled bush and she had solved the problem of keeping warm by wearing a fisherman's smock and black serge trousers.

'Mrs Howard wants to know if you are suffering from a wasting disease.'

'What did you tell her?'

'That you had lost the knack of being alive.'

He shrugged. He knew this was a lie: Mrs Howard dealt in commonplaces. She would not have understood the remark. Her husband Jem was a lobster fisherman: they both walked four miles to chapel every Sunday, singing heartily on the way home. To lose the knack of being alive was to be dead already in Mrs Howard's way of looking at things.

'Today, while you were out, a man called on the chance of enjoying a cream tea. He saw these very practical trousers, searched with his eyes for the breasts within my smock, blushed bright pink and beat a hasty retreat.'

'What kind of a man?'

'An Englishman.'

'I cannot stay here, Lucette,' Urmiston said suddenly. 'It solves nothing. It buys me nothing. I have treated

Mrs Bardsoe most unkindly. I was caught up in something that I could not control – I mean the other business I have told you about, the Paris business. I was too weak to bear it.'

'She will understand. Or rather, she will if you tell her everything. I have been waiting for you to leave, *mon cher*.'

'Have I made trouble for you, being here?'

Lucette laughed.

'You are my lodger,' she said. 'I have enjoyed your company. I like silence in a man. And you eat very little.'

'Don't tease, Lucette.'

'Was I teasing you? I am a solitary by nature. You are not. I shall miss you for a few weeks and then I shall forget you. Not entirely, but enough. I came here to forget, dearest Charles, and that is what I have done. You, I think, could stay here another ten years and still worry after London.'

'Is that what it is?' Urmiston wondered.

'After other people, then. People you know, people you have yet to meet. In Béziers I have a complete house with almost a hectare of grounds. I have not seen it for fifteen years. Perhaps I never will again. That is the difference between us. Having you here has been in effect a holiday. I had forgotten how important history is for some people, how much it explains.'

All this while she had been rolling them both cigarettes. She proffered his with a reddened hand, dabs of paint on her wrist.

'Come and see the studio for a last time.'

Her paintings were large. Though she lived by the sea, none of the canvases illustrated it or the local landscape. They were flower studies, intensely detailed, almost obsessively so. Nor was the light that fell on them that cruel, heartless clarity that seemed to Urmiston to belong specifically to Cornwall. These flowers seemed to stand bathed in gold. There was another inexplicable detail. All of them, in all of the paintings, had been cut. In the moment of their representation, they were already dying.

'You don't like them, do you?'

'They make me uneasy,' Urmiston admitted.

'But of course,' Lucette murmured. 'That is the right way to look at them.'

'Why do you paint this way?'

'I have no idea. One day Mrs Howard will come down to find out how I am and find me dead behind my easel. And then perhaps her husband will turn the canvases and use them to patch his boat. Or his roof, where it leaks.'

'I wish you would not talk that way.'

She laughed.

'Shall I tell you something, Charles? Remorse is a very indigestible meal. You have done nothing with which to reproach yourself. While it is still warm, you should take the bath out on to the lawn and scrub yourself free of Cornwall. And, if I may suggest, shave off your beard. I don't say this because you are in the least unclean, dearest Charles – you are in fact one of the most particular men I have ever met. No, you must think of it as a ritual of some kind. Preparations towards a journey.'

'You have been such a good friend, Lucette.'

'Oh, friends!' she laughed. 'What a store men set by friendship. I am not your jolly good egg, M'sieu Urmiston. I like you – and if it won't set you running off down the lane in terror – I even love you. But what is more, I know you. Friendship is for clubs, or public houses.'

He kissed her, standing on tiptoe to reach her lips. It was their first and last kiss: the singing in his ears was as real to him as the nap of her sleeve or the hands with which she framed his face.

'This is knowing someone,' she explained gently, as if to a child. Even his beard failed to conceal the blood that had rushed into his face. His ears burned like lamps.

'Someone is thinking of you,' she laughed, kissing him again on his forehead.

The next day he set off by cart to Helston, in company with four ladies and what seemed to be an itinerant village idiot. At one o'clock, he took the coach to Penzance, where the road to London lay along glistening iron rails. While he was waiting on the up platform, shivering a little from nervous anticipation, a day-old newspaper caught his eye.

Hagley had been discovered with his throat slit in a Bath hotel. The razor lay in his lax hand and there were no other signs of disorder. He was naked but that could be put down to circumstance. Inspector Todmarton deduced that the gentleman had risen from his bath and was about to shave when despair had overwhelmed him.

Todmarton was a giant of a man with a lantern jaw and very little imagination. There were four or five suicides a year in the city's hotel rooms and in his time on the force he had seen three other clerical gentlemen who topped themselves, two of them expressing doubts about the Trinity in notes propped against the mantelpiece. He was a chapel man himself.

There were one or two little anomalies. A guest towel was missing from the bathroom and on the carpet of the sitting room was the imprint of a shoe heel, outlined in blood. These were pointed out to Todmarton by the hotel manager, a Mr Bellamy. But then Bellamy was just the sort of supercilious sod that the Inspector disliked most in life. Everybody thought they could do a policeman's job better than the man in charge.

'I see a man with his throat cut, holding an open razor in his hand,' he boomed. 'That tells me all I need to know. My poor weak brain has, I believe, managed to grasp the essence of the matter. We are not in some Henry Ellis Margam novel here, Mr Bellamy,' he added spitefully.

Bellamy winced. It was in this very hotel that Guy Liddell had leapt from a first-floor window in *The Devil's Knapsack*, landing foursquare on Sir John Repington as he made his escape, the smoking gun still in his hand. It was an early Margam but he was inclined to make too much of it, especially when talking to persons of a literary bent.

'You don't think that at some point there were two people in this suite?' the manager persisted.

'Very grateful to you for your help, sir,' Todmarton said with maddening complacency. For emphasis, he pulled out a pipe from his jacket and lit it, sending clouds of smoke billowing. Looking for somewhere to dispose of the match, he returned it absent-mindedly to his pocket.

'I have arranged for the body to be removed to the morgue. My Sergeant Perkins will tidy up the details. But please, I beg of you, set your mind at rest. The Reverend did himself in. You get a feel for these things, you know.'

Bellamy went downstairs in a fury and snatched a sheet of hotel stationery towards him. His letter to Henry Ellis Margam was addressed care of his publisher. When it arrived in London, a young clerk found a second envelope and sent it along unopened to a poste restante address in the Strand. There Quigley picked it up as part of his daily duties. He was ambling back to Fleur de Lys Court when he was clapped tentatively on the shoulder by a familiar presence.

'Well I never!' he exclaimed, pumping Urmiston's hand with genuine pleasure. 'Loveaduck, if I didn't think you was gone for good.'

'I was ill, you understand, Captain, but I am better now.'

'And I all the better for seeing you, dear old lad.'

'I read that Mr Hagley has committed suicide in Wiltshire.'

'And good riddance to bad rubbish, as the saying goes. Look here, do you turn in at this old pub on the corner and wait five minutes while I fetch the memsahib. Which she will be as pleased as punch to see your ugly mug, no doubt about that.'

He peered at Urmiston and laid his hand on his shoulder.

'I see a touch of grey about the old temples. And a man sorely in need of something to blow out his kite, I would say. The lamb shank and a plate of cabbage for you before we go another half-hour!'

It was clear from the way he plucked at his moustache that he was preparing to say more. When he found the words, they came out shyly, with more delicacy than was usual with the Captain.

'Will you be going round to see Hannah Bardsoe later, at all?'

'If she will see *me*.'

Quigley chuckled. 'Oh, that's a good one! That's very rich. Which she has waited for you like a lovesick girl. Hands clasped, eyes to heaven.'

Mrs Bardsoe listened to the story of Urmiston's time on the Lizard with tears pouring from her eyes. They sat knee to knee, holding hands, pushed by love into an horizonless fog. She asked no questions, made no comment, but her eyes seldom left his.

'You see, dearest Hannah, how little I know about the human heart, how clumsy my actions have been. They are a very earnest and particular people down there and it was this that gradually acted on me. I have come back to ask your forgiveness.'

'As if it were needed,' she cried. 'You have nothing to reproach yourself with. I was sorely feared I would never see your kind face again but that was all.'

'I came back to tell you that I loved you,' Urmiston concluded, trembling.

She leaned back, astonished.

'Well, if there are happier words to be spoke this afternoon, I should like to hear them. I will tell you straight, Mr Charles, I love you back. Indeed I do. Body and soul, my dear.'

He looked around the parlour, savouring its supreme ordinariness. The china spaniels stood either side of the clock. Hannah's sewing basket sat in the corner and her table was littered with what seemed the very same muddle of drying herbs, the teapot, and a cheese dish big enough to house a cat.

'The picture,' he remembered with a sudden start. 'The picture from Paris.'

'And did you think I had chucked it out?' she asked fondly. 'You will find it over my bed and 'tis the last thing I see before I blows out the light.'

'I hope it is hung at the best height to show it off.'

'That is for me to know and you to find out,' she said, arch.

They were interrupted, as they knew they would be, by the arrival of Bella, bearing a huge cream cake. She was followed soon after by the Captain.

'Well,' Hannah Bardsoe said in a high state of playfulness, 'I hope I can call for a bit of a knees-up. And whyever not, on such a happy day?'

The shop bell clattered and announced a third guest, as unexpected as might have been Gladstone or the Prussian Bismarck. Murch stood in the doorway, dressed in a black tail coat, his neck decorated with a red snuff handkerchief worn as a cravat. By way of greeting, he merely nodded to the company, though giving Urmiston a brief and wry smile.

'Sit down, Mr Murch,' Bella said, absolutely astonished. 'However did you know to find us here?'

'Word gets around,' he said calmly.

'Another prodigal returns,' Mrs Bardsoe cried. Murch smiled again and walked to the least comfortable chair in the room.

'And where have you been then, Billy?' the Captain asked.

'Round and about.'

All this passed over Urmiston's head. He busied himself with the corkscrew, his face brick red with pleasure. He knew that when he was in this mood all the mirrors in the world began to lie. In them, he was transformed from a middle-aged man to the voluble, overheated boy he once had been at Christmas parties. He served cake, he tripped over Mrs Bardsoe's carpet and found even the slightest thing amazingly funny.

Only half an hour later, after a single glass of wine, Murch had gone.

TWENTY

Hannah bardsoe read the headstone with unselfconscious deliberation and then knelt and placed her posy of flowers at its base. Urmiston watched, feeling that he too was being watched. A cloudless but pale sky stretched back across the Channel, where the white horses pranced. Several close-hauled fishing smacks buffeted the waves. It was a cold day, with a biting onshore wind.

Coming back to Boulogne was entirely Hannah's idea – indeed, she insisted on it. She was a much better traveller than someone like Quigley and while she could be nothing but an Englishwoman, as described by her dress, there was a seriousness, an alert awareness that endeared her to the French. They had spent the morning walking round the fish market and taking an aperitif in a café that, while it was not exactly like the one Mueller had painted in Paris, was sufficiently romantic in her eyes.

Urmiston was used to people, even the best sort of people, treating France as some kind of zoo. But there was a calm and common sense about Hannah that he loved. At least in the district round about the fish market, she was as if at home.

'Well, if he isn't eating mussels!' she observed of their neighbour in the café.

'Would you like some?'

'Would I ever! And though I know you will take a glass of wine with yours, what I should like most is a glass of beer. For the shape of the glass as much as anything.'

When *la patronne* fetched the drinks and put the wine in front of her and the beer in front of Urmiston, Hannah switched them about with such a warm smile that he felt his heart would burst.

'Now it's at times like this that a body can say she's content with the little things,' she observed. 'Same as on the boat, were we not happy with that wicked old soup that would hardly stay in the plate?'

'You are easy to please, Hannah.'

'Maybe that's why you took up with me,' she suggested.

But their true business in being there was to visit Marguerite's grave in the Protestant cemetery. Borrowing from the quiet desolation and moreover as the only people present, their mood was chastened.

'Would she have liked me?' Hannah asked doubtfully.

'She was a parson's daughter from Wivenhoe,' Urmiston explained. 'Very shy, not at all the jolly person you are. And in her last years, too ill to take much note of other people. A good woman, Hannah, but in the end an unhappy one.'

'Well,' she said, 'I am glad we come. I truly am. Do you want a few moments alone with your thoughts, my dear?'

'No,' Urmiston said gently, pressing her gloved hand to his lips.

They turned and walked slowly away, her arm in his.

'And was it ever your thought to live here, out of England, Charlie?'

'Never once. Else, how could we have met?'

She reached on tiptoe to kiss him, her warm lips against his icy cheek.

'Now don't you go saying it was all in the stars,' she warned. 'That wouldn't be the right thing to say. No, not at all. Not today of all days.'

'It was chance, then. But a lucky chance, such as comes to very few men.'

'And you ain't ashamed of me for my common ways?'

'I have asked you to marry me,' Urmiston protested.

'Yes,' she said, chewing her bottom lip. 'That.'

She had given herself to him the previous night in a little commercial hotel, more anxious than she could remember since being a foolish young maid in Uxbridge. She had nothing to fear from his love-making, which was of such a dreamy nature that she took it to be an excessive form of politeness. But afterwards, cradling his head on her pillowy breasts and watching the moon through unshuttered windows, she began to cry.

'My dear,' Urmiston said with alarm. 'Whatever is the matter?'

She could not tell him that in the silent and modest minutes they had just spent she had seen, as clearly as the passing of the Lord Mayor's Show, the whole of his first marriage.

'My dearest boy,' she whispered, stroking his naked shoulder. ' Nothing at all is the matter and whyever should it be?'

'I have disappointed you.'

'What a wicked, wicked thing to say,' she howled, bursting into bad-tempered sobs. For good measure, she punched him on the breast-bone and snatched the duvet back to her side of the bed. She thought at first he too was crying but it became apparent that he was shaking with suppressed laughter.

'Right!' she said. 'We'll see who's disappointed.'

Pulling off her nightgown and kicking off the duvet, she straddled his narrow hips, the tips of her breasts dipping into his eyes. Her kiss, when it came, was like the brisk bang of a post-office date stamp on a letter. So much so, in fact, he feared for his front teeth.

Quite by chance, the Captain came across Murch in Cecil Court when he was going about a little piece of business (fifty or so fine bindings that had come into his possession in the usual way). He declared himself as astonished as the jack tar who married a mermaid.

'I don't see you for weeks on end and now bless me if we don't meet twice in ten days.'

Billy Murch was cagey, claiming to have been in Gravesend, visiting a former colleague in the West Kents, now down on his luck.

'And do I know this cove?'

'I shouldn't think so. I thought your mob was the 18th Hussars,' Murch said pointedly.

On the spur of the moment, the Captain invited him to a meal at the Coal Hole, suggesting they might stroll up west later on the old *qui vive*, the only two accurately pronounced words of French he possessed.

'Well, I am busy,' Billy declared. 'As I see you are.'

'Are we chums or are we not chums?' the Captain demanded.

'Let us say that we are,' Murch allowed, after a too-lengthy pause. 'Tomorrow night, then.'

When he set his mind to it, Murch could come it the toff with the best of them and appeared next evening in a frogged velvet jacket and fashionably narrow trousers, sporting a pair of boots that were almost brand new. The reason for this pride in his appearance was very evident, for on his arm he escorted Molly Clunn, known to both of them as a glamorous figure from a different world. And so much for a pal in Gravesend, the Captain thought bitterly.

Molly's glory days were past, as happens to music-hall artistes, though perhaps they were never as glorious as she allowed people to believe. Nevertheless, for someone born in Brewer Street above a pork butcher's shop, she had done well. In her day she had played to audiences at the Mogul in Drury Lane, at Gatti's, and across the river at the Canterbury, where she was famously retained for six consecutive weeks. Molly was taller than Captain Quigley and almost as tall as Billy Murch. Her hips were square and her shoulders broad. This physical presence dictated the kind of act she was known for. She was a comic singer and actor, one with enough fame for her catchword to follow her round. 'Well, this ain't like no saveloy I ever saw' – a line from a dire sketch – was still shouted at her in the street.

'Molly, if you don't look as lovely as ever,' the Captain exclaimed, dragging back a chair for her and trying to conceal his astonishment.

'And yourself, Captain?' she asked with just that touch of negligence that had made her a star.

'Bully, my dear, bully.'

Close to, he could see the lines etched either side of her mouth and the faint scrawniness of her neck. Her bosom was whitened with rice powder.

'And which hall are you working at the moment?' he asked gallantly.

'I buried my poor mother in January last and that has set me back, my word it has. I remember dear old Marie Collis telling me, right when I started, a fortnight out of this game and you are as good as forgot, as good as though you never had been. I mean in London, you understand me.'

'Molly's been starring in the circus,' Murch said.

'Yes, dear,' she muttered. 'Topping the bill with the Peking Kings and Walter the Talking Horse.'

'But only at the best venues, I wager,' Captain Quigley suggested.

'If you count Kidderminster and Stourbridge and the like. The truth is, boys, Molly's not as young as she was. I've known you chumps more than twenty years and I was on the halls even then.'

'Has it really been twenty years?'

'I knew *you*,' she flashed, pointing at the Captain, 'when you was merely Percy Quigley, market porter. Before you won your medals,' she added with a raucous laugh.

Wine for Molly, stout for the men. The conversation ranged over people they had known and music halls they had visited or played. While they talked, they ate. Patting her chest to aid her digestion, a cloud of white powder rose from Molly's busom, the marks of her fingers remaining in orange outline. A strand of her hair came down.

'I'll tell you the real truth,' she said as the waiter uncorked the second bottle. 'Old Molly's on her beam ends. If I had a gun tonight and the Peking Kings were to come in here to the dear old Coal Hole, I would shoot the little bastards stone dead, so help me God. They say people run away to join the life of the circus and it's true, we have one in the company now. But for the most part we are a sorry lot. Flotsam and jetsam, Captain.'

'Can we not come and see you?'

'Bicester's the closest I've been to London for six months. I'm only in town now because MacGilligan, the cove that owns the business, is down the docks taking delivery of an elephant. That they aim to run up to Paddington somehow and shove in a goods van to Oxford.'

'An elephant, eh?'

'Me and the beast to open the show. If he's got anything about him at all, the animal, I don't doubt he'll get top billing and I'll be on my way.'

'And this MacGilligan?'

'Like no saveloy I ever saw. Irish. The breath on him could pickle eggs.'

'Well, this is a sorry tale and no mistake. If I wasn't took up with business, I would make it my pleasure and bounden duty to bring you back into the halls under your old flag. Flying your old flag, if you follow my drift.'

All this while, Murch had been ruminating in his cross-eyed way.

'This new bloke you mentioned. The one run away to join you. Can't you make a pal of him?'

'Him! A toff who speaks with a mouthful of marbles? Who can't be taught even the simplest thing, no, not even to pull the right rope when the ring is being rigged? I don't think so.'

'He's a toff?'

'A true-blue toff. Spikka da German but he's about as much a fritzi as my old ma's chamber pot, God rest her soul.'

Quigley was about to say something but Murch laid his hand on the Captain's wrist. And not in the most friendly way either.

'What it is,' he grunted, 'me and Molly have it in mind to go up west for an hour or so. So shall take it kindly if you was to hop off.'

'Well, where are you staying, Molly my beloved?' Quigley asked.

'Only me and Billy know that,' she laughed. When she stood, she staggered.

'A breath of fresh air will set me right,' she said doubtfully. 'I aren't used to the bright city lights no longer. And me, who played the Canterbury for six solid weeks.'

'Would I be such a gooseberry if I was to come along with you?' Quigley asked hopefully.

'Yes, you would,' Billy Murch said, rising. Without knowing a blind thing about his transfiguration as Meinherzen, the way he handed Molly to the door was gentlemanly perfection.

The Captain supped off and for want of something to do, decided to go up to Paddington in hopes of seeing the elephant board the train to Oxford. It was a long shot but he had never seen an elephant. No call for it. However, someone had once told him that they took offence easily and ran amok at the smallest insult to their dignity. It would be worth the price of an omnibus fare to see that.

After a quick patrol round the darker parts of the station – smelling more of fish than elephant – and being told to garn off out of it by indignant porters, he gave up on the idea and strolled to a pub on the Wharf Road near Paddington Basin. There he stayed until chucking-out time, musing on Molly Clunn and the historic favours bestowed on him when he was a likely lad and she an altogether more reckless sort.

'You say she took a shine to you?'

'To me and no other.'

'And what's her name again?'

'Molly Clunn.'

'I never heard of her, mate.'

'And that's because you're an ignorant no-nothing get.'

The bloke was bigger than him but a bit slow on his feet. Quigley was wearing his best boots, however, and what they lacked in style they made up for in thickness of leather. A flying kick on the shins and a thumb in the eye worked their magic.

'I'll wait for you outside,' the Captain promised but legged it as soon as he got through the door.

Walking back towards Praed Street along the blackened walls of the station (one last gander, time spent on reconnaissance, et cetera) he was rewarded by seeing a grey and shambling giant being coaxed through some handy gates, attended by MacGilligan's men and a crowd of drunks and whores. A child walked past with some souvenir dung under his arm.

'Has the animal run amok yet?' Quigley asked.

'Drunk two buckets of ale, scoffed up half a dozen cabbages, give us his trumpet noise an' everythink,' the child said. 'Woman fainted, was carried down to St Mary's. Circus coves pissed as newts.'

The Captain pushed his way to the gates, where the elephant was of a mind to turn round and walk back to the pub for more beer. There was great shouting and jostling and cheers as MacGilligan was dragged this way and that by a chain hanging from the elephant's neck.

'This is prime,' Quigley said to a neighbour.

Since he had never met Bolsover, he did not recognize him, putting him down merely as a fat cove with fleshy lips, wearing a seal-hunter's cap, the earpieces tied under his chin. The man was so drunk – or perhaps elated – he clung on to the Captain's shoulders for a few seconds before moving away to aim a kick at the animal's wrinkly backside.

'That's the way,' a whore shouted. 'Show him who's master.'

Bolsover turned and flashed her a hideous grin.

'Absolutely,' he drawled.

TWENTY ONE

As if signalling the change of seasons, it rained for a week in London, turning the streets to rivers of mud and filth. Damp plaster and ruined carpets. Coal and more coal fetched up from the cellars. The air grew yellow and sulphurous and out of doors breathing became something only to be done through a scarf or handkerchief. The whores and horsemen were driven from Hyde Park and miseries that had remained invisible in the summer – because dispersed like dust and pollen – now became starkly obvious. Beggars and vagrants formed villages under the railway arches at Charing Cross, where they roared and fought in front of huge fires fed by park benches, beer crates, stolen barrows, even young trees.

Some stories of the incessant rain acquired an almost biblical significance. In Tooley Street, opposite the Tower of London, rats rose out of the cellars, at first in their dozens, then as a moving carpet of hundreds. Very few people actually saw this happen but the news of it spread like wildfire across the river. By nightfall, everyone knew someone who had seen this army, its battalions led by a grinning king variously estimated as the size of a rabbit, cat, or dog. The rats swam the Thames in a single compact mass and were last seen at dusk on Tower Hill, terrorizing pedestrians. Or in Leadenhall Street, or St Paul's Churchyard, according to the powers of invention in this or that pub.

Then, with the abruptness of an electrical switch, the weather changed. Cold air rushed in from the north, bringing with it dry, crisp conditions and morning frosts. Bella rose with the pale sun and walked each day as far west as Kensington Gardens. It was a pleasure to walk across grass stiffened with rime and among bare trees brought to a juddering halt by the cold, their arms outstretched. In the hotels along the Bayswater Road, wan lights burned with an almost Japanese delicacy.

On the second of these dawn walks, the only other human being Bella met was someone she recognized. The Foreign Secretary was picking his way by horseback across an empty Hyde Park. His face pinched red by the frost – and perhaps by the early hour – he touched the brim of his top hat to her with a laconic salute that had come down from Wellington's day.

It was an impressive moment. It occurred to her that perhaps this was how Meinherzen might receive the thanks of a grateful country, not with medals and speeches but by a single nonchalant gesture. It was not too late to interpolate such a scene. But then she shrugged her coat closer to her and went on.

At the beginning of the week, she had moved the manuscript of her novel back to Orange Street, where it was kept under the bed, the place anxious old ladies hid their best spoons and silver picture frames. The story's value to her was not that it was good but that it was finished. Meinherzen would have to make do with what he had been given, a final sight of Miss Fern Jellicott at the window of her train to Paris, before he turned and slipped away into the shadows of the Vienna Bahnhof.

The moment a Margam story was finished (which happened at more or less the same time every year) it was Bella's habit to move out of Fleur de Lys Court, leaving the office for Quigley to furnish as his winter quarters. It was an emphatic seasonal punctuation that suited both parties. For three months she barely picked up a pen. For his part, the Captain fetched in his bed and coaxed a draught from the chimney, cooked himself chaotic bachelor meals and entertained his cronies.

Winter was when Quigley made his real living. This year, within a day or so of Bella moving out, the office was stacked with two hundred orange and marmalade tiles from a garden path and the front door towards which it had led. Tucked in a corner under wraps was the sword drawn by Sir Henry Havelock in his conquest of Sind – or if not that sword, one very like it. Half a dozen naval cutlasses, stolen from the same house in Belgravia, were waiting similiar authentication. Easier to dispose of: a hundred brass stair-rods and their fixings.

The MacGilligan elephant made the letters pages of *The Times.* It fell out that MacGilligan's was the smallest travelling circus ever to acquire such an attraction and the owner was roundly castigated for his impudence. In a correspondence begun by an anxious vicar, very indignant men from the shires who had seen India wrote in to assure the Editor that the beast would die of pneumonia, run berserk and kill innocent bystanders, or simply pine away. A professor of zoology was more brutal yet: the elephant would starve to death for want of his native foodstuffs. Though he had come no further than a barn outside Maastricht and was as domesticated as the average cat, it appeared that Quigley had witnessed an historic moment in the long history of cruelty to animals in England.

'Seemed sprightly enough to me,' he commented. 'And according to Molly Clunn, nothing wrong with his stools or motions, neither. Not a merry beast, not jovial in his dealings with others, but then they never fetched him over for his sense of humour.'

Bella endured these reflections from the Captain on her last visit to the office, already horribly disordered by its translation to winter quarters. (She noticed with a pang that the mangle had gone, though it pleased her to see that the rosewood table that served her as a desk was struck out of harm's way.) Quigley was of course trying to throw a smokescreen over the embarrassment of having spoken to Bolsover without knowing who he was.

'Could any of you have done better on the night, I wonder? I think not.'

There was injury in this as well as bombast. It had been Murch who tumbled at once to the possibility that the toff who pretended to be German was Bolsover. And thanks to the romantic streak in Molly that responded to Billy's soldierly way of courting, there was an energetic spy in the camp. The only problem was that none of the information she gathered came back to Fleur de Lys Court. Murch had not been seen in London for more than a fortnight.

'Executing a long-range patrol, I don't doubt,' the Captain explained.

'It is all the same to me if he has emigrated to Canada.'

Bella meant this. Murch (and Bolsover) could go to hell. There were plenty of other things to occupy her. She was planning to take her manuscript to Frean in Boulogne and then rescue Marie Claude from Fern Jellicott's struggle to find her lost soul. The medium in Camberwell had suggested to Fern that it might be found in America, advice that was channelled through a two-day-old girl who had died in an Indian attack in 1832.

There was also the matter of Urmiston's marriage to Hannah Bardsoe. The two women met for tea at Gunter's.

'Well, these are nice prices, I must say,' Hannah whispered, secretly very impressed.

'Where do you and Charles intend to live when you are wed?' Bella asked.

'Right where we are now. He is teaching himself herbal remedies from books he has scratted together – books, mind you! – and says he wants no better life. We can call this the honeymoon period,' Mrs Bardsoe added with her usual realism, 'for if he sticks at it, it will surprise me no end. The good Lord knows it is a low trade. And if the clientele ever found out we was dosing them from *books*, the balloon would go up and no mistake.'

'But you are happy all the same?'

'Oh yes,' she replied with a shy glance. 'All that side of it's going very well.'

'Do you think you might ever leave London at all, Hannah?'

'Bless me, no. No more than you should ever let it cross your mind. You love Miss Anvil with a passion but leaving this dear old place for her sake would never do.'

She had been momentarily perplexed by Marie Claude when they met at dinner in Orange Street but rallied when the French girl complimented her on her laugh, which it was true would raise the dead from their sleep. About the relationship between the two women, Mrs Bardsoe had nothing to speak but praise.

'If she is not the most beautiful little creature ever to wear bangles,' she exclaimed admiringly. 'And what a fortunate child she is in knowing you.'

'You should remind her of that from time to time,' Bella laughed.

Hannah Bardsoe seized her moment.

'Charles is very anxious that we should not lose touch,' she said carefully. 'None more relieved than him to be done with this Bolsover business, for he often says he made a fool of himself over it. But would be highly mortified not to keep your acquaintance.'

'In these winter months I seldom stray out of doors. This is not to evade the question, dearest Hannah, for I hold you both in total esteem. But from now until Easter I shall grow fat and lazy at home.'

She saw at once she had said the wrong thing.

'Of course, I hope to dance at your wedding,' she added, flustered.

'Ho! As to that, I am talking the dear man out of a church wedding. It would not do, would not do at all. I am already as married to him as ever a woman could be and no form of words can make it otherwise.'

Bella went to see Urmiston a day or so later. She found him in the shop, wearing a baize apron and pounding a dark red mixture in a stone mortar.

'Cough medicine,' he explained.

'It smells delightful.'

'That is the peppermint oil. I don't understand how exactly, but we have also released something called menthol. The colour is a mere additive. People won't buy pills or lozenges unless they look dangerously red. May I present you with a box? They are perfectly safe.'

'You do look the complete article,' Bella said admiringly.

'The neighbourhood have taken to me. I am sublimely happy.'

'May I fetch a chair and watch you work?'

'No, come into the parlour and we shall have coffee and chocolate cake. Hannah is out. She will be sorry to have missed you.'

The big surprise was the change in character of Hannah Bardsoe's parlour. All the usual fixtures were in place but along the length of the only blank wall Urmiston had installed shelves, on which were housed his library of treatises and texts on herbal medicine.

He took his visitor out to inspect improvements to the scullery. He had been busy with saw and plane, scratch-building cupboards and hanging a new back door. There was a yard that housed the privy but was too sunless for even the most good-natured plants. Bella was amused to discover the mangle that had decorated her office in the summer housed in a new lean-to shed; but the pride of the entire street was surely the bird pavilion Urmiston had built Hannah, an intricate structure of dowels and fretwork mounted on a ten-foot pole.

'Did you know there was such a bird as a coal tit? We watch them from the bedroom window,' he explained shyly.

'But it is beautiful!' Bella declared. 'You have talents I knew nothing of.'

'My grandfather was a master craftsman, a wheelwright. He taught me a small fraction of what he knew.'

'There cannot be another thing like this in all London.'

Urmiston laughed. 'Hannah is at pains to point that out to neighbours.'

'How I envy you both.'

In the house behind them, the kettle began to sing.

'I believe I know why you are here,' Urmiston murmured. 'It is from something Hannah may have said at Gunter's. I do not wish to lose you, Bella.'

On an impulse, she kissed him.

'Never dream of it. You – both of you – are very important to me. This late business has changed me more than I realized. Let us go inside. There is so much I wish to say.'

But of course, once inside, she found herself tongue-tied. Her heart was too full to bring out what she wanted to say most: that she was jealous of the happiness she found in that crabby parlour and the dusty little shop, as if it had stolen her friends away from her. Urmiston understood, as clearly as if she had spoken aloud.

'There will be other occasions when you may need to call on one or both of us for help and support. I can't imagine what these might be, or how they will come about. But wherever and whenever you are in jeopardy, you may count on us. I think you know this.'

'In jeopardy?'

Urmiston smiled. 'Whenever Henry Ellis Margam next takes up his pen.'

*

'And how is Mrs Vickery?' Bella asked dutifully, mentioning Fern Jellicott's Camberwell medium. Marie Claude glowered.

'I have told you a thousand times it is not Mrs Vickery who speaks but Charity Caudwell, the spirit voice from Conestoga Springs.'

'And how is she? I mean, I know she is dead – obviously – and only two days old at that but how is she getting along generally?'

Marie Claude burst into floods of tears.

'I hate her.'

'Charity?'

'Fern!'

'Good!' Bella said cheerfully.

The summer trip to Cromer had been a disaster: something had happened that was never to be mentioned in Orange Street, no, not for a million pounds. But Fern was needy in a way that shocked even Bella. Almost every day a letter arrived for Marie Claude in a pale green envelope, many containing poems – or at any rate verses. These were opened, read on the spot and then flung into the breakfast-room fire, the recipient in floods of tears.

Bella's brief adventure with Philip Westland was likewise a secret – one much easier to keep. Since they parted at the end of the trip to Shropshire she had heard nothing from him. Lady Cornford, who made everyone in London her business, was quite certain he had gone back to Cairo, where he had taken a houseboat on the unfashionable bank of the Nile. Her sister Alice had it of a Captain Dunscombe, an unimpeachable source. But a gentleman overhearing this told Bella a few minutes later that Westland had been spotted in Mentone. Or perhaps it might have been Florence.

'At all events he is married,' he concluded, not without a pitying glance.

There are some things a woman knows for a fact. Westland married was as unlikely as the Queen in labour. Bella wrote to him twice care of his club, light, bantering notes that mentioned lemonade and skylarks. The composition of these tiny letters with their measured archness cost her more than a chapter of the book she had just finished. Well, Mrs Venn observed, when Bella wondered a bit too nakedly how Mr Westland was going on these days, he knows where you live, my dear.

'Look at me, child,' Bella said to Marie Claude. 'Don't grind your teeth but look at me. Miss Jellicott is an idiot. You can do better. Next Wednesday you and I will go by train to Marseilles and thence by steamer to Cyprus. For two months.'

'To Cyprus?'

'For two months.'

'But why?'

'Because I love you.'

Marie Claude shook her head gloomily.

'I know you don't love me.'

'Well then, because I am devoted to you. If you don't believe that either, because I would like to make you happy. It is the island of Aphrodite, Marie Claude. Peasants with huge moustaches will kneel in the road to worship you. I shall have you carried about on a golden throne.'

'We have never been away at this time of the year before.'

'More's the pity.'

Marie Claude considered some other objections to the plan and then rose and embraced Bella. That is to say she leaned against her, her lax arms round Bella's waist.

'And if I don't like it?' she asked with her usual petulance.

'I shall chuck you into the sea. And then I shall smoke a cigar and talk to the village elders about wine. And olives.'

'Is it because you are writing another story? Is that why we are going?'

'How suspicious you are! I do not care if I never pick up a pen again.'

Marie Claude smiled through her tears. She lifted her face to be kissed.

'Poor Mr Frean. You will break his heart. He will cry his eyes out until he is dead.'

Bella stroked the girl's hair.

'Perhaps he won't die. Perhaps he will buy a bath chair and be wheeled about Boulogne by some handsome young man in white trousers, remembering me as the lady who went to Cyprus for two months but stayed there for ever.'

For the briefest flicker of time, that actually seemed a possible outcome. But then Bella's realism came flooding back in. She was going to Cyprus to forget. Two months would be ample. After all, there was only so much to be said about olives.

'Will we stay in a hotel?'

'Would I waste you on a hotel full of old colonels and Egyptian widows? We shall stay in a villa I have rented, surrounded by cypresses, with a fine view of the sea. Now go upstairs and begin packing a few sensible clothes; and a great many more that are ridiculous. You will know exactly how to choose.'

The manuscript of the book lay parcelled on the table, neatly tied up by Mrs Venn with blobs of sealing wax on every knot. Tomorrow it would set off for France. And, she thought vengefully, if a certain section of her readership did not recognize Lord Bellsilver for who he was in life, then she was not the writer Mr Frean so often assured her she was.

Murch had the patience that went with living from time to time like a predator from the animal kingdom. His natural habitat was London. Cellar steps that gave a worm's-eye view of snowy pavements; mossy front rooms where the plaster clung to the walls with the last of its strength and the fires of strangers had been conjured over months and even years from floorboards and banisters; the stone huts of railway workers or nightwatchmen's ramshackle sheds. Yet unlike many Londoners, he had no fear of the countryside either. More resourceful than Quigley, less fastidious than Urmiston, he could adapt his mind to anything. It was not the journey but the destination that mattered. Murch believed in outcome.

Accordingly, for three days he laid up in woodland beside the road into Tetbury, waiting for MacGilligan's wagons to roll into view. A huge Gloucestershire sky grizzled overhead – not a heavy rain, more like a widow's inconsolable snuffling and sneezing. Murch's Snider-Enfield rifle, stolen from the same house in Belgravia that had furnished Quigley with a cavalry sword and half a dozen naval cutlasses, was a souvenir from the 1870 siege of Paris. Wrapped in sacking, it was the one reasonably dry thing in the entire wood, save for the three cartridges Murch carried in a pouch next to his heart.

True to the way Bella had imagined Meinherzen, Murch's self-possession was complete, or almost so. Never the man to reveal too much, inside him there was an indigestible crust of disappointment at the cards life had dealt him. Molly Clunn was merry, she was courageous even, but the romantic in Murch found itself thwarted by her raucous laughter and incurable habit of self-advertisement. They had spent some riotous evenings in High Street inns in godforsaken towns where Molly used these stolen moments to perform, as though upon a stage.

'Who's the miserable sod you're with tonight?' randy farmers would ask, pointing to Murch sitting a little apart, the one still thing in a whirl of music-hall song and what he saw as bumpkin revels. Later, in bed, she would collapse into sobs and promises.

'I'm no good, Billy. I can't hardly remember how a woman – I mean a real woman – behaves.'

In the dark, he silently agreed.

'If you was to get me out of it, say we started up a little business together in one of these towns, I could be so good for you. We would make a right team. Partners.'

She was used to his habits and did not scold when he failed to reply.

She ran on until she was too exhausted to speak any more and then slept, her mouth ajar, her fists opening and closing.

For his part, he lay on his back, wide-awake. Without him knowing it, Bella had sent him this way before – with

Constanza, Duchess of Vrac, another chatterbox a little too fond of the wine. In the novel, the accommodations had been far superior to those of the Fox Inn, Norton Parva: a marble-floored bedroom that boasted a sunken bath. But the mood had been the same. Constanza was a spoiled creature, the consequence of having inherited too much money far too soon. Meinherzen let her down gently, slipping out of the Duchess's bed and shinning down a trellis to be sure, but leaving behind on the pillow a single rose.

The originals for characters in fiction never recognize themselves. *The Widow's Secret*, when it came to be published, would be one of the few books Murch read from cover to cover, though more as an examination of technique and craftsmanship than any interest in the story. Murch in the act of reading was much like Urmiston running his hand down the grain of a choice piece of walnut or admiring a particularly well-seated mortice and tenon. It was an exercise for the eye. Here in the woods, he bivouacked against a dry-stone wall during the hours of darkness and felt the same satisfaction in a well-made thing.

Now, at last, Molly Clunn came striding along the road into Tetbury. She was singing loud enough for the sound to carry to the wood in which Murch lay: the song was a favourite of hers – 'I'm always the one that's last out the door.' Behind her the rest of the circus rumbled in five gypsy caravans, each of them with smoke rising from the chimney. The elephant ambled in the shafts of the first. A man – MacGilligan – sat on its back blowing a trumpet. One by one figures jumped down from the other caravans. But no sign of Bolsover. Or not yet. Murch studied the little convoy carefully and began undoing the sacking that covered the Snider-Enfield. It released a sudden and very agreeable tang of machine oil, as exciting to him as the smell of cooking.

A few children came out from the town to greet the circus which obligingly paused on the high-arched viaduct that led into the town over some ancient watermeadows. The elephant came to an obedient halt, drums and fifes were added to MacGilligan's trumpet: the zanies in the company began to leap and caper. More of the curious came down past the church and on to the bridge. The music resolved itself into a jig.

Bolsover came out of the third caravan, dragging on an embroidered felt overcoat. He joked with the children, whirling several round by the wrists. Although Murch had never seen him before, constant questioning of Molly had furnished a description that was unmistakable. He opened the breech of the rifle and inserted a cartridge warmed by the heat of his skin. He estimated the range at two hundred and fifty yards. The bolt closed.

You could say that Bolsover was being given his chance. Two hundred and fifty yards was hardly a distance but Murch knew he would be extremely lucky to get off two clear shots. In the Crimea, he had downed a man at nine hundred paces, bringing him the approbation of Lord Raglan himself (a vague wave of the hand from behind an olive press, the Commander-in-Chief's horse cropping unconcernedly as clods of frozen turf flew round his head as his master nibbled on a ship's biscuit). But the Crimea was an old story and the Russian battery commander Murch had sent into eternity was dust. Two hundred and fifty yards, some would say, constituted a sporting shot.

Bolsover was a clumsy circus hand. He was the butt of the troupe, their grinning but hapless dancing bear. A clown darted up and jammed a cap with antlers on his head. The townsfolk laughed as he jumped on to the parapet and skipped his way along it. Murch lowered his rifle. His target was dancing out of range. His breathing remained perfectly steady. Perhaps the only sign of his heightened tension was that the sound of music and laughter coming from the viaduct seemed to reach him from under the sea, distorted and very, very faint. He swallowed.

Bolsover turned and began dancing back again, clapping his hands over his head like a child on a lawn. His antlers bobbed, his coat flew out into wings behind him. And then, abruptly, he was blown off the coping as if by a sudden and savage gust of wind.

The report of the rifle boomed down the valley a fraction of a second later. Panicked, the elephant ran on into town, scattering the crowd. Screams, shouts; even hysterical laughter from those who wanted it all to be a showman's trick. There was a fifty-foot fall to the water-meadow and some credulous people were hanging over the parapet to see whether and when the stupid fat man would rise up again.

Up in the woods, towards which the shrewder of the locals were looking, Murch stood, rubbed his thighs and shins to restore some warmth to them, and sauntered away. Never the man to waste a single unnecessary gesture, he walked casually to the pit he had dug for the rifle, dropped it in and scuffed the soil and leaves over it. There was a gate at the end of the copse and he climbed it easily and calmly. A pheasant rocketed up from a hedge. He loped along the field's edge, jumping puddles, disappearing over the brow of the hill. Rooks who were stalking in the furrows rose in a lazy whirl and settled again. The sky pressed down.

Now read the first chapter of the next
Bella Wallis mystery

THE CAPTAIN'S TABLE

ONE

London, one late August afternoon in 1876. Hyde Park is busy with people, the better sort strolling on the dusty paths, herding their children gently in front of them. From time to time these family groups are overtaken by men in frock coats who have given up their carriages and are taking the air at a brisk pace. In this way one might encounter someone like Lord Hartington of the War Office, moving at a suitably military clip and trailing two or three secretaries behind him. At the sound of the great man's approach – and Hartington does not stint but comes on like a cheery yet urgent tornado – gentlemen raise their hats, the parasols part and boys in sailor suits stand to attention. The better sort (or maybe only the more impudent) salute.

So it is also along the sanded carriage drive that runs around the edge of the park. On a mild and windless day such as this is, men of affairs, peers of the realm, half-pay admirals, dowager duchesses and distinguished foreigners roll gently past under the trees. The public likes to congregate in knots to watch them. There is a sudden flurry of hat-raising – the Queen's youngest son, Prince Leopold, is seen to be taking the air, looking well, according to some bystanders, looking drawn and hunted to others. The ladies with him in the royal landau are identified as Lady Breadalbane and Sir Henry Ponsonby's good-natured wife, Mary.

Prince Leopold's mama, if she ever got wind of such innocent pleasures, would at once put a stop to them: she has it in her head that her boy is an incurable invalid, quite as likely to fall out of his carriage as to enjoy its easy motion. As everyone knows, there is something wrong with his blood and even the slightest accident with scissors might threaten his life. He has the anguished sympathy of those who watch. There is a scattering of applause and one or two muted huzzas. A recent story tells how, when in Oxford for the funeral of Dean Liddell's dearest daughter, Leopold took a white rose from his buttonhole and laid it on the coffin. There was gallantry in this gesture but also some real emotion. None of Victoria's other sons could have done such a thing – or not with such unassuming grace.

The Prince, who has impeccable manners, raises his hat a little, just a very little, at the warm reception given to his carriage. His smile is soft and diffident. Lady Ponsonby, who sees everything and knows everyone, dips her head in grateful acknowledgement of the crowd's kindness. Tonight, a hundred or so gentle souls will speak about their encounter with Prince Leopold as though he had stepped from the carriage and shaken each of them by the hand. This pale haemophiliac, with a student's beard and uncertain blue eyes, is somehow their connection to what makes England great.

But by far the larger number in the park today are men and women from another world altogether. They sprawl, they drink, they fornicate. Hundreds of empty bottles reflect the sun and the dusty grass is stiff with broken glass. From time to time the police sprint after thieves or form in knots to prevent a breach of public order, as, for example, when a ragged file of former soldiers pass, playing battered instruments. They are almost too drunk to stand, these men, and their behaviour insults the few scraps of uniform they wear. Their intention is to reach the mamas and their children, the better to wring their hearts. The police have drawn truncheons to prevent them.

There are people here who have been turned off from distant factories, agricultural labourers who have not seen work for months, dismissed servants, French and German exiles, beggars, whores and bully boys. The hubbub that is carried on the sultry breeze comes in part from hundreds of them bathing in the Serpentine, as near naked as makes no difference, roaring like seals, copulating, occasionally fighting, just like seals.

Foreign visitors are amazed by these sights, but to Londoners it is just another day in the park. In Berlin, in the Tiergarten, such a spectacle as these nameless and faceless beasts that roam and bicker on the tawny grass would be unimaginable. In Paris, the Jardin du Luxembourg is cleansed of the unwelcome and the unwaged by that same French sense of propriety that also ensures the pollarded trees are as near identical as possible and the iron benches aligned like parade soldiers.

Here in London, the rich pass among the poor with something like equanimity. Mortice locks and insurance policies are one form of defence; that nebulous idea, the

Law (meaning the courts of justice, the treadmill, bread and water) another. Most of all, a Londoner of the better class will tell you that it is only very occasionally one has to meet the lower classes face to face. Even a hundred yards makes a difference.

The afternoon wears on, the parasols twink and slowly disappear. In an hour or two the roads around the park will be filled with traffic on its way to very different addresses. In some of the more popular streets and squares, there will be a queue of vehicles waiting to discharge elegant and perfumed guests, not at a little distance from their destinations, but immediately outside the front door. The human animals with whom they shared the afternoon are forgotten. This is a different – and most would say – a better world.

On this particular autumn day, Mrs Bella Wallis was saying goodbye to her godson, Jack. Earlier they had been to Shepherd's studio in Long Acre, where the boy was photographed in his spanking new ensign's uniform, doing his best to look worldly and as far as was possible, languid, one arm cocked against a white glaze jardinière. His right boot was planted on the head that decorated a tiger rug and an occasional table bore books and a rolled map. Young though he looked, he carried off this make-believe well, with one sorry exception. The moustache he had been ordered to grow by his adjutant was too sparse and pale for the camera: with the greatest tact Mr Shepherd suggested some judicious darkening. There were blushes and indignation at this but Bella held his chin firm and applied a very little rouge, so that Ensign Starling was captured for posterity in his blues, a thirty-guinea sword at just the right angle, his boot on a tiger's head – and a red streak across his upper lip.

'You look very well, sir,' Shepherd smiled. 'If I may say so, a credit to your regiment.'

'He sails for Capetown tonight,' Bella said, busying herself with a handkerchief at Jack's upper lip. Though she had been a widow for more than ten years, and had not seen her godson for five, she could all the same feel the heat of childish lust coming off him. His excited breath fanned her cheeks. Bella sighed. The new subaltern, like most of his kind, was a danger to shipping.

She offered him early dinner at Fracatelli's but he asked instead to go back with her to the house in Orange Street. As they walked, he gave her his arm.

'You really are most incredibly beautiful,' the boy blurted as they crossed the road into St Martin's Lane. Bella laughed.

'Why, Jack, that isn't often said of me.'

'I should so like to kiss you.'

'May we not take the thought for the deed?'

He followed her glance and saw a dishevelled figure saluting them both. The man wore a faded red tunic of ancient cut and concertina canvas trousers. Dundreary whiskers decorated a face heated by drink. To amuse passers-by (at any rate to his own satisfaction) he was marching with one foot in the gutter and one on the pavement.

'Who is that?' Jack asked, alarmed.

'I have no idea,' his godmother said in a very guarded tone.

'But he seems to know you. If not, if he is merely being importunate, allow me to deal with him.'

'You'll do no such thing.'

The old soldier, if that is what he was, laid his finger along his nose, straightened his back and executed an extravagant right-wheel into New Row. Jack stared after him in amazement.

'That fellow has the impudence of the devil.'

'Yes,' Bella agreed grimly.

'But does he know you?'

'His name is Quigley, these are his streets and he has quite as much right to walk in them as anyone else. And you, my dear, are nineteen years old, take ship for Africa later on tonight and must try to learn not to be such a confounded owl.'

'I beg your pardon,' Jack said, perking up his chin and blushing to the roots of his hair.

Though he knew London hardly at all, Orange Street was not very much his idea of a good address. Starling had been warned by his mother that dear, dear Bella was quite the woman of mystery, which to Mrs Starling was the same as saying she had a wooden leg. The faintly raucous street Bella lived in was mystery enough to Jack, as was the house itself, shabby on the outside but wonderfully calm and elegant within. Bella's drawing room was small but – to his young eyes – perfect. The blue-grey walls were set off by some very good paintings. Once seated (or sprawled, remembering to cross his legs at the ankle as did all the fellows in the mess) he was calmed by a glass of very good claret and the present she made him of a leather writing wallet.

'I wish to apologise for my earlier behaviour,' he said with stiff formality.

Bella jumped up and kissed him on his forehead. 'You are such a chump, dearest Jack. We are friends, as much as more or less complete strangers can be. By midnight tonight you will quite forget me. That is entirely as it should be. In three weeks' time you will be at the Cape, cutting a dash with your fellow officers and letting the adjutant win at billiards.'

He laughed. What he saw in front of him was a woman in her early forties, with wonderfully grey eyes and a humorous mouth. There was a magic about her, not least because she lived alone with the sort of self-possession his own mother lacked completely. The dusty old fool they had stumbled across in St Martin's Lane was a poser, to be sure: what on earth was his god-mother doing by being able to name such a dreg? But there was a bud of commonsense in Ensign Jack Starling that would grow and blossom in time – far, far beyond this present moment – to adorn a general's rank. He saw that he was dealing with a real person and not some cypher.

He toasted her across the rim of his glass. 'Well,' he said gallantly, 'I apologise for wanting to kiss you but insist upon describing you as the most beautiful woman I have ever met.'

'Spoken like a gentleman.'

And then he was gone, in a flurry of cabs and trunks. It would not have broken his heart but might have piqued him to know that within an hour the beautiful Bella Wallis had more or less forgotten his existence. She read, she yawned, she ate a plate of cold cuts; and as the night drew in, lit lamps. In order not to shock her godson she had abstained from smoking in his presence but now she lay back in her favourite chair with her shoes kicked off and a cheroot smouldering in a saucer.

The boy Jack was her sister-in-law's child, from happier days. Then Bella had lived in some style in Hertfordshire with her husband Garnett. When he died, she moved back to London and set about reinventing herself, not as a society lady and certainly not as a grieving widow. There were no children of the marriage and not much money left to her in Garnett's will. She lived quietly. Though for a giddy year or so she was embroiled – and that was the very word for it – with the beautiful and childlike Marie Claude D'Anville, represented to the wider world as her companion, Bella Wallis was one of those lucky people who have an exact idea of who they are.

She was someone who could live alone and not shrivel like an apple. Marie Claude was gone, more or less amicably; and while there were plenty of men only too willing to take her place, Bella enjoyed her own company. There was a pleasure to be got from listening, as now, to the sighing of the house as it settled for the night: the bumps and creaks and faint gurgle of water in the pipes that was as familiar to her as conversation.

'Ah, but where are her wellsprings?' an intelligent woman had once asked. 'What is the source of this perpetual refreshment?'

No one knew. At eleven by the clock, Bella flung her arms back over her head to ease her spine and walked upstairs, unbuttoning as she went. She unpinned her hair, scooped water into her face and eyes, completed her undressing and slipped naked into bed.

If there was one being who could bring down the walls she had built around herself, whose genial good nature could beguile her more than any other man she had ever known (and that included her late husband), he was not in London tonight, and probably not in England either. Philip Westland shared her own knack of seeming to walk alone. They were lovers in the strictly technical sense – an exuberantly romantic weekend in Shropshire – but had circled each other since like sun and moon.

Bella fell asleep with his name upon her lips. And then woke at two, cursed roundly, padded downstairs and found – by feeling gently along the mantelpiece – a pasteboard invitation. She took it upstairs in the dark and laid it on the second pillow to remind herself in the morning, before diving once more into dreamless sleep.

As for Jack Starling, he lay on his back in a cabin hardly bigger than a wardrobe, his mouth filled with bile and about as far from sleep as was the English Channel from the Cape of Good Hope. A choppy head sea, though it barely troubled the massive three-decker he was sailing in, had uncorked smells that did nothing for the stomach. For three hours he had taken his farewell of dear old England with his head in a tin basin.

Bella was both right and wrong about Philip Westland's whereabouts. He was out of England but on his way home. He was in fact in Calais, talking none too willingly with a man called Alcock from the British Embassy in Paris. Alcock was a former naval commander with some of the brusquerie of that profession.

'You saw our friend in Cognac, I believe,' he suggested.

'I saw the man you sent me to meet, yes.'

Westland's attraction to both men and women was a shambolic sort of charm. He was tall but maybe a stone or so overweight. His expression was frank and unflinching but could be misunderstood as slow-wittedness. Alcock, for example, who suffered under the delusion that he could tell a man's worth by the way he picked up a wineglass, or a spoon, considered Westland a bit of an ox.

'How was he?' he persisted. 'How was our friend?'

'I wonder why you keep calling him our friend,' Westland mused. 'The feeling is not reciprocated. But, to answer your question, he is very well aware of the interest taken in him and responded accordingly.'

'Ha! He was on the qui vive, shall we say?'

'I think weary resignation is a better description.'

'There is a young wife, I believe?'

'There is indeed. Her name is Laetitia.'

Alcock chewed his lip for a moment or two.

'You gave him the Ambassador's letter?'

'I gave him the letter you gave me. I might as well have given him a handful of gravel scooped from the hotel grounds. I must tell you, Commander Alcock, I am about as fitted for this sort of business as a one-legged bosun.'

'Bosun? Why do you say bosun?' Alcock cried sharply.

'Don't the best bosuns have two legs?'

Alcock lit a cigarette. This fellow Westland was either some sort of simpleton or had just said something very deep. 'You have managed a very small but quite significant piece of intrigue for your country,' he explained. 'And I think you should be proud. I will not trouble you further tonight, Mr Westland. I believe you catch the early boat?'

'That is so.'

'I hope we may call on your services again.'

'Oh, I shouldn't bother,' Philip Westland murmured. 'The French postal services can do as well, or better. And, of course, with them you get to keep the stamp.'

The man's an idiot, Commander Alcock decided. This impression was reinforced when they stood to shake hands. Westland overtopped him by more than a foot. He would not do, the commander noted to himself. Would not do at all.